Buried Crimes

ALSO BY MICHAEL HAMBLING

THE SOPHIE ALLEN BOOKS

Book 1: Dark Crimes
Book 2: Deadly Crimes
Book 3: Secret Crimes
Book 4: Buried Crimes
Book 5: Twisted Crimes
Book 6: Evil Crimes
Book 7: Shadow Crimes
Book 8: Silent Crimes
Book 9: Ruthless Crimes
Book 10: Brutal Crimes
Book 11: Hidden Crimes
Book 12: Vicious Crimes

Michael Hambling

BURIED CRIMES

Detective Sophie Allen Book 4

JOFFE BOOKS

Revised edition 2024
Joffe Books, London
www.joffebooks.com

First published in Great Britain in 2016

Cover art by Nick Castle

ISBN: 978-1-83526-891-9

To my parents, Nora and Bob.
Always supportive and always remembered.

To the memory of the late William S Bennet (died spring 1980, Girvan, Ayrshire). Bill was an intelligent and supportive friend and colleague who made a major contribution to my early adult life. He died tragically young.

PROLOGUE

Midnight.

Leaves, damp bark, stone, dew-covered petals, all reflected the silvery sheen of moonlight. Even the soil in the garden seemed to shimmer with a metallic glow, except for a patch of newly turned earth. Its blackness swallowed any light that fell upon its surface, like a dark star. In the centre stood a newly planted butterfly bush, a figure in miniature, protruding from the shadowy earth. It was less than fifteen inches tall. Its erstwhile home, a plastic pot, was lying to one side of the patch, upturned next to a garden fork spiked into the ground.

The late-night gardener stood back from the freshly turned bed and looked at the results of the past hour's efforts. Droplets of perspiration, shining in the moonlight, ran down a pale face and onto the chin, spattering the dark blue jacket. A cat wandered by and paused nervously for a while, tail twitching, hearing the sound of laboured breathing. The gardener leant heavily on a spade and looked around. Nothing disturbed the silence of the cool night. The figure stood looking down at the newly planted bush for several minutes before slowly gathering the tools together and walking back towards the house. The terrible task was completed.

CHAPTER 1: THE BUTTERFLY BUSH

Friday night and Saturday morning

Midnight.

A creak. Possibly an old timber contracting in the cool night air.

Jill Freeman lay awake watching the fuzzy outline of the moon through thin curtains. She could hear and feel Philip, her husband, gently breathing beside her, in a deep slumber. In the moments before he fell asleep, he'd told her how contented and happy he felt. She and Phil had moved to the house in Dorchester ten months previously, in early summer, along with their two children, Karen and Paul. It was the kind of house that families such as theirs could usually only dream about. An old, detached dwelling in one of the town's leafier areas, a throwback to an earlier century. It sat among a hotchpotch of Victorian, Edwardian and Georgian buildings.

Finch Cottage had seemed like heaven for the family of four, after their cramped and noisy terraced house in Bristol. Some of the neighbours were undoubted snobs, but it was a benign kind of snobbery, harmless. And anyway, the area was close enough to permit the Freemans to maintain regular social contact with their Bristolian friends. They were a cheerful and gregarious family who, given time, would fit in to their new social environment. A benevolent great-aunt of Jill's had recently died and left them a substantial inheritance. She would have approved of their use of the money. They had bought property in an upmarket area, and invested the remainder of the cash wisely.

Jill and Philip were good parents, ambitious for their children. They had married rather later than average, in their late twenties. Now they were fairly fit forty-year-olds, active and careful of their health. Philip was tall and slim. Despite his fair hair, he tanned easily. His freckles multiplied now that he was spending more time outside in the open air. Jill was rather more fit than her husband, but she was shorter, darker and of a heavier build. Karen, the twelve-year-old daughter, was tall, fair and slim whereas the ten-year-old son, Paul, was dark, heavier and shorter like his mother.

The cluster of houses in their immediate neighbourhood, close to St Paul's church, were all attractive detached properties with sizable gardens. Their new home had been somewhat neglected by its previous owners in recent years, so the Freemans had planned to renovate. This was why Philip had fallen asleep so easily. He had completed the redecoration and fitting of the lounge (sitting room, as the neighbours called it), and they had celebrated by inviting some old friends who were on holiday in Dorset, for dinner that evening. It had been unusually mild for early spring and the four of them had been able to sit with the French windows open, showing a view of the sunset. The Freemans were pleased with their redecoration. Phil's new job was based in the local town planning office, and his contact with developers and builders had helped him in his DIY work. Their dinner guests ran a small building firm, and Philip had tapped into their knowledge. Bob Walker had helped Phil refit the kitchen before they moved in. He had complimented the Freemans on their choice of decor.

In bed, Philip had talked of his plans for the following day. He would start work on the garden. Many of the trees and shrubs required pruning after several years of unrestricted growth. He was planning to move a buddleia to a more open, sunny position where it might attract a greater number of insects. Then he had turned over and closed his eyes, falling asleep almost instantly.

Jill continued to lie awake, uneasy thoughts swirling around in her head. It wasn't until well into the silent, early hours that she finally fell into a fitful sleep.

* * *

The next morning Philip was in the garden with Karen. He had decided to go ahead with his plans to move the aged, gnarled buddleia, despite the light rain that had started falling during the night. The ground was now sticky and wet, and both were dressed in old clothes and boots.

'Why's it called a butterfly bush, Dad?' asked Karen.

She had finished clearing away some weeds and other debris from the area around the shrub. She stood, leaning on a fork. Her father had begun to dig a trench around the roots, preparing to lever out the plant.

'The flowers must be attractive to them. Not just butterflies. Lots of other insects too.'

'How much longer will it take?' the girl continued. 'I thought we'd be finished by now. I'm getting tired.'

'Not too much longer. The preparation always takes longer than you expect, and we've done all that now.' He looked up at the grey sky. The drizzle was starting to turn into a definite downpour. 'You start at the other side,' he added. 'Let's try to get it out before we get completely soaked.' He wondered about postponing the final stage of the work, but looked at their mud-caked clothes. It would be easier just to work on, and then clean up with a bath or shower.

'There's an old bit of rug or something under this end, Dad,' Karen said. 'The fork keeps getting stuck in it.'

'Take the spade and chop it downwards to clear whatever's there. It should come out then.'

Philip kept digging, his damp shirt beginning to stick to his back. He heard his daughter suddenly gasp, and looked up. Karen stood with her mouth open, her eyes riveted on the object she held out. Decayed and rotten fabric had partly fallen away from the lump she had freed and picked up. It revealed the bones of a small, human hand severed at the wrist.

Philip looked at his daughter in horror. She had turned deathly white. She stood, mouth agape, staring at what she was holding, as if unable to let it go.

'Drop it!' he hissed urgently.

She looked at him uncomprehendingly, then dropped the hand. She moaned once and began to topple over. He caught her limp body before it fell to the ground, hugging her to him as he carried her back to the house.

* * *

The streets around Finch Cottage had rarely seen such activity. Within a few minutes of Philip Freeman's emergency phone call a squad car had arrived, followed shortly after by a doctor called out to treat the shocked young girl. Karen was pale, and shivered in uncontrollable spasms, still gasping with occasional sobs. She sat, hunched forward, wrapped in several layers of blankets in the warmest room in the house. White knuckles showed the tightness of her grip on the covers. Her thin, white face looked pinched and tearful.

The doctor was present for just five minutes. He talked to Karen, administered a mild sedative and suggested a warm bath followed by a spell in bed. Her father declined a sedative for himself, opting instead for a hot shower and a cup of tea.

'She's a lovely girl,' said the policewoman as Jill led Karen upstairs to the bathroom. Two constables had made a quick inspection of the excavation spot before the older one had returned to the house. Her younger colleague remained outside watching the site, sheltering from the pouring rain in the garden shed. She had spoken to her headquarters by radio, and then talked to Karen and the doctor before he left.

'What do you think?' Philip asked, once his daughter was out of the room.

The policewoman shrugged. 'Can't say. There is still some old rug or carpet visible, but it's impossible to say how much. We'll just wait until the forensic team and the officer in charge arrives.'

'It could be entirely innocent, I suppose. There are meant to be remains from an old battle all around here.'

'But they wouldn't have wrapped the body in a carpet, sir,' she answered. 'It's likely to be quite recent. But as I've said, it's not worth speculating at present.' She took a cup of tea out to her colleague. The rain was falling more heavily now.

* * *

It was falling in torrents as Detective Chief Inspector Sophie Allen stood gazing out from her office window. Her hands were thrust deep into the pockets of her fashionable cardigan. The weather matched her current mood, which was somewhat dark and brooding. She stared at the view stretched out below her second floor window: deserted pathways awash with water. After all, it was a Saturday morning. Who would want to come to work on a morning like this, unless they had to? Well, she'd only called in to collect some paperwork to take home. There was no point in planning any outdoor activities on a morning like this. The door opened and an administrative assistant walked confidently into the room, only to stop suddenly when he realised that the small office was not empty. Sophie looked round.

'Sorry, ma'am. The light wasn't on, so I didn't think anyone was here.' The young man hesitated, apparently unsure what to do next. He waved the single sheet of paper that he held in his hand. 'The chief's office asked me to put a copy on your desk ready for Monday. Last month's provisional figures.'

Sophie merely nodded, so the young man dropped the paper on the desk, then backed towards the door. 'Do you want me to put the light on, ma'am?' he asked.

Sophie sighed. 'You might as well. I'd better have some light so I don't take home the wrong report.' Before she could return her gaze to the damp scene outside, her telephone rang. She picked it up and listened to the message. As she listened, she stood taller, her green eyes opened wider and the frown vanished. She played with an earring and pushed a few loose strands of pale hair back behind her ear.

'No, I'll go myself,' she said. 'Who's there at the moment?' She listened. 'Get back to them. I shouldn't take more than fifteen minutes. And arrange for a forensic team, will you? Make sure there's an outdoor specialist included. They can move in as soon as the pathologist has finished. Until I decide what we're dealing with, we treat it as suspicious and do it properly.'

She replaced the receiver, swung her waterproof jacket from the back of her chair and hurried out of the room.

* * *

Water dripped from trees and bushes, and poured from the gutters. It ran in rivulets down the windowpanes at the rear of the house, obscuring the view to the garden so that everything looked distorted and out of focus. The traditional "April showers" had arrived with a vengeance. The wind was gaining strength, plucking some twigs and a few early leaves from some of the garden trees. A couple of these blew onto the windowpanes, where they stuck as if glued on by some mischievous child.

The family, and the neighbours, watched from their various windows as the police team arrived by degrees. First, another pair of uniformed constables, then several groups of plainclothes officers, followed by the forensic squad who erected a tent-like structure over the area where Karen had made her macabre discovery. It was clear who was in charge: the middle-aged woman wearing pink wellington boots, which clashed somewhat with her olive-green waterproof jacket and trousers.

The find was devastating for Philip and Jill Freeman. They weren't horrified in the same way as their daughter. Instead they felt a deep and sad unease that their new home, their dream paradise, had been so swiftly and utterly changed. It had become tainted by what their garden had revealed.

The gloom and despondency in the house and garden seemed to establish itself as each hour passed. In a brief flash-back, Philip had realised that the skeletal hand was only half the size of Karen's. The thought haunted and appalled him.

* * *

'It's a curious sort of job this, isn't it, Sophie?' The speaker stood under the awning looking at the severed hand, now wrapped in plastic, lying on a shallow tray. He turned again to the woman who stood beside him.

'What do you mean by job? This particular crime? Or this line of work?' Sophie Allen had often worked with Benny Goodall, but their friendship stretched back much further to a time when they'd been housemates while at university. Sophie had been studying law and Benny medicine. He was Dorset's senior pathologist, and Sophie had sometimes wondered whether he did nothing in his life but wait to be called to another murder scene. But she couldn't judge him harshly, considering how her mood had lifted on receiving her own call an hour earlier. We're both just a little too macabre, she thought.

'My job. Routine medical work most of the time. Often utterly tedious, working by the book, and following procedures set in stone. But this type of nasty deed . . .' he waved his hand, 'it's grimly interesting. I know it's a bit nightmarish, but it's fascinating at the same time.'

Sophie looked at Goodall as he stood in the liquid ooze, his wellington boots caked in mud. He had a lively gleam in his eye.

'I hope you didn't say anything like that within earshot of the family, Benny. They'll be shocked enough as it is. I wouldn't want them going over the edge.'

'No, no, no. Only the proper official manner to members of the public. Now, do you want to take a closer look? I can't do any more until we free the rest of the skeleton and get it back to my place.'

Sophie nodded to the SOCO unit who started to clear the soil from the stump of the buddleia and dig around the damp and malodorous rug. The butterfly bush was cut off at ground level, and soil was carefully removed from its roots and deposited in bins for later examination. There were frequent pauses while photographs were taken.

Soon the disintegrating remains of the rug were exposed, revealing a skeleton, complete apart from a missing hand. Roots from the shrub grew down through the ribcage. The skeleton was small.

'Young boy. Probably about six or seven years old,' Benny said, watching the progress of the forensic unit with interest.

Sophie merely nodded. She was concentrating, trying to fix the image so that she could recall it later. There was little smell, none of the putrefying odours associated with a more recently decayed corpse.

'How long do you think he's been there?' she asked finally.

Dave Nash, the senior forensic officer, replied. 'A long time, I'd guess. Possibly twenty years or more.'

'What?'

'Not much doubt about it. That bush has been pruned back hard several times, but its stump and root system are undisturbed. I'd guess that it was planted here as a young shrub, placed deliberately on top of the body. You can count the growth rings yourself. It's got to be about that long, give or take a few years.'

Sophie looked again at the stump. Nash was right. The top section of the bush, which lay off to one side, had obviously been cut back on several occasions. 'Is there any other evidence to support that length of time? Other than the growth rings?'

'Just circumstantial at present. The state of decay of the rug. The consistency of the surrounding soil. We can't confirm until we get everything back to the lab. As you can see, we're keeping all of the soil for examination. Once we've removed the body, we'll take the soil from directly beneath it. It may have residues from the body.'

'Was he clothed do you think?' asked Sophie.

'Almost impossible to say at the moment. Any clothes he was wearing would have decayed along with the rug. But there might be trace residues of clothing along with the rug debris. If so, we'll be able to spot them in the lab analysis.'

'How do you plan to get him out?'

'We'll cut through the rest of the roots and clear the stump away. The rug looks fairly complete underneath him, even though it is half rotten. We'll try to get a plastic sheet below it, then lift everything out in one go. If it works.'

Sophie stood looking down at the sparse remains for some time. Then she said, 'okay, Dave. I'll leave it to you.' She turned to Goodall, who was just about to leave the shelter of the awning. 'When will we know more?'

'There's not much to examine, so you'll get the initial report in a few days. I may call in my friendly local bone specialist for some help. She might spot something that I'd have missed, although it could add a couple of days. But you're in no immediate hurry for this one, are you? No one is going to be breathing down your neck after twenty years.'

Sophie stared coolly at him. 'You know me better than that, Benny. Whoever he is, however long he's been lying here, he'll get my full attention. He deserves nothing less.' She left the tent.

* * *

Sophie turned her back on the section of the garden that had hidden the corpse for almost a quarter of a century. Her young, ginger-haired detective sergeant stood waiting for her outside the awning.

'So this is where we start thinking, Barry,' she said. 'Why would someone bury the body of a young child in such a way?'

'Manslaughter? Murder? It's got to be something like that, ma'am,' Marsh answered. 'If he'd died of natural causes he wouldn't have been wrapped in a rug and dropped into a hole in the garden. And my guess is that the bush was deliberately planted over the body to prevent it being disturbed. Whoever did it had a strong reason for keeping it secret. I wouldn't have thought that poverty would have been a problem either, not in a house this size. The owners must have been pretty well-off by any standards.'

Sophie was silent. Then she said, 'I don't like cases like this. They don't fit the normal patterns — you know, husband, wife or jealous lover. But when it's a youngster I get this creeping sensation that seems to warn me to be doubly careful. I'm getting it now. But there's little we can do until we get the full details back from forensics. Once we know more precisely when he was put there, we can start looking through the missing-persons records.'

'What are you going to tell the press?'

'Just the bare facts at present. I'll release more as and when required, once we have the forensic and pathology reports.'

Barry Marsh looked at his boss as they stood in the rain. Her eyes looked dark, almost black. Several droplets of water trickled slowly down her pale cheeks.

'You look worried, ma'am.'

'It's unusual, Barry. There are no set procedures for a body that's been undiscovered for this long. We'll follow the usual procedures as far as seems sensible, but after twenty years it's almost an historical crime. The chances of getting witnesses, clues or any useful statements are pretty remote.' She paused. 'But that's not what bothers me. I just hope that it's a one-off and that there aren't any more.'

She turned on her heel and walked back towards the house, with Barry Marsh following.

* * *

Sophie nursed the mug of tea in her hands before taking another sip. She looked at Jill and Philip Freeman, who were sitting together opposite her on a sofa. Both looked pale and drawn. The afternoon light was beginning to fade and Jill reached out to switch on a table lamp beside her. The soft light seemed to help them relax a little.

'The body will undergo further pathology procedures and all of the soil will be sent for complete forensic examination. They'll sift it thoroughly for clues and analyse anything they find.'

'Twenty years, you say? That's unbelievable,' whispered Jill.

'But likely, from what we know at present. We counted the rings on the stump. It didn't look as though it had ever been disturbed, in which case the body has been there as long as the bush.' She took another sip of tea. 'I know you've only been in the house a few months. What do you know of its previous history?'

'Not a great deal,' responded Philip. 'We bought it at Easter. It had been empty for some time. We decided not to move in until we'd refitted the kitchen, rewired all of the electrics and got the plumbing done.'

'Did you do all of that yourself?' asked Sophie.

'No, just the kitchen, and I did that with a friend who's a builder. We had the wiring and plumbing done professionally. And we've just finished this room. We plan to work our way slowly through the house, room by room.'

'What kind of state was it in?'

'Poor. It was very run down. The roof and exterior walls were fine, though all the timbers needed a lick of paint. But nothing had been done to the inside for years. As far as I know there was an absentee owner who rented it out. It was put on the market when she died.'

'You don't know who inherited it? The person who decided to put it on the market?'

'No. It was all handled by a solicitor.'

'It was a local solicitor,' said Jill. We've probably got the name somewhere if you need it.'

'Yes, that would be useful. DS Marsh here will get it from you. How is your daughter now?'

'She's asleep at the moment. She was in shock, so the doctor gave her a sedative. You don't need to speak to her, do you?'

'I would like to, if you agree. I don't mean just now, I wouldn't dream of disturbing her sleep. But she may want some reassurance and, once she recovers, she might want to know what we are doing. It will help her come to terms with it. I'll call round in a couple of days, once I have some news. Would that be alright? We'd really like to have a quick look round your house, if you'll let us. We need to get a feel for the place, to see the rooms and their positions in relation to each other. It won't take long, I'm sure.'

They started in the large, south-facing kitchen. Its window looked out onto the back garden and the forensic team still at work. The kitchen had a walk-in pantry and a utility room. The two doors were set beside each other in a wall to one side. Sophie glanced inside the pantry and Barry looked into the utility room. He called to her.

'Ma'am! There's a door at the far end.'

'Steps to the cellar,' explained Philip Freeman, who was standing behind the DCI. 'The only thing we keep there are some storage boxes that we haven't got around to opening yet. The door's locked but there's a key in it. The light switch is on your left just on the other side of the door.'

Marsh led the way down the wooden steps and flipped the switch. A dim bulb shed a poor light on a grubby-looking room. The three of them stood on an area paved with plain concrete slabs. The far half of the cellar was not floored and consisted of hard-packed earth. Several sealed packing cases stood beside them, set against the wall. The rest of the cellar was empty, its brick walls showing remnants of a pale, possibly white paint. The air smelled musty and old.

'It doesn't seem damp in here at all,' the owner volunteered. 'The boxes are as dry as when we first moved in.'

Sophie nodded. She looked around her, then indicated that she had seen enough.

The rest of the ground floor, a dining room and study, was spacious and well furnished. After a quick look in each room, the trio moved to the upper floor where they had a peek inside each of the four bedrooms, including the one in which Karen was sleeping. A pull-down loft ladder at the far end of the landing allowed them easy access to a sizable attic, floored and neatly stacked with boxes.

'They're all ours,' Philip explained. 'It was empty when we moved in. In fact the whole house was empty. There was nothing left in any of the rooms. One of the neighbours told us that the owners used a house-clearing agency, and they'd been told to either sell or dump everything.'

Sophie turned to Marsh. 'It might be worth following that up, Barry. We'll talk about it later.' They returned to the kitchen, where Jill Freeman joined them. Sophie was about to ask her for more details about the house when her mobile phone rang. It was Dave Nash, the forensic team leader, still outside. She listened, keeping her expression blank and her eyes fixed on her sergeant's face. She nodded to the Freemans and went quickly out of the house into the garden. Barry Marsh struggled to keep up with her. There was no doubt now. It had to be murder, surely? She entered the tent to a line of grim faces.

'Are you sure?' she asked.

Dave Nash was standing at the bottom of the pit, to one side of it. He nodded. Sophie moved to the edge, peering at the place Nash was indicating. There lay the unmistakable shape, now partly uncovered, of another decayed rug, similar to the previous one. Nash flipped it aside to reveal a small set of arm bones, neatly folded across a child's ribcage. A second body, lying hidden under the first one.

'This one's a young girl, Sophie.' Benny Goodall's normally cheerful face was pale and set. He said nothing else. What else was there to say?

CHAPTER 2: LOCAL HISTORY

Monday morning

For once, the police investigation proceeded smoothly. It was purposeful, but there was none of the tense urgency that usually accompanied the discovery of a murder victim. In this case there was no need for rapid action to prevent the perpetrator from slipping away. Sophie had decided she had three avenues open to her: tracing the ownership history of the property, sifting the forensic evidence, and examining old missing-persons' files, once the year of death was confirmed, assuming that records went back that far. She stayed in overall control and, as usual, liaised with Benny Goodall, allocating the missing person trace to Barry Marsh, her second-in-command, and the property investigation to Rae Gregson. She also had access to some local Dorchester detectives and clerical staff to aid with immediate investigations. Police resources would not stretch to a larger team until a lead opened up. The twenty-year-old crime was not high profile. Local Dorset newspapers would probably carry the story on their front pages, but the nationals would tuck it away inside, if they bothered to report it at all. Sophie presumed that would change as further details came to light.

Sophie gave the local background research to Rae Gregson, the most recent addition to her violent crime unit. Rae was a keen and thorough investigator, willing to put in the extra effort that often yielded the clue that would crack a problem. Sophie knew that Rae loved digging in records and documents, fleshing out the bare bones of an investigation, exactly what would be needed in this case, with its lack of witnesses and current evidence.

Rae set to work immediately. She visited the Estate Agency that had handled the sale of the property. The young receptionist at the office was cheerful and helpful, but Rae thought the manager's surliness was due to more than just a Monday morning hangover. He kept her waiting for almost ten minutes before seeing her, despite having no other visitors, and his answers to her questions were monosyllabic. She forced herself to restrain her impatience, and was finally rewarded with a look at the file on the Freemans' property. She noted the address of the vendor. It confirmed what Jill had told them two days before. The house had been sold on behalf of a solicitor's practice in Salisbury.

'Now, Mr Adams, I'd like to pick your brains if I may,' she said lightly. 'I'd expect someone in your position, as the manager of a local estate agent's, to know a little about the history of properties in the local area. You might be able to save me a great deal of work. I need to identify the occupants of that house for some time back. I suspect that, in recent years at least, it saw a rapid turnover of tenants. Can you help?'

'We didn't handle the lets on that property,' he said.

'Fine. In that case can you tell me who did?'

'No. I don't know. Its recent sale is the only time we've had to deal with it. I can't help you.' He clasped his fingers and rested his chin on them, looking at her coldly.

So that's it, thought Rae. He's probably read me. Prejudiced bastard. She realised she wouldn't get any more from him, thanked him politely and left his office.

On her way out she spoke to the young receptionist. 'Is he always like that?'

'Oh yes,' came the reply. 'Don't think it's you. I'm only temping here. No one lasts more than a few weeks in the job, as far as I can tell. He used to own this business, but was forced to sell to one of the big chains during the property crash. He's resented it ever since. I don't think he'll last much longer.'

Rae was annoyed with herself. It was a problem she shared with many other transgender people. She assumed that any rudeness and friction directed her way was due to prejudice against her trans nature. Yet, more often than not, it was just some grumpy person who was rude and unpleasant to everyone.

'Is there anyone else whose brains I can pick about the history of the houses in the area? There's no other estate agent, is there?'

The receptionist thought for a while. 'There's a lady who worked here for a long time. I can remember chatting to her when I worked here once before. She retired a couple of months ago. She'll be as good as anyone. I don't know exactly where she lives, somewhere behind the High Street I think, but her name is Margaret Court.'

'Like the tennis player?' asked Rae.

'Yes. And she played tennis herself as a youngster. She'd even won some cups at the local club, so she told me.'

Rae borrowed the local telephone directory, and quickly found an address for a John Court in Honeywell Lane. This was a side street running at right angles to the High Street. There was a good chance that this was the correct address. She thanked the young girl for her time and left. She walked the hundred yards or so to the junction with Honeywell Lane. The rain had eased, so she left her umbrella rolled up in her shoulder bag. Number forty-seven was at the end of a smart terrace. An elderly man was working in the well-tended garden, putting out some summer bedding plants. Rae halted at the gate. He looked up as she approached and smiled.

'Mr Court?' she asked.

'Yes. How can I help you?'

'I'm looking for a Mrs Margaret Court who used to work in the estate agent's office. Have I got the right address?'

'Yes. That's my wife. I'll get her for you if you'd like to come in. Who shall I say is calling?'

'DC Rae Gregson, Dorset police. I'd like to pick her brains if she'll let me.'

The man opened the gate. 'She'll enjoy that. She's a fount of local knowledge. I'll take you round the back if you don't mind. My feet are a bit muddy.'

Rae followed him around the side of the house to the back door, where he ushered her in ahead of him.

'Margaret!' he called. 'Someone from the police to see you.'

She heard a woman's voice, and the man turned back to her. 'She'll be through in a minute. She's tidying up. We had a visit from our grandchildren over the weekend. Would you like a coffee? I'm about to put the kettle on.'

'That would be great, thank you.'

He pulled a chair out for her at the table, and put down a plate of biscuits. Margaret Court came into the kitchen just as he finished pouring three mugs of coffee. She was a tall, slim woman with an alert expression. She looked a little worried. Rae introduced herself and began to explain why she had called.

'I visited the estate agent's office to see if they could give me information about the previous owners of a house in the area. One of the staff recommended that I visit you.'

'Well, I hope I can help, but I'm not sure how. What house is it you're interested in?'

'Finch Cottage. I need to identify as many occupants as possible.'

'How recent?' The woman looked puzzled.

'For at least the last twenty-five years if I can.'

'We saw the activity up there yesterday,' Mrs Court replied. 'We took our grandchildren to the park after lunch. They were fascinated by all of the cars, vans and flashing lights. People were saying that a body had been found. Is that right?'

'Yes. I can't give you any further details except that it had been there a long time. That is why we need information.

Were you still working at the agency when the house was sold last June?'

'Yes. It was one of the last sales I was involved with before I left. A lovely house, and nice gardens too. They were a pleasant family who bought it. I dealt with some of the paperwork.'

Rae sipped her coffee. 'I've seen all of the official records at the agency, but do you know any other details? Anything about the people who lived there while it was being let out? The previous owners? Anything would help. I'm trying to build up as full a picture of its history as possible.'

The older lady nibbled at a chocolate biscuit. 'It was empty for about six months before it was sold last spring. Before that it had been rented by three families — furnished, I think. But in each case the lease was only temporary. I can't give you much in the way of detail because we didn't handle the lets. This is just what I know from general chatter.'

'I'll need to write this down,' said Rae, opening her notebook.

Margaret Court sipped her coffee. She talked slowly, as if checking each memory as it came to light. The three lets had each been for periods of between six and eighteen months, administered by an agency in London that specialised in homes for long-stay visitors from abroad. As far as Margaret Court knew, two of the lets had been to foreign diplomats and one to a visiting academic.

'But these were all in the past eight years,' she added. 'Further back than that is a bit difficult. I've a feeling that it might have been owned by an actress at one time, and also the manager of a small shipping line that ran from Weymouth, but I can't be absolutely sure. I need some time to get my thoughts together and to try and remember the rough dates. Would that be okay?'

'Of course. You can think about it and let me know when you're ready. I'll come back to get the details.' Rae finished writing and handed over her card. She saw that Margaret had been watching her.

'You've taken a lot of care over your appearance,' the older woman said. 'I have to congratulate you. One of our nephews is trying to be a woman. He's not half as convincing as you. He's called Andrea now.'

'Is this relevant?' Rae responded, irritated. 'I'm not a he, and I haven't ever truly been one. I'm a *she*, as your Andrea is. Maybe it's time you digested that.' How much longer would it take for people just to accept her and other women like her without the need to make some comment? It was getting infuriating. If this woman had someone transgender in her family, surely she should know that endless comments, no matter how well-meaning, aren't welcome.

'I'm sorry. You're right. It's just that Andrea struggles so much to fit in. And no matter how hard I try, I keep remembering the boy he was.'

'Probably an unhappy boy,' Rae replied. 'Even though he would have tried desperately not to let it show, it would have been there, I know.' She closed her notebook and put it in her bag. She looked at her watch. 'Thanks for your help, and please get in touch if you remember anything else.'

She stood up, turned and walked out of the room more quickly than usual. Had she been too sharp with Mrs Court? Well, it was too late now.

What should she do next? She drove back to the police station to continue checking on the house's history by phone. She had enough information now to get started.

* * *

Barry Marsh was back at Finch Cottage checking on the searches that were going on. Ground-penetrating radar had been brought in, but it had not shown any other bodies buried in the garden. He'd brought in the dog unit that had proved so useful the previous year in the search of Charlie Duff's land in Poole, but this too had revealed nothing. The bodies of the two young children were the only ones there.

Thank God for that, he thought. Saturday's discoveries had been grim enough, without more being found. He watched the technical team pack their kit away, then walked across to join Dave Nash in the forensic tent. A few bags of soil from the rudimentary graves were still stacked neatly to one side, awaiting transport to the labs. Barry had watched the large bulk of materials being dispatched earlier. It would take the forensic team some time to work their way through the soil removed from the immediate area of the double grave. He wondered if the process could be automated in some way. Probably there was no substitute, in the early stages anyway, to manually sifting the soil, with observant people looking for anything out of place.

Marsh returned to the incident room at Dorchester police station. The computer systems should have been readied by now, prepared to start receiving the mass of data that would inevitably accumulate. In the boss's absence, he would need to check that the administrative staff had structured the systems properly. DCI Allen had gone to London mid-morning, but had said nothing about the reason for her visit. His was not to reason why.

CHAPTER 3: THE WORST THING

Monday lunchtime

Harry Turner sat in a small alcove sipping his pint and wondering why he'd agreed to come. He'd cancelled a lunch date with a couple of cronies from the local chess club in order to be here. Maybe lunch date was the wrong term to use. In reality it had been more like an informal agreement to meet over a drink. He looked out of the window at the busy London traffic queuing up outside on its way past the bulk of Waterloo Station, taxis stuck behind a bus, forced to stop mid-road to unload passengers because a bakery van was parked in the bus pull-in. As he finally passed the van, the bus driver gave it a cheery wave. Surprising, thought Harry, wishing that some cheer could be directed his way.

He took another sip of his beer and fought his way back through a forest of memories, to the final weeks before she'd left. The increasing sense of desperation that had engulfed him in those last days had taken him unawares. It had been obvious that she'd eventually move on, that her time with him would be limited, so he should have been prepared. But the human brain is a funny old thing, he thought. You can rationalise and reason things through until you've kidded yourself that you'll cope, but when absence has become a reality, it knocks you for six.

He missed everything about her. Her smile, her sense of style, her ability to say just the right thing and reflect back at him the very ideas that were formulating in his own brain. Her willingness to take risks, her determination and drive. No one had ever replaced her. No one could, not in his view. And in those bleak months after she'd left, he'd dragged himself home every day and wondered how he would cope. But, of course, he had. Just like she'd told him he would.

'Harry,' she'd said, 'don't be stupid. There'll be others. You attract talent, really you do.'

And she'd flung her arms around him and given him a long, farewell kiss on the cheek. If only she'd known. If only she'd realised what he'd really meant when he said he would miss her terribly. That he was referring to things that went deeper than the superficial words could convey.

He could still remember the perfume she favoured. The heavy, dark, musky scent seemed to coil around her, particularly on that last day. He could almost taste it, all these years later.

He felt a hand on his shoulder. So it wasn't his brain playing tricks, she still wore the same perfume.

'Hello, Harry.'

He glanced up as she slid into the seat opposite. Would he be able to speak? Could his lips open? Would any sense come out of them?

'You're looking well,' she continued.

He responded with a nod and pointed at the brimming glass of beer on the table in front of her.

'Got one in for you.' There. He'd finally said something and it hadn't been gobbledegook.

'Thanks. I'm grateful, Harry. Not just for the beer but the fact that you're willing to meet me like this.'

He took another sip. Maybe it would be alright, after all.

'It's a pleasure, Sophie. I told you when you left that you could always come back to me for advice if you needed it.'

'Yes, but that was fifteen years ago. A lot's happened since, to both of us. Particularly to you, now you've retired. I always knew how lucky I was in having you as a boss, Harry. It's not just that you were the best in the business and were willing to share your thoughts with me. It was the fact that I could see the way the other bosses treated young women coppers. You were different. You never tried to lay a finger on me, not ever.'

'But I did have feelings for you, Sophie. I never let on. Did you know?'

'Yes. I guessed. There were clues. And I didn't know what to do. I had Hannah just about to start school, and Jade was a baby. Martin was struggling with some appalling classes at his school. And I'd always thought of you as a father figure, as well as my boss. It frightened me.'

He lowered his eyes. 'I knew you'd never known your father, so I guess I slipped into that role a bit too easily. Maybe it was just so comfortable that I didn't realise it was turning into something else.' He took another sip of beer. 'Anyway, water under the bridge. You moved on and got on with your life, as was right and proper. And Archie Campbell added the finishing touches and turned you into the detective you are today.'

Sophie reached across and rested her hand on his.

'But you'll always be my first and most important mentor, Harry. I couldn't have done it without the start you gave me. I owe you everything.' She picked up the menu card. 'Shall we get some food? This is my treat.'

Sophie took their order to the bar.

When she returned to her seat, she asked, 'how's Sheila?'

'She died six months ago. Heart attack.'

'Oh God, Harry. Why didn't you let me know? Christ. I'd have come to the funeral, you know I would.'

'That's what I was afraid of. Sheila dead, and you appearing. I just couldn't have coped. I swore everyone to secrecy so that you didn't hear about it.'

'Shit. This isn't going the way I wanted it to. I thought it would be simple. We'd have a drink and something to eat. I'd pick your brains for a while, then we'd say goodbye and I'd catch my train back to Wareham. But now this.'

'Don't worry. It wasn't a surprise when she had the final big one that took her. She'd had a sequence of small ones that everyone said were warning signs. But she ignored all the advice, and kept smoking and drinking. She always knew better than the experts, in health matters as well as everything else. She nearly drove me mad.'

'But you still loved her.'

He nodded. 'She gave me our two children, and they're wonderful. Both married now. In fact I'm a grandfather, so life isn't all doom and gloom.' He paused. 'I hate to say it, but I don't really miss her as much as I should. I suppose we slowly drifted apart, particularly in the final years. She wouldn't leave the bottle alone. Everything was becoming impossible.'

Sophie didn't answer immediately. 'I bet you're a brilliant grandfather. Just like you were a brilliant dad. Matthew told me, years ago. I always thought he was like you.' She touched his cheek. 'I buried my own father last winter, Harry. I found out what happened to him.'

He nodded again. 'I heard later. I was away on holiday in Greece at the time. Archie Campbell was down here for a conference and we met for a couple of drinks. He told me all about it. I really don't know what to say.'

'Maybe we should just get down to business. We're getting ourselves embroiled in the past and I came to see you because of problems in the here and now.'

They talked as they ate.

'Child-killing, Harry. That's why I need to pick your brains. I know it was after I left, but you became the Met's expert on child murder. And it's that I want to know about. I just can't visualise what went on. My brain seizes up and I start to panic when I try to think about it. Why's that, Harry? Is it just me, or does it happen to others?'

'It's the worst thing. It's the most terrible thing we can ask our minds to think about. Maybe we all react in different ways, but that's the reason for it. We're emotional beings, we humans. We've evolved to care and protect our children. Our brains are unable to cope with the thought of murdering a child. It can just leave us in a horrified pit of emptiness if we let it.'

'So how do I cope? I can't ask my team to get on with it if I can't work through it myself. What can I do?'

'Do what I always trained you to do. Blank it out. Once the investigation starts in earnest, go emotionally cold on it. Don't let yourself imagine the victims and their lives unless it's in a productive way. Treat it all as data. Once it's over, and you've got the killer safely locked up, then is the time to relax and let some emotion in.' He chewed on another mouthful of salad. 'Yours is an historic case anyway, Sophie. That's if my guess is right and it's those children's bodies in Dorchester?'

Sophie nodded.

'Okay, so it'll be easier. It was, what, fifteen, twenty years ago?'

Another nod.

'So you won't have to meet any family members whose emotions are raw and bloody. Time will have softened the memories. So it's just you, and you've got to stay on top of it.'

'But they were both so young. The boy could have only been about eight at the most. And the little girl was about the same age, we think. They've been down in that hole for longer than they were alive.'

'Exactly. I know you, Sophie. I know you can do this.'

Sophie shook her head. 'I'm not who I was, Harry, not now. Not after that business with my father last year. Part of me went missing when I discovered the truth about him.' She looked into his eyes. 'I'm scared that I can't do it anymore.'

'I'll be here if you need me. I can even pay a couple of visits if it would help.'

'Oh Harry, that would be wonderful. I've never felt vulnerable like this before. Why's it happening?'

'It's not just you. It happened to me a couple of times, but I never told anyone. Maybe it was the cause of the rift between me and Sheila, part of it anyway. I brooded on it and she couldn't reach me. Don't let that happen to you, Sophie.'

'I'll try not to. Anyway, Martin wouldn't let it.'

'Well, that's good. Now let's finish the food and you can let me see what you've got on the case so far. What train are you getting?'

'Not sure. There's one every half hour, so it's not a problem. I may not be going directly back anyway.'

They were just finishing their lunch when Harry had his idea.

'I found it useful to speak to people in social work or child protection when I first took over the unit. I don't mean as part of any investigation, just to get a feel for the realities of violence against children. Maybe you could do the same. Someone who's not connected with the case who'll be able to give you some support if things seem to be getting too much. Is there anyone down your way that you know? Someone with experience in dealing with vulnerable children?'

After a long pause, Sophie's face lit up.

'My grandfather!' she said. 'He worked for Gloucestershire council, in charge of social issues. It was called something else back then. He's in his late eighties and when he retired he did voluntary work for a children's care charity for many years. It would be ideal. It would give me an excuse to see him and get him involved. I know he came across some pretty dreadful things that he won't talk about. This would benefit both of us. He's always complaining that I work too much and don't see him and my grandmother often enough. I wonder if I could see them this evening? I'm meeting Hannah for an afternoon coffee here in London, so I could check train times to Gloucester, and possibly see them this evening rather than going directly back to Dorset.' She glanced at her watch. 'I'd better be off.'

She stood up and gave her first boss a hug and a peck on the cheek. 'Harry, you've been so helpful. I'll be in touch, I promise.'

Harry Turner watched her walk smartly away and through the door where she quickly disappeared into the crowd. He couldn't begin to sort through the whirl of emotions this meeting had stirred in him. One thing was sure. If she did ask him for more help, he'd be ready. It was time to dust off some of the personal case notes he'd made years ago while investigating similar crimes, thrust into the back of an old cupboard at home. If his instincts were correct, she'd need all the help she could get on this one.

* * *

Rain was beginning to fall as Sophie emerged from Russell Square underground station and crossed the road to the modern shopping complex in Bloomsbury. She paused in the entrance to the café and spotted her elder daughter sitting at a small table near the door, waving to her. The rich smell of coffee was closely followed by the delicate scent of Hannah's perfume as the two women hugged each other.

'Mum, you look a bit flushed. Are you okay?' Hannah asked as they sat down.

Sophie and Martin's elder daughter was now in her third year at Drama College and was beginning to pick up one or two acting roles in suburban theatres. Her parents had been rather surprised when, at her fifteenth birthday party, their quiet daughter had announced her intention to become an actress. She had never changed her mind and was now making a great success of her college course. She was blonde, like her mother, but more slightly built than the rest of the family. She had started to make a name for herself playing the role of young, vulnerable women. In fact, as her parents knew all too well, she was as tough as well-tanned leather. Sophie smiled at her daughter.

'I'm fine, honestly. It was warm on the tube. And Harry Turner kept plying me with beer at lunchtime. I tried desperately to resist.'

'I vaguely remember him, I think. How old was I? About four or five?'

'When we were here, yes. But he did pay us a short visit when we were in the Midlands. He was on some course, and came over for an evening. I think he read you some stories before you went to bed.'

'Was he the one who made Captain Haddock sound as if he was from deepest Somerset?'

'That's it. Although he veered from west country to Irish, sometimes in the same sentence. I found it hard to keep a straight face, but he did try.'

'How is he?'

'Sad. His wife died in the summer. I could see that he misses her terribly, even though he didn't admit it. That's the way of things, Hannah. Anyway, have you decided what you want? I'll just have my usual coffee, please.'

Hannah ordered from the lurking waitress. 'Would it help if I saw him occasionally?' she said. 'Maybe somewhere like this for coffee? I remember calling him Uncle Harry.'

Sophie smiled. 'Yes, that's right, you did. I'm sure he'd appreciate it, if you could find the time.'

'I saw a short report about your current case in one of the papers this morning. Is it likely to be a tough one, do you think?'

Sophie shrugged and took a sip of her coffee. 'We can't tell at this stage. It might not even be murder, though why anyone would bury the bodies of two children in a garden for any other reason is beyond me. But I have to keep an open mind about it.'

'Okay. I won't ask any more. You said on the phone just now that you're off to see your grandad in Gloucester to tap into his knowledge. Aren't you a bit worried about getting them involved? I mean, they are a bit frail.'

'Do you think I'm using them? Is that what you mean?'

'Well, since you've put it so bluntly, yes. You can be a bit unscrupulous, Mum. We both know that.'

There was a brief, strained silence.

'Well, since you've brought it up, your great grandfather did say some time ago that if he could ever help, he'd really like to. And I did think about it before deciding. I even phoned your dad to get his opinion. Okay now?'

Hannah shrugged. 'Maybe. I do trust your judgement, Mum. Just treat him gently, please.'

Sophie laughed. 'Stop lecturing me, Hannah. You sound like my mother. I'm starting to get worried about my old age. You'll be watching me like a hawk, I can see. Anyway, I love those two old people far too much to put them under any pressure. You must realise that.' She looked into her daughter's eyes. 'I'm not the person I was, not after last year.'

'Hmm . . . I haven't seen much evidence of it. You can still be pretty single-minded. Maybe bloody-minded would be a better word. I might look like you, but Jade's got your personality. Absolutely. To a tee.'

Sophie gave another wry laugh. 'Can we change the conversation now? I wasn't prepared for such a lecture. Tell me about your current boyfriend. Well, as much as you want to tell me.'

CHAPTER 4: BE AT PEACE

Monday evening

'What I need, Grandad, is background. I need to talk to someone who has worked with troubled families and has been involved with cases of child violence on a professional level. I can get statistics and case histories from our own county records. I can get an angle on the subject from books, but there's nothing like talking to someone. I got a lot of help from my old boss, Harry Turner. I saw him today in London. He only saw things from a police perspective, in the course of investigations. He suggested I speak to someone involved with social services, and I thought of you. That's why I phoned. Are you sure you feel up to it?'

Sophie's grandmother, Florence, was tidying things away in the kitchen, leaving them to talk over coffee. It was little more than a year since Sophie had discovered the existence of the elderly couple, her long-dead father's parents. They were both frail but enthusiastic about helping Sophie and her family wherever possible. They had no other descendants.

'Of course I'll try to help, my dear, although my brain is a lot slower than it was. It might need a while to get it into gear. What kind of things do you want to know?'

'Just tell me about some of the worst cases. What the family background was, how the children coped or failed to cope. Relationships between the parents. You might want to leave out the Wests, though. I'm not sure if I'll ever be ready to hear more about that level of evil.'

'I'm not sure that my experiences in the county social support department would be of much use. I didn't really deal directly with the children under threat then. What would probably be of more use is the more recent work I did after I retired, for the charity. Would that be suitable, do you think?'

'Try me. Tell me about any cases that stick in your mind.'

Sophie's grandfather settled his thin frame back into his chair, looking thoughtful. 'There was a young boy with a stutter. His father was a tough, brawny type, keen on sports, whereas the boy was slightly built, shy and introspective. The man made his son's life almost impossible, subjecting him to constant taunting for not being a "proper man." Whenever the mother spoke up on behalf of her son, she got an earful. The father didn't use any physical violence, just constant, demeaning comments.'

'What happened?'

'The mother came to see us, and we talked the father into attending a couple of sessions with us. We pointed out that things would just continue to get worse if he didn't alter his unreal expectations for his son. He was the cause of the boy's stutter and lack of confidence. He claimed he didn't realise it. Things improved once we made him realise what he was doing. He started to hold back a little. I don't think he ever became close to his son, but at least the boy became less anxious and got his stutter under some kind of control.'

'So that one turned out well?'

'From our perspective, yes. I couldn't say what happened later.' James closed his eyes. Sophie thought he might be nodding off, but then he began to speak again.

'Another case involved a teenage girl, abused by her mother and the mother's boyfriend. It appeared to be sexual, but of course it was all about power. They forced her into all kinds of unspeakable acts just to see how far they could go, as far as we could tell. We put her into care, of course, and they ended up in prison, but those experiences will be with her forever. And that's the saddest part of it all, the fact that these children will never be able to forget. She seemed so brash on the outside, but you only had to talk to her for a few minutes to see just how vulnerable she was. I can still picture her now. Her face was so pale and tired. But that wasn't due to physical exhaustion or loss of sleep. She was almost broken by her experiences.' He looked at his granddaughter. 'Like us, in some ways. Haunted by the past and what happened to Graham.'

Sophie stood up and went to put her arms around her grandfather. 'At least you have me now, Grandad. And the girls. I'm like you. I spend all my time wishing things had been different. It's like I'm hammering on the granite walls of a huge castle with my bare fists, knowing that I can never break them down. I never knew him. I wish I had known him. He was my dad and your son, and we just have to accept what happened. But I have you two, and you have me. That'll have to do, won't it?'

The old man's eyes were moist. Sophie held his face between her hands. He nodded and seemed to pull himself together.

'I'm alright,' he whispered. 'You're right. We have you, his daughter. And that will do just fine. Let's carry on, shall we?'

She forced a smile and nodded, kneeling on the carpet in front of him, stroking his dry, gnarled hands.

His voice dropped almost to a whisper. 'There was a child sex-ring. They organised young girls for abuse. Even boys at times. I've never liked talking about it.'

'They were caught, though? Did the prosecution succeed?'

He nodded. 'The problem was no one ever knew how far it extended, or how many other children had been involved. They were all vulnerable, you see. From care or foster homes.

Not that any foster parents were involved, the checks were too thorough. But the group had some kind of access to contact details and we never got to the bottom of it. I think about five were caught, four men and a woman. But I know that the local police team suspected more.'

'It's unusual to target both girls and boys, isn't it?'

'It was a business. It looked very much as if they picked children to order. It was just . . . horrifying. We couldn't believe it when we found out what had been going on.'

'What happened to the children?'

'They went back into care until they were old enough to look after themselves. We tried to keep an eye on them but most of them wanted to get away from the places that reminded them of what they'd suffered. How they are coping now, all these years later? Well, your guess is as good as mine. A lot of them will still need counselling. If they've got any sense, they'll still be getting support if they need it. But how many of them are in a position to seek it? Not many, I would think.' He paused. 'They were traumatised at the time. That would have faded over time, but it never disappears completely.'

'They didn't kill any of the children, did they, Grandad?'

'No. Around here, it was only the Wests that did that, and you said you didn't want to talk about them.'

'No. Is there anything else that I should know about?'

James thought for a while. 'Yes. You probably know about this already, but just as a fact. The youngsters often feel an enormous sense of guilt. They think they are somehow to blame for what's happened. They feel ashamed. The feeling of shame fades and alters as they grow older. Then they start to feel a deep, burning anger and can experience long periods of depression. They are often unable to trust anyone again. They feel set apart. Their whole life may be dominated by the awful events they experienced as youngsters. If you meet them as adults, you have to remember this.'

'I think I understand,' said Sophie.

'But so much will be different now, because of the internet. It's so much easier for abusers to get organised, and find others like them. The internet allows them to talk — and hide. What is it they call it? The part of the internet that's totally unmonitored? It was on the news a couple of days ago.'

'The dark web. It's hidden from view, apparently, and most people aren't aware of its existence. I can't tell you much about it, Grandad, but I do know there are several agencies that try to monitor what's going on there.'

Sophie got up, leant forward and kissed her grandfather's brow. 'Bless you. This has all helped me so much.' Florence came slowly into the room.

'Are you sure it's alright for you to stay over for the night, Sophie? It seems strange to me, being on your own without Martin and Jade. It's this modern life, isn't it?' Her grandmother seemed bemused.

Sophie smiled. 'Yes, it is. But we're used to it, Gran. I suppose it's the downside of us both having such high-powered careers. But neither of us would want anything else. Anyway, it's so lovely being able to stay here with you both, just me. Martin and Jade will be fine at home. They're both better cooks than I am.'

'Well, you have a choice, dear. You can use the room you've been in before, when you've stayed over with Martin. Or you can have the single, the one that was Graham's. It's up to you. It's been used lots of times, of course. Jade slept in it when you all came to stay at Christmas.'

Sophie understood the implication of her grandmother's words. She had been offered her father's room for the night. It would be the final step.

'I'll use the small room, Gran.'

* * *

Sophie looked around the room, decorated in pale green. There were tasteful, geometrically-patterned curtains that matched the furnishings, and a carpet in mottled green. The room smelled clean and well-aired. Her father's room. Her father, who had disappeared before she was born, and who she'd mistakenly hated throughout her childhood and teenage years. That hatred had led to a breakdown the previous year. Perhaps this was the final opportunity to settle her restless thoughts, to finally put to rest the churning emotions she felt about the person who had, on occasions, dominated her thoughts while growing up.

'Be at peace, Dad,' she murmured. 'I love you.'

She stood in the centre of the room with her eyes closed. After a while she picked up her travel bag, which she had left on the floor near the door. Slowly, she unzipped it and took out her wash things and a nightdress, borrowed from Hannah that afternoon. She went to the small bathroom. Soon she climbed into her father's bed and fell into a deep sleep.

CHAPTER 5: BULLYING BY PROXY

Tuesday morning

'Was your trip to London worthwhile, ma'am?'

Sophie looked closely at Barry Marsh. He returned her gaze with a smile. The question had been a genuine one.

'Yes. I didn't explain very well, did I? I left in a bit of a rush yesterday. I decided to visit Harry Turner, the best copper I've ever worked with, to pick his brains. He was my first boss at the Met, and I haven't seen him for nearly fifteen years. He's retired now, but one of his jobs after I left was to head up a new unit specialising in violent crimes against children. This team developed the procedures we all follow today. Then I visited my grandfather who worked for a child protection charity after he retired. It was worth it. I feel a lot more comfortable now. I needed some background, Barry. You know what the tabloid press are like when it comes to violence against children. They smell the kind of story that can increase their sales by thousands, so they watch us like hawks.' She glanced at her watch. 'We'd better get the briefing started, even if we don't have much to discuss at the moment. Has Matt Silver been in touch since the weekend?' She saw the look on Marsh's face and stopped. 'Is there something you need to tell me?'

'It won't be the super in charge, ma'am. He had a serious cycling accident yesterday evening while he was training for a charity triathlon and he's in hospital with several fractures of his right leg. The word is that he'll be laid up for some time.'

Sophie noticed something in Marsh's tone. 'So who's replacing him? Who'll be overseeing us at headquarters?' But she was already beginning to get an empty feeling in the pit of her stomach.

'DCS Dunnett. The word came from the top brass this morning.'

'What? But he's been gone for six months. He was helping to set up a Home Office training exercise. I thought it was going to be a permanent move. What's he doing back here?'

Marsh grimaced, aware of the friction between his boss and Neil Dunnett. 'I don't know the full story, but Matt Silver hinted that the placement was cut short because of a lack of progress.'

'Why doesn't that surprise me? So we're landed with him again. Find a swear box, Barry, and move it to my desk. I think I'll be in need of it. When can we expect to see him?'

'He phoned just now and said he'd try to pay a visit this afternoon, but would confirm later.'

'Right.' Sophie thought quickly. 'I want you with me when we meet, Barry. I'll explain later. Let's get going.'

Sophie listened to the reports from Rae Gregson, Barry Marsh and the local Dorchester detectives, then discussed her plans for the day. She finished with a reminder.

'You may think that because the bodies were in the ground for twenty years or so, the press won't be very interested. Nothing could be further from the truth. There was a lot of interest at the press conference yesterday, most of it from local journalists. Once the post-mortem results are published and if it becomes clear that those poor children were murdered, which I think is a distinct possibility, then all hell will break loose, and quite rightly so. If a society can't protect its most vulnerable members, its children, from sadistic violence, then it's a poor reflection on that society's core values. So, everyone, we'll have the press on our backs all the time. They'll be remorseless, particularly in the light of all the other child abuse scandals of the past few years. So you must be meticulous. Everything must be cross-checked and double-checked. Everything comes to me. And no talking to anyone outside the team, not even your family. There are to be no leaks of any kind. Leave all contact with the press to me. Understood?' Everyone nodded but Sophie knew that, sooner or later, information would leak out. It was too much to ask human beings to remain totally silent about their work. Some were almost certain to talk to their spouses or other close family members at some time, particularly if they'd had a bad day. Then it would all depend on that second individual's discretion.

Sophie nodded to Marsh as she walked away, and left her office door open for him.

'You know there's been a problem between me and the DCS, don't you?'

Marsh nodded.

'I hope it doesn't resurface, and he just allows me to get on with the investigation without too much interference. We've managed to keep out of each other's hair since the Charlie Duff case, and even then he kept his distance, so maybe he's changed. But in case he hasn't, I want you to be in on our meetings whenever possible. You'll have to leave if he asks you to, but otherwise you should stay. I need a moderating influence. I try to behave reasonably in front of junior officers, so it'll help me not to lose my temper and step out of line.' She smiled grimly at Marsh's perplexed expression. 'It's a matter of self-protection, Barry. Now there's a new Chief Constable, I've lost friends. Presumably Dunnett will be based back at headquarters all the time and will be working hard to make allies, whereas I'll be out of the office on the case. He might feel like flexing his muscles again, so I need to be prepared. Okay?'

'No problem. I'm sure it'll be fine, though. You may be worrying about nothing.'

'Let's hope so. But remember the old saying: forewarned is forearmed. And act accordingly. How about a coffee before we go and visit Benny? And sometime, when you're not busy, could you find out how they managed to get a machine that makes such good stuff? Did they pull strings or what? We could do with one like it in our corridor at HQ. Everyone would be forever grateful to us. Think of all the favours we could call on if we offered people this rather than the muck that passes for coffee over there.'

* * *

The two small skeletons were laid out on adjoining benches in the pathology lab at the Dorset County Hospital. Benny Goodall stood looking at them as the two detectives entered the room. He wasn't smiling. Sophie gave him a hug.

'There's not much I can tell you,' he said. 'No fractures, no scars, no unusual marks of any kind. We've gone over the X-rays with the proverbial fine tooth-comb, but nothing much has shown up. There is residual organic tissue on some of the bones, but nothing that can help determine cause of death. We've analysed parts of the surrounding tissue for traces of toxins but, again, nothing showed up. In short, we're no further forward than we were two days ago when they were dug up. You'll just have to wait for DNA profiling to come back. That's unless you want me to put them in for more detailed scanning, but it will cost.'

Sophie thought for a moment. 'So there's no evidence so far of any maltreatment prior to death?'

Goodall shook his head. 'None. That doesn't mean it didn't happen, of course. But the X-rays don't provide any evidence one way or the other. Maybe your forensic team will have more success with their examination of the fabric and soil residues.' He attempted a weak smile. 'Sorry, Sophie.'

Sophie looked down at all that remained of two children who had probably run, skipped and played their way through their short years on earth. Well, she hoped that they had had happy childhoods at least. They would have been in their mid-twenties by now if they'd lived, only a few years older than her two daughters. What had happened? Had the two children been related, or were they strangers to each other? Had they even met? It was entirely possible that their deaths had occurred weeks, even months apart. The real problem was that she still had nothing to go on. No evidence of mistreatment, no traces of drugs or poisons, no suspicious marks on those thin, fragile bones. The only positive outcome from Benny's examination was that there was nothing for the reporters to work themselves into a lather over. Which meant that Neil Bloody Dunnett was likely to be the only awkward individual breathing down her neck — in the short term anyway.

'Do you have anything at all for me to go on?' she asked. 'I need something to get me started. Teeth?'

The pathologist shrugged. 'Nothing unusual. Both sets of teeth were pretty good. We'll do a detailed dental analysis, of course. That might help with identification.'

She looked again at the two skeletons. 'You're holding something back, aren't you, Benny? It's staring us in the face and you've deliberately failed to mention it. Is this some kind of test?'

'No. I decided to wait until the DNA results come back. It could just be coincidence. After all they can't be identical, can they? Not with one being a boy and the other a girl. I knew you'd spot it, with them laid out like this, side by side. But it is a bit uncanny.'

Sophie turned to her assistant. 'I wonder if that reconstruction expert is still around, Barry. She seemed to be a bit of an expert on head shapes. You remember? We used her to build up an image of our suspect in the Donna Goodenough case. The trouble is, then she was working with people's memories of what he looked like. This is different, working from skulls, but I've seen it done in clay. I wonder if her software does it? Could you try and track her down later to check?'

Marsh nodded.

'And no mention of the possibility that they were twins, not even to the team. Not until we get the DNA results. Okay?'

She turned back to Benny Goodall. 'Yes, please do the additional scans. I'll probably have someone from on high complaining to me about the extra cost, but I need to know. How long will it take?'

'This time tomorrow. I'll slot them in for an overnight session, when the scanner's not being used on any patients.'

* * *

Detective Chief Superintendent Neil Dunnett arrived in the office during the early part of the afternoon. He asked to see the incident board and stood in front of it for several minutes, his bulk blocking much of the display from view.

'Not much to go on, is there?' he said.

'Cases like this are always difficult, sir. There are rarely any real clues with remains that have been in the ground this long. My gut feeling is that it'll be a long and difficult investigation, but we'll get there. If these children haven't died naturally, and that's what my instincts tell me, then we'll get to the bottom of it.'

'You went to London yesterday, I hear. Why was that? It wasn't on your schedule. I checked. Did Matt Silver know?'

'Of course. I discussed it with him on Sunday morning, just before our press conference.' She looked at her temporary boss, picking her words carefully. 'No one has much experience of this kind of crime, Neil. I don't just mean on this force, but everywhere. I felt the need to pick the brains of the country's acknowledged expert on child murder, even though he's been retired for a while. I met him for lunch near Waterloo.'

'And he saw you? Only two days after the bodies were found? I'm impressed.' And he really was, Sophie could see. She managed to keep a straight face.

'Contacts, Neil. I have lots. I'd like to call it a kind of old boys' network, but since it involves me, I can't, can I?' She smiled innocently. 'It's my background, Neil. I've been around a bit. I had fairly long spells in the Met and the West Midlands. I can call on favours owed. I also went to Gloucester yesterday evening to speak to my grandfather. He was director of a support charity for abused children after he retired, and chatting to him was also helpful.'

'So it was worth it?'

'Yes, absolutely. I knew it would be. I'm now much happier with my own ability to run this investigation. I'm much better prepared for the tensions that will surface.'

'You're expecting problems?'

'They're inevitable. We're dealing with two children whose bodies were dumped in the ground twenty-odd years ago. It isn't just the press and the public who will get wound up about it. The team will feel it too. I need to be on top of it all.' She paused. 'You'll be wanting to chair the press briefings, I imagine, in Matt's absence?'

She saw the flicker passing across his face. He liked his moments in the public eye.

'Yes, I can certainly help you out there. When's the next one due?'

'Once we get the full details from forensics and pathology. There's no point in scheduling anything until then, not unless we uncover something dramatic meanwhile. I've asked for the two skeletons to go for detailed bone scans. The X-rays showed nothing. So, should we arrange the next press release for Friday, say?'

'Okay.' Dunnett looked around the room. Only Sophie and Marsh were within earshot. 'I'm concerned that your DC, Gregson, might not cope. With the background he . . . she has, I mean. There must be some instability, surely? In some ways it's a shame you lost young Pillay last year. Where is Gregson, by the way?'

'Out putting together the history of the property. Who lived there and when. Chasing up neighbours.' She paused, thinking hard. 'What do you mean about her background, Neil?'

'The fact that she was a he until recently. Wasn't it obvious what I meant?'

'How did you know? As far as I'm aware you hadn't been told, and neither was Matt. He might have guessed because he's met her fairly regularly, but as far as I'm aware, you haven't. She arrived after you started your secondment. The only people to officially know about Rae's background are myself, Sandie Blake in HR and Jim Metcalfe, as ACC. Oh, and Barry here as her immediate superior.' She stared at her boss. 'Has someone been talking? If so, procedures are quite clear. Whoever it was needs to be reminded.'

'Don't you tell me what the procedures are. I bloody well know what the procedures are. I've just been with the Home Office for months working on new training programmes and it included equalities legislation,' said Dunnett.

'So you know that your suggestion that Rae isn't up to the job simply because of her background breaks every principle of recent parliamentary acts. You might have been working on training programmes, but I was there before you, translating the legal principles into practical procedures. I have a degree in Law, Neil. That's why I was on that first panel. You must have seen my name on the action plan, surely? Why do you think you were in the follow-up group? The Home Office wanted to maintain the link with Dorset.' She paused to catch her breath. 'None of that really matters. What is important is that Rae's background should not be made public and should not be used as an excuse for unwarranted judgements about her. She's a first-rate detective with great potential and that's all that matters.'

Marsh broke in at this point. 'I agree. I've been very impressed with her work. She's much better than I was at her age. She's never given me any cause for concern.'

The two senior officers stood glaring at each other. Then Neil Dunnett turned on his heel and left the room.

There was a silence.

'What was all that about?' Marsh said.

'There's something going on in that nasty little brain of his. He didn't even pick up on the fact that I'd arranged for further scans. That's unusual since it will inevitably add to the cost. So what was he thinking about when I mentioned it? I didn't like what he said about Rae and I didn't expect it. I just hope it isn't the start of something serious, because we've got enough on our plates as it is.'

He's obviously anti,' Barry said quietly. 'What can we do?'

'We just keep supporting Rae as long as she's with us and doing a good job. I think he's prejudiced against women generally, let alone a trans woman like Rae. I thought so a couple of years ago when I had my first brush with him, before he realised who I was. It wasn't pleasant. He's a bully who likes to pick on people he thinks are weaker than him. Unfortunately for him, he picked on me. He ended up with egg on his face, and he's kept well clear of me ever since. He probably won't try it on with me again, but he's feeling out Rae as a possible substitute. Bullying by proxy.' She looked at Marsh. 'I'd hoped we could relax as far as Rae's concerned, after her triumph last autumn, but I was clearly being overoptimistic. What concerns me is that Dunnett used to chair the promotions committee before he went off on secondment, but they didn't fill his role with anyone permanent. Now he's back I think he'll slot in again, which is a problem. I was hoping that Rae might consider taking her sergeant's exams sometime in the next few years. I think we can read his comments as a warning shot.'

'But her position is protected by law. That's what you said just now.'

'Technically you're right, Barry. But in practice so much depends on the boss's day-to-day attitude. He or she can deliberately make life difficult for an individual, as some trans people discover to their cost. Rae's happy with us, and we're happy with her. But all Neil Dunnett has to do is initiate some kind of redeployment process under the guise of efficiency savings. He could shift her to some job where she would be side-lined, needled and made to feel unwanted. It's in his power, that's the problem. We live in insecure times, all of us.' She sighed. 'I'll phone Sandie Blake about the possible leak. If someone at HQ is gossiping, they need to be stopped. But it's pointless to speculate too much and we've got this current case to focus on. I want to see how Dave Nash's team are getting on over in forensics. Do you want to come?'

* * *

The set of labs housing Dorset's Forensic Unit was a hive of activity. In one of the rooms soil taken from around the two bodies was spread out on every available bench. Items of potential interest were accumulating in a set of trays, each fragment labelled with a card. The largest and probably the most important collection held fragments of clothing and associated fibres. Sophie peered at some of the items through a microscope. She noticed something pink amidst the dirt.

'From around the girl's body,' Nash explained. 'It appears to be cotton, and we think it may have had a pattern on it. A blouse or dress, maybe?'

'Could be,' Sophie answered. 'You'll need to judge how soft the fabric was. If it was very soft, it could have been a nightdress or pyjamas. The thing that would help most, I suppose, would be if a label could be found. You know, with the shop it came from, or washing instructions. Labels are sometimes harder-wearing than the clothes they're attached to.'

'I don't think my team are likely to miss anything, Sophie.' Nash sounded a little put out.

'I wasn't implying that, Dave. Goodness, why is everyone so touchy today? Maybe we all worked too hard over the weekend and need a break.' She looked at another tray, holding a small, steel link. 'That's a link from a bracelet, isn't it?'

'Yes. We think the rest was ordinary steel and has rusted away, leaving the link clip. It was only found a couple of minutes ago, so there might be more from the same bag of soil.'

'Anything from the boy yet?' Marsh asked.

'Nothing of any importance, even though I've got half my team working on the samples from around his body. A few clothing fibres, that's all.'

'Well at least it doesn't look as though they were naked,' said Sophie.

Nash shrugged. 'Does that help in any way?'

'Psychology. If it was a stranger, it wouldn't matter to them whether the children were clothed or not when they dumped them in the hole. If it was a family member or someone known to them, they'd be more likely to bury the children with clothes on. It doesn't prove anything, of course. But it provides a pointer.'

'Do you think they were buried at the same time, Dave?' Marsh asked. 'Well, it looks that way at the moment. There was little difference in the compactness of the earth around them, and no obvious layering. The two rugs show the same amount of disintegration, so my current guess is that they were put there together. Only a guess, mind.'

'Okay, but we'll keep our minds open about it,' Sophie said.

She looked at the forensic chief. 'The cellar. It's been niggling away at me ever since we went down there on Saturday. The floor seems to be of hard-packed loose material, maybe earth, maybe something different. Most of it is covered in closely laid paving slabs, but the section at the far end is open. It didn't seem damp in there at all, just chilly.'

'You want me to take a look?'

'I need to cover every possibility. Would it be possible to take a few samples from the soil patch and do some analysis? But what traces could there possibly be after twenty years? What kind of things would we be looking for?'

Nash shrugged. 'I don't know, but I'm not a forensic archaeologist or an analytical chemist. In this kind of situation, we contact the experts. We can call in our friendly archaeologists from Bournemouth University, and the analytical squad from Southampton. Problem solved, though it will cost us. Do we have the money?'

Sophie frowned. 'Leave it with me. I'll have to do a bit of schmoozing. At least Jim Metcalfe is still in post as ACC, so I have one ally. What you could do meanwhile, Dave, is to contact those people and see if they think it'll be worthwhile. Find out if there could be any traces if those poor kids were held in the cellar for any length of time. Then get back to me. Okay?'

Nash nodded. 'I'll do what I can.'

CHAPTER 6: FACES AND SKULLS

Wednesday morning

'Yes, I can do that.' Louisa Mugomba was talking to Sophie and Barry Marsh in the incident room. 'It was always going to be the next logical step for the software and I have a prototype ready. All I need are the detailed measurements for each skull.'

'They were due to be scanned first thing this morning, so we're expecting the results any minute now,' Marsh said.

'Right. Send me everything, including the visual images from the scans and X-rays. It all helps.'

'This will be really useful, Louisa,' Sophie added. 'If we can create some kind of likeness and publish the images in the press, then maybe it will stir someone's memory. It's just about the only avenue open to us. There's not much else to go on. How's your work being funded, by the way? Still by the Home Office?'

Louisa shook her head. 'That money dried up with the completion of the last package, the one I used with you a couple of years ago. It got me my doctorate, by the way.' She stretched out her legs and rubbed a knee. 'I bruised it at the weekend playing hockey for the university . . . Anyway, the money for this stage is coming partly from the EU with the UN funding the rest. They want to use it to help identify the bodies of mass murder victims who've been buried during conflicts. You know, for war crimes investigations. That's why I'm still in post at Southampton. I've got a year's grant as a post-doctoral researcher. It fell into place nicely, because it's exactly the kind of project that will help me land a permanent job somewhere, maybe in forensic archaeology. I never imagined that I'd end up in this line when I was doing my first degree in computing and software design, but I love it. I'm using my skills to do something really worthwhile.'

'How does the programme work?' asked Marsh.

'The first stage recreates the skull as a three dimensional image. I'll use the scan data as the input for that. Maybe I should consider developing an input method that takes the scan data directly, but at the moment I'll have to enter the figures manually. Once I have the image, I'll compare it to the photos of the skull to check that it's right. Then I start adding muscle and other soft tissue. I get help with that from one of the medics who has worked with me on the programme. Finally we add skin and hair. That's where we have to use some guesswork. In your case, we don't know what the hair looked like, nor do we know the skin tone, so I may have to produce a range of images for each of the heads. I'll get them emailed to you and you take it from there. Okay?'

'Sounds good to me,' Sophie replied. 'And if the result is anything like the image from that previous programme, it'll be a real bonus for us. It was so good that it refreshed my memory as well as one of my team members.'

'Really?'

'Yes. It helped us so much. He'd been lurking in the crowd outside the police station — trying to judge whether we'd fallen for his tricks, I suppose. It helped us to nail him.'

'Is that common? Hanging around during the investigation?'

'Oh yes. A lot of criminals have huge egos. In their minds the world revolves around them and their desires. They really do feel much more important than anyone else. Their feelings, their needs, their resentments always take priority. And checking on the police's progress, or lack of it, helps to feed their overinflated opinion of themselves. It's quite astonishing, the number of killers who even volunteer to help with searches of the area where a body might be found. Not that it will happen in this case, twenty or so years after the event. Deaths like these leave so few clues.'

Louisa frowned. 'I did realise that this was an unusual case and would need a lot of sensitive handling. It's quite shocking, isn't it? How do you manage?'

'We just get on with it. What else can we do?' Sophie shrugged. 'We have to solve the crime, just like any other. But it isn't like any other, we know that. So we make sure we're always aware, always careful about what we do and how we act.'

Louisa nodded. 'By the way, since the software is still under development, I'll categorise your request as a test case. It won't cost anything.'

'That's a relief,' Sophie replied. 'I can see that money's going to be a problem with this investigation, since it all happened in the dim and distant past. The powers that be consider it high priority, as you can imagine, but the budget will be smaller than for a current murder investigation. And we don't even know that it is murder. There could be other reasons for them being buried like that.'

Louisa wrinkled her nose. 'I can't think of any that are anything but bad. Who would ever do such a thing?'

Marsh heard a beep from his computer and went to check on an email message. He came back a few minutes later carrying a print-out. He handed the pages to the computer software specialist. 'The two sets of skull dimensions. I've forwarded the email to you as well. Remember — it's all confidential.'

'Of course. Just like last time. I should have some news for you in a couple of days. Is that okay?'

'Fine, thank you. Let us know if you need more information.'

Barry Marsh saw Louisa out of the office. He returned to continue the planning, but was interrupted by Sophie's desk phone. She listened, frowning in concentration. She wrote down a phone number and replaced the handset.

'Curiouser and curiouser,' She looked up at Marsh. 'Apparently the vicar at St Paul's phoned in a few minutes ago and asked if I could go round and see him. He might have some information about the investigation, but he didn't say what. Let's go and see what he has to say, Barry.'

* * *

The minister at St Paul's parish church was a soft-featured, kindly-looking man with iron grey hair and twinkling eyes. He smiled at the two detectives, shook hands and invited them inside.

'I'm Tony Younger, the parish vicar. I hope that this visit won't be a waste of time for you. I've been worrying about it ever since I saw the news about the two children's bodies in that local garden.'

'So, exactly how do you think you can help us, Mr Younger?'

'It's about some poems that were sent in for the parish magazine. We've always encouraged our parishioners to submit stories, essays and verses that might be uplifting or that have a faith-based theme. It's always nice to have an input from ordinary people. It makes it more interesting than just being a list of what's on and when.'

The detectives followed the vicar into his study. 'So these poems were in your magazine?' asked Sophie.

'Well, that's the point. I never included them. They were unsuitable for a monthly parish newsletter. I never really knew what to do with them. They were sent in anonymously so I had no way of contacting whoever sent them. I just hung onto them in case their author ever contacted me to ask for them back. They never made much sense to me, although I could tell that the writer was suffering some kind of mental anguish.

I even put a request in the magazine a couple of times, asking for them to contact me, but I never got a response.'

'When was this? When did they arrive?'

'About seven or eight years ago. There was nearly a year between them. I always wondered whether the person would have sent more if I'd published them.'

'And what makes you think they're relevant now?'

'I suggest you read them. I think you'll spot what made me think of them when I saw the news on Saturday.'

He passed across a clear plastic wallet containing a couple of sheets of paper. Sophie pulled on a pair of latex gloves, extracted the top page and studied it, slowly. What she read made her shiver. She had felt the same overwhelming sense of self-loathing herself, just a year before. This person was down in a dark pit of despair, unable to see a way out. And there it was, the reference that had made the vicar suspicious.

She handed the first page to Marsh and picked up the next one. Further outpourings of self-loathing, but again a relevant reference.

Sophie turned to the minister. 'You were right to contact us. I'll need to take these. Who else has touched them, apart from you?'

'My late wife, when they first arrived. They've been in my filing cabinet since then.'

And there haven't been any more? Nothing remotely similar?'

'No. That second one was the last. Maybe by then whoever wrote them had worked through the problem.'

'You said your late wife, Mr Younger,' Marsh interjected. 'Did she pass away recently?'

The vicar nodded. 'Three years ago. Cancer.'

'I'm so sorry to hear that. You have our sympathy. It must have been a terribly difficult time for you.'

'It still is. The sense of loss never goes away.'

There was a silence. Sophie took the two sheets of paper and slid them back into the folder.

'I can see why you never published them. Whoever wrote them seems to have lost his or her soul,' she said.

The vicar nodded slowly. 'I know. I understand that sense of desolation now, after the loss of my wife.'

'Do you think it's likely that they come from one of your parishioners? Would anyone else be sending you material for the parish newsletter?'

'Well now, there's the problem. We don't just restrict circulation to our churchgoers. We deliver one to every house in the area, right up to our parish boundary. It costs a lot of money, but we had a specific donation for that purpose left to us in a will. So they could be from anyone living in the area, not just one of my regular parishioners. I do get some non-church stuff and put it in whenever I can, as long as it's suitable. That was a condition of the funding bequest.'

'Who else knows about these poems, Mr Younger?'

'No one. Chrissie and I decided that we'd keep them to ourselves.'

'Please keep it that way. Certainly for the time being.'

CHAPTER 7: POEMS OF DESPAIR

New Home For Old Rugs

Are you happy there, down in the soft earth, down in your new home?
Have your patterns faded?
Have your tufts peeled apart?
Have the stains soaked away?

Are you happy there, down in the soft earth, down in your new role?
Acting like swaddling clothes?
Holding them tight?
Entrapping their souls?

Are you happy there, down in the soft earth, encasing their bodies?
Like pupal skins
Waiting for metamorphosis?
Two ghastly, rotting parcels?

* * *

Who Am I?

I live a spectral life, empty of meaning.
I inhabit a ghostly world, vacant of substance.
I pore over old memories, and retch at my actions.
I think of their grave, and pray that it stays closed.

Dear God, who am I? What evil being spawned me?
Not my mother and father, kindly souls both.
More the evil monsters that dwell beyond imagination,
Pouring out their filth into this world, a muck that sullies everything it touches.

I am poison, I am toxic.
My name is Death, my face is Medusa.
My breath is sulphurous, my spit is arsenous.
My body drips vileness upon the ground.

And still those two poor parcels call out to me, call my name.
What does their long-dead mother say, howling in the mist?
Does she still search for her babies among the lost, dead souls?
I am destined for the devil to consume, an end that is too good for me.

CHAPTER 8: YOUTHFUL TRAUMA

Wednesday afternoon

Lorna MacIntyre leaned forward in her seat and spoke quietly to Karen Freeman. The young girl sat opposite her in the small interview office.

'Your parents are right to send you back to school, Karen. One day of absence was enough, as I said to you yesterday. You may not think so. You may think it would be better for you if you had another couple of days off, but it's not the case. I spoke to the principal on Monday after your parents phoned in, and we all agreed about it. Even your parents, when I called them back later.'

Karen was tearful. 'But I just can't concentrate on anything, Miss MacIntyre. And I keep thinking everyone's looking at me. I hate it. I hate being here.'

'We all realise that you're having a terrible time. But being in school gives you the chance to take your mind off what happened at the weekend. If you try to concentrate on your work as best you can, the horrible feelings you have will slowly fade. And we are taking your situation very seriously. Mrs Taverner asked to be kept informed of how you're getting on, because we all care about you. She'll speak to you herself if you want, but she thought I'd be best placed to have a quick chat with you each day, since I'm your form teacher.'

It was lunchtime at Dorchester High School, and Lorna was giving up half of her valuable free time to see the troubled youngster, still clearly upset by the events of the past weekend. Martin Allen, her boss in the Mathematics department, who was also the assistant principal, had stepped in to run her weekly "Catch Up On Maths" club for younger pupils so that she could have some time with the young girl and talk through her problems. Martin had been adamant. The girl should not be told that he was the husband of the police officer in charge of the investigation into the two young bodies found buried in the garden of her family home.

'Not a good idea,' he'd said. 'It will backfire if we tell her that. She'll think I'm always watching her. She's got enough on her plate anyway, poor kid. We need to help her to forget. I don't want anyone else to know about Sophie either, just you and Claudia Taverner. And for God's sake don't let the girl's head of year know. Sharon Blake is the biggest gossip in the school.'

Lorna had been surprised. 'Doesn't she know what your wife does?'

'No. And I want it kept that way. Sophie bumped into Sharon last year at some liaison meeting at County Hall. She'd been taken by our esteemed previous principal, God bless her cotton socks. There was a bit of a clash between Sophie and our ex-leader. I don't think Claudia's predecessor came out of the encounter very well. Since it was only a few weeks after Sharon started here, it has probably stuck in her mind. I have a reasonable working relationship with her at the moment and I don't particularly want it to suffer. I think it would if she found out.' He grimaced.

Lorna looked up. Karen Freeman was watching her. She smiled at her pupil. 'You've got all the help you could ever need here, Karen. Just try to stay calm. All your teachers know that you've been through a trauma, though they don't know the full details. Your close friends know a little about it, and they all promised to be supportive. I said to you yesterday that we're all glad to see you back. Just remember that you're among friends. Are you getting support from anybody else?'

The young girl nodded. 'The police have arranged for me to see someone tomorrow after school. She'll be coming to the house. And we all get visited by a policewoman who's good at listening.'

'Well, if you need to talk while you're in school, just come and find me, any lunchtime or break time. Okay?'

She patted Karen's shoulder.

'How did it go?' Martin Allen asked when Lorna returned to the maths department office.

She sighed. 'As well as could be expected. I feel so sorry for her. It must have been awful. How on earth does your wife cope with it, having to deal with these things all the time?'

'That's a question I often ask myself. I always thought she had a layer of impenetrable psychological armour, but I've become less sure of that in recent years.' He glanced at the clock. 'Two minutes to afternoon registration. We'd better be off.'

* * *

Jill Freeman had left work early so that she would be home when her daughter arrived back from school. Paul, two years younger than his sister, was already in the lounge watching television when the front door banged shut behind Karen. She sniffed the air: cakes. She dropped her bag and walked through to the kitchen.

'It's only fruit scones, Karen. I haven't had time to do anything more complicated. But the first batch is cooling on that rack, so you can have one if you like. It'll be an hour or more before Dad's in for dinner.'

Jill rinsed the last of the dishes and watched her daughter spread jam thickly onto a scone and take a large bite. Thank goodness, she thought. Things are beginning to get back to normal.

'How did school go today? Were things any easier?'

'It's horrible. I keep thinking people are looking at me, then when they see me looking back, they look away. I keep thinking they're talking about me.'

'It will just be your imagination, Karen. Your friends are really nice, aren't they? Certainly the ones I've met. You don't think that about Jamila and Rachel, do you? And they're your closest friends. Haven't they been friendly enough since you went back yesterday?'

The girl sighed. 'I suppose so. And it's not them, it's the others.' She paused. 'Oh, I don't know. I just feel sad all the time. I feel like crying. I cried today when Miss McIntyre saw me at lunchtime. I tried not to, but I couldn't help it.'

'It's not a bad thing to cry, Karen. It helps to show how upset you are because then other people will try to understand a bit better. How did the talk with Miss McIntyre go?'

'Okay, I suppose. But some of the other girls found out and they were looking at me when I went into registration.'

'Maybe you could ask Jamila and Rachel to wait for you outside Miss MacIntyre's office next time. Then you wouldn't be going into registration on your own afterwards. How does that sound?'

'Okay.' The girl finished eating her jam-covered scone.

'Will you and Paul be alright watching the telly for a short while? I need to pop out with an important message for someone. Okay, sweetheart?' She watched her daughter anxiously. Karen merely nodded absentmindedly, spread some jam onto another two scones and took them through to join her brother in the lounge. Her mother smoothed down her skirt, checked her appearance in the hall mirror and slipped out of the front door. Some things just couldn't wait.

* * *

Theresa Jackson was the family liaison officer assigned to the Freeman family. She was a young Dorchester-based PC, dedicated and keen to do well in her chosen career. She visited Finch Cottage early each evening in order to talk through any issues that the family raised, and to keep them up to date with developments. This particular evening, Wednesday, would be problematic for her, though. She had made a date with her current boyfriend to celebrate his birthday in one of Dorchester's upmarket restaurants. She had decided to drop in on the Freemans during the late afternoon instead. Karen, the family member of greatest concern, should be home from school by then.

Theresa turned off the main road and drove into the quiet, tree-lined area where the Freeman family lived. She suddenly noticed that the woman walking quickly around a nearby street corner into a secluded cul-de-sac was the Freeman mother, Jill. But why was she acting so furtively? Every few paces she glanced back over her shoulder. Theresa slowed and pulled her car close to the kerb where she watched and waited.

The door of a parked car, a red VW Golf, opened as Jill approached and she slid quickly into the empty passenger seat. Theresa thought she could just make out the hazy shapes of two figures embracing, or was it her over-vivid imagination? She noted the car registration then moved her own car back into the traffic lane and drove on to Finch Cottage. She rang the front doorbell and waited the few seconds that it took Karen to answer the door, safety chain engaged.

'Hello, Karen. Can I come in? I'm a bit early today, aren't I?'

Karen smiled weakly and closed the door in order to disengage the security chain. Theresa was glad to see the youngster looking markedly more cheerful than on the previous three days. She followed Karen through into the kitchen.

'Mum's just popped out for a few minutes. She won't be long.'

'Who else is home, Karen?'

'Just Paul and me. But we're okay, honestly. Do you want a scone? Mum's just made some and they're lovely with her strawberry jam on.'

Theresa looked around the room. Everything safely tucked away, with no apparent hazards, she noted. 'No thanks, I'm going out for a meal tonight with my boyfriend. I can't afford to ruin my appetite, can I?'

Karen looked at her. 'Is he nice?'

'I think so. Otherwise he wouldn't be my boyfriend. Where has your mum gone? Did she say?'

'Not really. She just said that she had an important message to give to someone. She made sure the doors were locked.'

'So, how has today gone? You're looking a bit better. Did school go quite well?'

'I think so. I was telling Mum I still think people are talking about me, but my form tutor talked to me again at lunchtime and I suppose I don't feel as bad as I did.' She paused. 'It's okay as long as I don't think about it.' She shuddered. 'I held that hand, those bones. I could feel them, all cold and wet. And to think that the rest of the body was down there too. Ugh.'

She didn't cry. This was a first in Theresa's experience.

'Shall we go through and see your brother?' she suggested.

They walked through to the lounge to join Paul, who was intently watching the latest instalment of an adventure series on television. Without taking his eyes off the flickering screen he reached out and took a jam-covered scone from the plate Karen held out to him.

'Are you okay, Paul?' Theresa asked.

'Mmmm,' he replied.

'Well, that's alright then.'

Karen rolled her eyes at Theresa. 'He's always like this when the telly's on. It's like talking to a robot.'

Theresa looked around the room. It was the first time she'd been able to do so in the absence of one or other of the Freeman parents. Family photos were displayed prominently on several surfaces, along with a few ornaments. They all looked happy enough in the photos. They had always appeared to be a close-knit family when she'd talked to them, but was that just a careful deception? Had Jill, the mother, always been slightly distant? Even if that was the case, was it relevant to the reason why she, Theresa, was here? She would mention her concerns to her bosses, but she couldn't see how her observations could affect the case.

Ten minutes later she heard the front door open, and Jill's head appeared in the lounge doorway. She put her hand to her mouth when she saw Theresa sitting with the children.

'Oh!' she gasped. 'You're much earlier than usual.'

'Don't worry, Jill. I've only been here a short while.' Theresa gave the mother a reassuring smile. 'They were safe. Karen is very sensible and knew what she had to do. You weren't being negligent, if that's what you're worried about.'

'Even so, it must look bad.'

'Compared to some of the things I've seen on my home visits? You have no idea. I said don't worry, and I meant it.'

'I only popped out to the shops for a few minutes.'

'Okay. Karen's looked after me, and even offered me scones and jam. You've been busy in the kitchen then?'

'Yes. I took most of the afternoon off so that I could be here for when they came home from school. They usually go to friends' houses for an hour or so, but I wasn't sure that would be for the best at the moment. It'll only be for this week, though.'

She was calm again, Theresa noticed. She tried to remember what Jill did. It was something managerial, she was sure. That would explain how she regained her composure so quickly. What had she been doing when she went out? There were no shops anywhere near the street where Theresa had spotted her, and Karen had told her that her mother was out giving someone an important message. Why the change of story? Theresa was intrigued, but said nothing. It was probably not relevant, anyway. As Jill went to make a pot of tea, two pairs of eyes followed her. Both held doubt and suspicion.

CHAPTER 9: SIX AVENUES

Late Wednesday afternoon

Sophie Allen and Barry Marsh stood in Dorchester Hospital's Pathology laboratory looking down on two white examination benches. On the sterile surface of each bench a set of small skeletal remains were arranged. During the two years they had been working together, they had become used to visiting Benny Goodall on his home territory. They had seen numerous bodies in various states of decay spread out before them, but this was different. Two children. Each skeleton was complete, each a perfect example of a young human's bone structure.

'Well, Benny, is there anything more you can tell us, now you've had the scans done?'

He shook his head. 'I'm still not certain. There are no definite marks, no healed fractures or lesions. No obviously suspicious scar marks that would indicate physical violence, but there are a few shadowy areas that I can't quite make out. The girl's cheekbones. The front of a couple of ribs on the boy. The problem is we don't know how much these might be due to natural degeneration, with them being in the ground so long. It can't be used as direct evidence that would stand up in court, it's all too unreliable.'

'What about their ages?' asked Marsh.

'We think they were both about seven when they died. A couple of forensic bone specialists have been in to see them, and they thought so too. Interestingly, they both also thought they might have been twins. Apparently there are clues in the shape of the skull and some joints. This is only conjecture, of course. The DNA profiles will provide definite proof and you won't know the results of that until, when?'

'Next week,' Sophie replied, her eyes on the two skeletons. 'So there's nothing much for us to go on at the moment?'

Goodall shook his head. 'No. If they were murdered, it wasn't down to any hard blows. And I don't think they were badly mistreated, not over a prolonged period of time anyway. The bone density is good, so they were both well fed and probably had good general levels of fitness. If they were killed deliberately, it was due to soft tissue damage. But let's face it, most child murder is by smothering, strangulation or the like. We can't rule those out, nor can we rule out poisoning. What I mean is, the pathological evidence gives no direct clues as to the cause of death. Sorry.'

Sophie didn't reply. She was thinking about all those things that make a child's life so special, so unique in the memory. Was there anyone alive who still mourned for these two poor souls, who still remembered them as infants and toddlers? She looked at Barry.

'I can guess what you're thinking, ma'am,' he said. 'I feel it too.'

She sighed. 'Okay. You've done what you can, Benny. We should get going. We'll need to think of other avenues that might lead us to their story.' She reached out and, with a gloved finger, briefly touched the forehead of each skull in turn, as if making them a silent promise.

* * *

Back in the incident room, Rae Gregson had been working on a chart that listed the occupants of Finch Cottage, stretching back to the middle years of the twentieth century. Linked to it were similar charts that showed who had lived in the two neighbouring properties. This had been easy for the house to the west of the cottage: the couple still living there had owned the attractive, detached house since 1980, and had been very helpful in identifying many of the residents of Finch Cottage itself. They had never had a good view of the garden, though. Tall shrubs and trees close to the fence had always obscured their view. The list of residents for the cottage on the east side had several gaps. The chart for Finch cottage itself was nearly complete, but it had one yawning gap: a four month period at the start of 1995. The only thing the neighbours had been able to remember was that the occupiers during those few months were reclusive. They'd only met the mother twice and had seen children on just a couple of occasions. They'd assumed that the father worked away from home.

Rae's task had not been made any easier by the fact that the estate agency that had handled the cottage rental had long since gone out of business. It had proved impossible to find any paperwork for that period. The people renting the property during those months had never registered on the voters' roll. Council tax had, of course, been paid by the landlord. The knowledgeable neighbour had told Rae that she thought all administrative work for the property lettings had been carried out by the agency. The owners, whoever they'd been, would have known next to nothing about the occupants.

Rae got up from her chair and walked to the window. She stared out through the trees, across the Weymouth Road to the large public car park opposite. There's got to be a way around this, she thought. But what? She watched as a family crossed the road into the car park. The parents were loaded down with shopping bags, desperately trying to keep hold of their two children. Seeing the youngsters triggered a thought: maybe she should temporarily give up trying to trace the house's occupants, and start work on the local schools. She would start with the local primary school. Rae reached for the phone.

* * *

'You're asking a lot, aren't you?' The head teacher looked at Rae over the reading glasses perched on the end of her nose. 'That's a long time ago. There's nobody left on the staff from those days, not even the school secretary.'

'There's a chance they might have been twins. That's why we wondered if someone might remember. It might have stuck in someone's mind. You wouldn't still have any records dating back that far, would you?'

'No. It probably predates the time when we computerised our data, so the records would have been on paper. Anyway, we're not allowed to keep data that long, computerised or not. It would break the Data Protection Act, wouldn't it? We get rid of it all every couple of years, which is what the law requires. I'm sorry I can't be more helpful.'

As Rae left the office she was waylaid by the secretary. 'You might want to speak to Tina Wroughton. She's the senior dinner lady, and has been here for more than twenty years. She knows a lot of the children really well. It's worth a try before you go. You'll find her clearing up in the kitchens.' She glanced at her watch. 'You've probably got about ten minutes before she leaves.'

Rae hurried across the small playground to the kitchen. She could hear the clatter of cutlery being sorted and put away.

'Hello?' she called. 'Tina Wroughton? Hello?'

A fair-haired lady in her late fifties came to the door, wiping her hands on her apron. Rae explained why she was there.

Tina frowned. 'Goodness, that was a long time ago and my memory isn't what it was. But Pat, the secretary, was right. I suppose I have been here a long time. Probably too long. And I do get to know a lot of the kiddies. You can't help it, serving up their lunches day after day. Clearing up the mess they leave.' She laughed. 'But twenty years ago? I'm not sure. Do you fancy a cup of tea? The kettle's just boiled, and it might help to get my brain working.'

They sat in the kitchen sipping from mugs, while Rae watched the frowns criss-crossing Tina's face. At last she looked at Rae.

'You know, I think there was. A boy and a girl. Twins. I couldn't say how long ago, but it was ages. They were here, then they were gone. Very sudden, I think. That's all I remember. George Bramshaw would have been headmaster at the time. He retired about five years ago. He might remember.'

'Do you know if he lives locally?'

'No. He moved back to Salisbury when he retired. It was where he came from originally. I suppose he'll still be there.'

Rae thanked Tina for the tea and information and left. Salisbury. It would be, wouldn't it? She knew she'd end up back there one day, but it could have waited a bit longer, surely.

* * *

'So, as far as I can see we have six avenues open to us, though we're still waiting for the results of three of them. That's the children's DNA, the skull and possible facial reconstruction, and the forensic examination of the grave area. That last one should be in soon I would think, though I don't know what it will be able to tell us. Meanwhile, we have Rae's chart of previous occupants, these poems and this retired head teacher, if he's still around.' Sophie was perched on the corner of a table, summarising the day's developments.

'He is, ma'am. I managed to track him down just now and phoned him. He's available tomorrow morning. In Salisbury, where he lives.'

'Can you take that, Rae? Phone the locals to let them know that you're in town. Maybe do that just now? Didn't you used to work in Wiltshire?'

'Yes.'

Sophie saw her expression. 'Rae, if you're not happy about it, I can get someone else to do it.'

'No, ma'am. Leave it with me. I'll be fine, honestly.'

Sophie nodded. 'Barry, can you chase up the forensic people? They should have sifted through all that soil by now. It's Wednesday, for God's sake. They've had the stuff since Saturday.'

'It's what you said, ma'am. It's not a current case, so it's probably been pushed further back in the queue. And I don't think Dave Nash would have made that decision. Someone higher up decides the priorities.'

'Well, if something doesn't come in by the end of the week, I'll start complaining. That leaves these poems.' She pointed to the plastic wallet. 'I've been thinking about them since we left the vicar's house. I've been trying to recall the lessons I had at school on analysing poetry. In terms of their technique, I'd guess they're competent at an amateur level, but aren't the work of a serious poet.'

'Why's that?' asked Marsh.

'They lack subtlety. They're too . . . in your face. The most important thing for the writer was letting out his or her emotions, maybe after years of suppression. They had more of a therapeutic than a literary value. That's my guess.'

'But some of the words sound quite technical, ma'am.'

'Arsenous in the second poem. Containing arsenic. Clever, I thought. Particularly as a counterpoint to sulphurous, which comes immediately before it. They're certainly not written by an ignoramus, that's obvious. The author is most definitely knowledgeable about poetry. And the imagery and feel is very twentieth century. Were they written by the person we're looking for? I'd say yes, probably. The mention of rugs and parcels, death and babies. It's just too close. So how do we go about using them?' She paused, thinking. 'Barry, can you identify any local poetry or writing groups? We'll probably be looking for someone who was living on this side of Dorchester since they chose the local parish newsletter, but we can't be absolutely sure. Someone middle-aged or older I'd guess, but not necessarily so.'

Just then Theresa Jackson came into the room. She stood, rather nervously, just inside the door. Sophie beckoned to her. 'What is it?'

'Something for you only, ma'am,' she said. She followed Sophie into her office, where she told her about Jill Freeman's strange behaviour.

'You were right to tell me, Theresa, and well spotted. It probably has no bearing on the case, though. In fact I can't see how it can be connected. But you do need to bear it in mind, as the family liaison officer. If she's seeing someone and it comes out into the open just now, with that young girl in such a state, you may have your work cut out. Do a check on the car registration so that we have it on record but don't follow it up any further, okay? Please let me know if the situation changes.'

As the young constable left the office, Sophie's phone rang.

It was Louisa Mugomba. Sophie listened carefully, asked a few questions, then replaced the handset. She stared at it for a while, then walked to the main incident room.

'I've just had Louisa Mugomba on the phone,' she told Barry and Rae. 'And she's come up with a real puzzler. She fed all the dimensions from both skulls into her software, and they indicate the strong possibility that the two children were at least partly Asiatic. Apparently there are clues in the shape of the cheekbones. She warned me that some experts dispute that racial background can be accurately identified from the skull shape, but we now have to consider the fact that the children were not of European origin.'

'But does that alter anything, ma'am?' Rae asked.

'Of course not. But if it's also suggested by their DNA profiles, it may help us to identify them more easily. And that's still our first priority. Once we know who they were, we can begin to puzzle out what happened to them.'

CHAPTER 10: SALISBURY

Thursday morning

Rae changed down a gear, rounded the tight bend and started the descent towards the village of Coombe Bissett, nestling cosily in the Ebble valley. She always thought Salisbury started here, with the cathedral spire visible even from this far away. It felt weird coming back. She'd spent almost a year in Salisbury, as a very unhappy, apparently male detective battling against the demons of gender dysphoria. She would have preferred to forget this part of her life, but here she was. Salisbury is one of the most beautiful cities in the country. The people are friendly and cheerful, showing that amiable, gentle approach to life that is so typical of the West Country. Rae's feelings about the place were entirely due to her own history, and to the small-minded personality of one of her bosses. The man hadn't even been local. 'That tosspot from Swindon,' as some of the local beat officers had described him. Where was he now? She'd heard that he'd moved on, and was a Chief Superintendent somewhere. God help the poor souls who worked under him.

The traffic slowed to a crawl for the last mile or so, but the delay was almost worth it. The stunning bulk of the cathedral dominated the city centre and its glorious spire glinted in the morning sunshine. For me it even beats the nearby Stonehenge, thought Rae. This is the more perfect example of humanity's creative genius.

Rae turned off the ring road and headed for the eastern suburbs, arriving several minutes early. She sat in the car, gathering her thoughts, then picked up her bag and made her way through a bright-red wooden gate to the front door.

The man seemed almost to twinkle at her.

'I saw you coming,' George Bramshaw said. 'I was in the front room and spotted your car draw up. You didn't need to wait out there. You could have come straight in.'

The hint of mischief in his eyes matched the smile playing at the corners of his mouth. Rae looked around her. The hallway gleamed at her, slightly quaint and spotlessly clean. He waved her through into a small, neat sitting room. A pot of coffee, several mugs and a plate of biscuits were set out on a low table.

'Sit down, please. I don't get attractive young visitors very often, so this is a treat for me. You'll need to remind me what you want to know. I've forgotten already.' He smiled at her.

She guessed that he hadn't forgotten at all, but was teasing her for some reason. 'There were two children who might have gone missing from your school about twenty years ago. They could well have been twins, aged about six or seven. There's also a chance that they might have been Asian, wholly or partly. Possibly Chinese or something like that.'

'Ah yes, now I remember what you said on the phone. I'll pour us some coffee and tell you what I dredged up from my rather blurry memory. Have a biscuit if you want one.'

Rae selected a chocolate-coated biscuit and took a bite, suddenly hungry.

'Good choice. They're one of my favourites,' Bramshaw said, watching her take half the biscuit in one mouthful. 'I do recall something about two children who might be the ones you're looking for. But first, can I ask you something about your boss? The detective chief inspector you mentioned on the phone? Sophie something?'

Rae paused in her chewing, puzzled. 'DCI Allen. Why?'

'Because thirty-five years ago I think I may have taught her in her primary school, in Bristol. She would have been about ten then and I was in my second teaching job after qualifying. If it is her, and I think it is, Sophie Carswell would have been her name then. I found out that the Sophie I remember had gone on to study law, joined the police and has ended up in Dorset. Is it her? Did she come from Bristol originally? She was the brightest child I ever came across in that school. She knew her own mind, though.'

'Could be. I'll mention it to her when I get back to Dorchester, shall I?' Rae didn't want to give too much away. Was he trying to winkle out personal information for some reason? 'If it is her I'm sure she'll be in touch. If not, I'll let you know. Is that okay?'

'Of course.' He took a sip of coffee. 'Now, I've been giving a lot of thought to what you said on the telephone, and I may be able to help you. There were two children, twins, a boy and a girl. They were half Chinese, as you wondered. I only met their mother, and she was English. The boy's name was Kenneth and the girl's Jasmine. They were with us for only one term, in about 1995, although I'm not absolutely sure of the year. But for the life of me I can't remember the surname.'

'Maybe it was a bit hard to remember if it was Chinese.'

'But I don't think it was. Chinese, I mean. I have a feeling that the surname they used was British. Anyway, they left suddenly at the end of term. I seem to remember the mother saying that she was moving to America.'

'Which term do you think it was?'

'The fact that it stuck in my mind suggests that they didn't start in September. I don't think they left at the end of the school year. My impression is that they were only with us during the spring term and left at Easter.'

'Can you remember anything about them? What they were like as pupils?'

He paused, evidently thinking hard. 'Well, they were only with us for about three months, remember, so we wouldn't have found out much about them in that short time. As far as I recall they were a really nice couple of kids. The boy played piano and the girl flute. They did a duet for us at one of our assemblies. That's how I remembered them after you called yesterday. It had stuck in my mind. They were talented for a couple of eight-year-olds.'

'And you didn't ask why they left?'

'Well, I'm pretty certain that the mother told us when they started that they'd only be with us for a few months. She then came in at the end of term and confirmed that she'd just landed a job somewhere else, so they'd be moving during the holidays. She took some of their work with them, along with a summary report for their new school.' He put down his coffee. 'Anyway, you haven't told me why you want to know about them. I suppose it must be something fairly serious.'

Rae looked at him, astonished. 'You mean you don't know? You haven't guessed? Don't you watch the news or read the newspapers?'

'I've been away for a fortnight's holiday, a cruise in the Caribbean. I only got back the day before yesterday. Why?'

'Last weekend we dug up the bodies of two small children in a back garden in Dorchester. They'd been there for about twenty years. I assumed you'd guessed the reason for the call.'

His face turned pale.

'Oh God. That's dreadful.' He took a breath. 'And you think that's why they didn't come back to school? That something happened to them and they didn't get to their new home? That's awful beyond words. This is a complete shock.'

'If the mother was English, the father was probably Chinese, at least partly. You didn't ever meet him?'

Bramshaw shook his head. He seemed to shiver. 'No,' he whispered. 'There was never any indication of a father being around for the children. None ever appeared at any event we held, as far as I can remember.'

Rae finished her coffee. 'We have a facial reconstruction expert working on their probable appearances. Once it's complete I'd like you to see the images, just to confirm. We may be barking up the wrong tree entirely, and if so we need to know.'

He nodded. His cheerful demeanour had vanished without trace. 'Is this the kind of stuff that your boss, my Sophie Carswell possibly, has to deal with?'

'Perhaps not always quite as harrowing as this case, but broadly, yes.'

'How does she cope?'

Rae shrugged. 'Mental toughness. We have to try to shut out our emotions, and just get on with the investigation.'

'It must take a toll, though.'

'Possibly.' Rae was unwilling to say more. I've only just met the man, she thought to herself.

'Please tell her I was asking about her. If it is her, will you ask her if we can meet?'

'Yes, I can do that.' Rae stood up. 'Thanks for giving me your time, and for the coffee and biscuits.'

'Just a minute.' Bramshaw disappeared into the kitchen, and came back with the rest of the biscuits, still in the tin.

'For her, even if it isn't her. And you. You both deserve them.'

* * *

Rae looked around her at the ancient, stone walls and listened to the chatter of voices. She was in the refectory of Salisbury Cathedral, one of her favourite places to eat, and had just finished lunch. She looked across the table at Stevie Harrison, one of her ex-colleagues. He was using a crust of bread to wipe the last remaining traces of gravy from his plate.

'You always did enjoy your food, Stevie. I'm surprised you haven't ballooned to twice your size since we last met.'

Harrison laughed. 'Sharon won't let me. I'm only allowed chips once a week and I have to count the calories and exercise every day. It's like I'm living in my own private police state.'

'Is it worth it though?' Rae smiled.

'Oh yes. I feel good about myself and I do get my rewards. She's really hot – in every way.' He winked at her.

'I should be horrified at such a comment, but I'm not. I'm happy for you.'

'Nothing yet for you in the romance department? Or is that too personal a question?'

'No, it isn't, not from you. And no, nothing yet. The problem is I just don't know what I want. Now I'm a woman, I don't know whether I want a straight relationship with a man or a lesbian one with another woman. I think my mind is still sorting itself out and getting to grips with the new me. But time is ticking by.'

'Get stuck in, Rae, that's my advice. Life is for living, after all. It wouldn't be the end of the world, would it, if you dabbled a bit and found something wasn't for you? What's to lose?'

Rae nodded. 'It's partly because I'm so happy with my life. I'm kind of basking in a warm glow all the time and I don't want to spoil it. It's such a new experience for me, being happy in my own skin.' She drained her tea. 'Where is he now by the way, the Swindon Tosspot?'

'I'm not totally sure. He went for promotion about the same time as you left the team. It's unbelievable. How can someone keep getting promoted just to get rid of them? You'd think it was a made-up story. What's the quickest way to shift someone like that out of harm's way? Give him a quick promotion into yet another desk job. Last rumour I heard was that he was applying for a post in Dorset. He had nowhere left to hide in Wiltshire. He'd pissed everybody off, from the Chief Constable down to the tea-ladies.'

Rae tensed, horrified at the thought that her erstwhile nemesis was working somewhere near her. 'What? I didn't know that. Are you sure?'

'I've no idea where he actually ended up. They'd have been nuts to take him on, but he went somewhere. That's all I know. We had a night out to celebrate after he'd gone.' Stevie suddenly looked dreamy. 'That's where I got off with Sharon. She was in the same pub, with a couple of friends. The luckiest night of my life. That's what she keeps telling me.'

Rae laughed. 'Is it true?'

'Probably, yes. She's a woman and a half, I can tell you. Not size-wise, she's dinky. But every other way.'

Rae looked at her watch. 'I'd better be going, Stevie. It was great meeting up like this. Can we do it again if I'm up this way? Or maybe have an evening out? It only takes me an hour or so to drive from Wareham.'

'Yeah, why not? I had visions of you looking like a bloke in a frock, you know, sitting with your legs apart, but you look brilliant. I'd never have known if I hadn't already, if that makes sense. I could bring a couple of pals along. You never know. You might fancy one of them.'

Rae laughed. 'Let me think about that, okay?' She leant across, gave him a peck on the cheek and left the restaurant. There was a lot to think about, not least that she'd have to find out whether Stevie's news about the Tosspot was correct. Was her honeymoon period in Dorset over so soon?

CHAPTER 11: SMOKING IN THE SHADOWS

Friday morning

St Paul's Parish Church was an old building with an air of quiet grace. Before the installation of an effective central heating system several decades earlier, it had been well-known for its chilly interior. The current minister, Tony Younger, had made it his priority to make the building more welcoming, and the main improvement had been glaringly obvious: to counteract the incessant winter cold. His efforts had made a difference, with attendances at the regular Sunday services bucking the national trend and actually increasing.

He was in the church now, paying a quick visit before breakfast in order to have a few words with the cleaner. But the figure standing looking at some of the plaques was certainly no cleaner. He waved as he recognised who it was.

'I wondered who you were at first,' he said. 'It's unusual to get visitors this early in the morning. Are you here for any particular reason, Chief Inspector?'

'Not really. I didn't have time to pop in and explore after I saw you a couple of days ago. I just wanted to get a feel for the place. It's not a problem, is it?'

'Not at all,' he answered. 'Particularly since Dorothy, the cleaner, should be around somewhere. Visitors are always welcome, whether I've already met them or not. I try my best to operate an open-door policy, although that has its problems. But if a church is not accessible to people when they most need it, can it really fulfil its purpose? We keep the heating on low all the time during the winter for that reason. If some of the town's poor and needy can escape from the chill outside by spending an hour or two in here, then that's fine by me. And when some of my less charitable parishioners raise objections, I remind them that we are Christians and have a duty to look after those who are less fortunate than ourselves.'

'That's very worthy, Reverend,' Sophie said. 'If I were religious, you'd have my complete agreement. Sadly, I'm not.'

'Sadly for who?'

She sighed. 'Sadly for my appreciation of old churches. It restricts my opportunities somewhat, although that's largely due to my own guilt complex. Well, one of my guilt complexes. I have so many that I've lost count.'

'You sound as if you need an opportunity to unburden yourself. Not that I'm offering you a session. You're not one of my parishioners, and I'd be afraid of what you might tell me.'

'Don't worry. I've had therapy, and not all of it was helpful. But some sessions did help. They didn't remove my guilt complexes, but at least I've learned to live with them. Could you show me around? That's if you have the time of course?'

He relaxed a little. 'Yes, of course. But only on condition that you have some breakfast with me afterwards.' He glanced at his watch. 'I have about ten minutes to spare before I need to eat, then I have a morning meeting. It's Friday, so it's bacon sandwich day. Does that sound okay? I have it all ready in the kitchen.'

'That's the best chat-up line I've heard in ages,' said Sophie. 'What woman could say no to an invitation like that? My husband only cooks me porridge in the mornings. Maybe a personnel change is in order.'

Tony Younger grinned boyishly. Usually all he had to deal with were the humdrum concerns of his parishioners. Conversing with this very attractive, intelligent and self-aware woman was like a breath of fresh air, particularly at this time in the morning. He took her arm and led her into the depths of the church for a "whistle-stop tour," as he put it.

* * *

When she heard the main door open, Dorothy Kitson had quietly moved out of sight behind a column. The church cleaner watched the vicar and his visitor make their way towards the altar. She slipped off her shoes and tiptoed to a side door, slipping out into the chilly morning air. Chief Inspector? Was that what he said? What was she doing here, walking around with the vicar, arms linked like that? She slid back into her shoes and quietly made her way around the outside of the church building to the secluded north end. There she hurriedly pulled a cigarette out of a packet in her coat pocket, lit it and drew in several lungs-full of the calming smoke. She hadn't expected this. But then, she hadn't expected any of it. It was all a nightmare. What should she do? She realised that she was crying. Great streams of tears slid down her face and landed on her work overall. She took out a tissue and blew her nose as quietly as she could. It would be a disaster if they saw her, and the vicar brought that policewoman over to chat. She shrank back into the shadows behind a buttress and waited, shivering. She lit another cigarette.

* * *

'Ma'am, I've just traced another resident of Finch Cottage from nearly eighteen years ago. I've been in touch with her and she'd be happy to see us, this morning if we want. She still lives in Dorchester, but down-sized to a smaller house after her husband died.'

'Good work, Rae. Get on with it as soon as you can so that we can either log it as possibly useful or reject it completely.

By the way, well done for yesterday. I know I said so in our briefing, but it might end up being the best line of inquiry we have. If you hadn't bothered to search out that dinner lady on Wednesday afternoon, we'd be nowhere.' Sophie looked more closely at Rae. 'Are those new glasses you're wearing?'

Rae nodded. 'What do you think? They're only for close work.'

'They suit your colour really well, and the style is just right for your face shape. Maybe I should get you to talk to Jade. She might need to wear glasses, and she's not happy about it. We're going clothes shopping tomorrow morning and I was intending to steer her past a couple of opticians' shops, just so that she can see that there are some stylish ones out there. Maybe I don't need to with you looking so good in them.'

How does she do it? Rae thought as she collected her coat and headed towards the car park. In just a minute or two of conversation, she's made me feel special, needed. God knows what this unit would be like if someone like the Swindon Tosspot was in charge.

She drove north, pulled up outside a bungalow on a quiet side street and made her way up the path. She was greeted at the door by a stout woman in her late fifties, peering at her through pebble lenses.

'Come in, dear,' she said.

Jessica Hart ushered Rae into her living room.

'Mrs Hart, I'd just like to check a few facts with you about the time you lived in Finch Cottage. I think you were there in 1996, is that correct?'

'Yes. It was spring when we moved in, May.' She looked at Rae. 'Those children's bodies. Were they there when we lived in the cottage?'

Rae nodded. 'It looks like it. They were probably there about twenty years, but we're still waiting for confirmation from the experts.'

Jessica's hand went to her mouth. Her voice was muted. 'I can't believe it. It's such a lovely place but it was hiding a nightmare like that. I haven't been able to sleep properly since I found out. But I never liked the cellar. It made me feel nervous. That's why I phoned in. I hated going down there, but I never knew why. I've never felt like that about other cellars. Whenever I looked at that metal ring set into the wall, I shuddered. It was creepy.'

Rae looked at her in surprise. 'I don't think we spotted that, Mrs Hart. Where was it?'

'It wasn't easy to see. It was in the far corner, quite far from the light. It would be easy to miss.'

Rae made an entry in her notebook. 'Mrs Hart, from what you've said, you didn't own the cottage. Do you know who the owners were?'

'No. Our contact was the agency in town — Murchison's. They had an office just off the High Street. I don't think they're there anymore.'

'So, whose name should I look for in the records, Mrs Hart? I noticed it was you on the report I found.'

'It was my name on the rental contract. Bob was just no good with anything official, so I always looked after that side of things. I worked in the office at one of the big stores so I coped better than him with paperwork.'

'And how long did you live at Finch Cottage?'

'We moved there in 1996. Bob lost his job and we couldn't afford the mortgage repayments on the house we owned. I got a job in a shop in town. We stayed there until the autumn a couple of years later. By then I'd been promoted to supervisor and Bob found a job with a local joinery business. We wanted to save for our own place again, so we moved to somewhere smaller and cheaper. Finch Cottage was lovely for the boys but the rent was too high.'

Rae waited. Eventually she said, 'is Bob still here, Mrs Hart?'

Jessica said quietly, 'he was killed in a work accident. I got a good settlement through the courts because the firm were negligent. That's why I've got this little place now. But it's no compensation for the loneliness or the sadness, is it? I still work, just for the company really, but only part-time now.'

CHAPTER 12: CAFÉ CHAT

Saturday morning

'Mum. All these clothes. They're so, well . . . middle-aged.'

Jade was looking critically at the rails displaying some of the latest spring styles for women.

'In case you hadn't noticed, Jade, I am middle-aged, or fast approaching it.' Sophie continued to half-heartedly slide the hangers apart.

Her daughter snorted. 'You'll never be middle-aged, Mum, not even when you're sixty. We know you too well. This stuff,' she gestured expansively, 'is just not *you*. Not yet anyway. What we need is a boutique. Somewhere with clothes that are a bit edgy. Not this stuff. You wear this kind of gear to an old folks' home or a funeral.' She took the few items that Sophie was holding and put them back on the rail. She wagged her finger at her mother. 'These clothes are not for you. Really and truly they aren't.'

Secretly relieved, Sophie admitted defeat. 'Okay. Let's do it your way, but remember it's work-wear I'm looking for. Take me to the shop of your choice, Little Miss Fashion Expert. Show me what you think I should be wearing when

I head off to work each morning. A short, flimsy, skater skirt perhaps? Gold lamé hot-pants? I give in.'

'Stop it, Mum. People are listening. This is getting embarrassing.'

The two women left the department store and walked along the street. This isn't going as I planned, Sophie thought. She looked at her watch and gasped. 'I wanted to be finished by now,' she complained.

'You can't rush these things, Mum. You should know that by now. Someone in your position needs to choose the right clothes very carefully. You're a role model, you know . . .' Jade suddenly realised that her mother was no longer listening and had stopped moving. They'd just passed a café and Sophie was peering in through the window. She grabbed Jade's arm and pushed at the door.

'Coffee time,' she announced loudly as she pulled the teenager inside. They made for the nearest empty table and sat down. A waitress came over to their table and took out her order pad.

'Hello, Lily,' Sophie said. 'I thought it was you when I looked through the window. What are you doing working here in Dorchester?'

Lily Dalton peered at Sophie and then her elfin features broke into a broad smile. 'Chief Inspector! It's nice to see you. I applied for that job you told me about, at the café in Wareham, but it was taken. But the owner also has this place, and she offered me a job here. It wasn't very convenient but after what you said, I thought I needed a clean break. I took the plunge and moved here.'

'Well, you're looking a lot more relaxed than you were last autumn. Has the move worked out well for you?'

'So far. Early days still, I suppose, but I like it here. I'm sharing a small flat just outside the town centre. And I've made some friends.' Lily paused. 'Are you on that case with the two buried children? I suppose I shouldn't be asking you about it, but it makes me shudder. Most of the customers are talking about it. I tell them I know the person who'll be running the investigation, but I don't think many of them believe me. I don't suppose you can tell me anything?'

Sophie gave her a wry smile. 'Uh-uh. Can we order some coffee, please? And a couple of cream cakes?'

Lily wrote down the order. One of the customers passed them on her way out. 'Bye Dorothy,' said Lily. 'One of our regulars,' she explained.

Once the waitress had left them, Jade leaned over and whispered to her mother. 'That was a bit curious, Mum. That woman who just left was happily reading a magazine until she heard the words, "Chief Inspector." She stared across here, saw me watching, then gulped down her drink and hurried out. She deliberately kept her back to you all the time. Peculiar or what?'

Sophie laughed. 'Maybe she's been dodging her tax payments, Jade, or she's been smuggling illegal immigrants into the country. Or maybe she saw the time and realised she was late for something. There could be any number of reasons for why she wanted to hurry out. Don't get paranoid.'

'Well you didn't see the look on her face.'

'And I also know that if I'd acted on even half of the times you thought someone was behaving in a suspicious manner, much of the population of this country would be behind bars. Or, more probably, I'd be out of a job.'

When Lily arrived with their coffees Jade asked about the woman who'd just left, ignoring her mother's glare.

'Dorothy? She comes in here a couple of times a week, but I don't know much about her. She told me she does the cleaning for St Paul's church and does cleaning and ironing work for some people who live in that area. I don't even know her surname. Why?'

'I think she dropped a handkerchief. Look, under the chair.'

'I'll keep it for her. She'll be in next week sometime.'

The waitress moved away, out of earshot. 'Jade,' hissed her mother, 'that was unforgivable. For goodness sake, what does it take to get through to you?'

'I'm just being a good citizen, helping the police. Honestly, Mum, she really was acting weird. At least you know something about her now. St Paul's. Isn't that where the kiddies' bodies were found? And she's a cleaner in the area? I bet she's hiding something.'

Sophie held her head in her hands. 'God, this is a nightmare.'

'Actually, Mum, I do need your help. It's something quite serious, at school. I've dug a bit of a hole for myself, and I don't know how to get out of it.'

Sophie shook her head slowly. She sighed. 'What is it this time?'

'Well, you know that I'm a prefect and we encourage younger pupils to come to us with their problems if they're not sure about going to a teacher? I look after a couple of year seven classes. They're the youngest groups in the school. I've been doing some work at lunchtimes with them about FGM, you know, the way many girls get cut in some African countries. It's because of Hannah coming to Dorchester with the charity group to give that talk on Sunday. She asked me to help publicise it. I've been using a few of the posters that she sent. You remember that Dad took some in to his school? Anyway, one of the girls came to find me yesterday afternoon after school was over. She's a little black girl and she's worried about her best friend, Safiyo. Safiyo has discovered that her family are taking her back to Africa next week for a short visit. She's convinced that the visit is to get her cut. Apparently Safiyo is terrified and doesn't know what to do.' Jade paused. 'The problem is that to get the story out of Asli, I had to promise I wouldn't tell any of the teachers. But if I don't do something, the poor little thing could be taken out of the country and mutilated. I hardly slept last night, worrying about it. What can I do?'

'It's a child protection issue, Jade. In a case like that, any responsible adult who becomes aware of the problem is legally obliged to report it. Verbal promises made to a child no longer have any weight. You're technically not a responsible adult, so the law doesn't apply to you. But you've told me now, so I have to act, and I have to do so right away, without delay. I'll need the details from you, including all the names, so get your brain in gear.' She looked at the clock on the wall and took out her mobile phone from her bag. 'So much for our retail therapy.' Sophie shook her head.

'Sorry, Mum.' Jade looked worried. 'So what will happen? Will she have to go into care? That would be awful.'

'It's unlikely. The child safety officers will probably get a court order issued forbidding her parents from taking her out of the country. They'll probably visit with the police to make sure the order is enforced, and in case family members try to resist.'

'So she's likely to stay with her family? Isn't that dangerous?'

'Not usually. The council people will assess the risk, but with FGM a court order is usually enough. It's better for the girl to remain at home with her parents. The problem is cultural, and the parents often mistakenly feel they are doing the right thing.'

'Would it help if I came along? I feel responsible somehow.'

Sophie thought about this. 'I don't think that's realistic, is it, Jade? It's thoughtful of you, but let's leave it for the right people to deal with it.'

'I know she's going to be really upset.' She looked mournfully at her mother. 'Can't you be the police presence? Then I could be around and there'd be a familiar face.'

'No, I couldn't. It has to be one of the designated team. I can't break the rules, Jade, not even for you.' She consulted her watch, and then tapped in the number on her phone. 'This could take some time, so we might have to skip the rest of the morning. No boutique, I'm afraid.'

Jade sighed. 'Let's face it, Mum. That wasn't going to work anyway, was it?'

It only took half an hour to make the arrangements. Sophie knew who to contact and Jade was at hand to supply the details.

'Maybe I'd better pop round and see little Asli later,' Jade said. 'She'll hear about it soon enough, but it might be better coming from me. I hope she won't be too angry with me.'

'Jade, why do you think she told you about it? Clearly she wanted you to do something. What was the point in telling you otherwise? Particularly if she's seen that you're linked to the anti-FGM campaign at school. By all means go and see her, but don't be apologetic. She did the right thing in telling you, and you did the right thing in telling me. Though I don't see why you couldn't have gone to one of your teachers yesterday afternoon, instead of waiting until now.'

'I told you, she made me promise not to tell them. Anyway, we were in the bus queue and I'd have missed my bus. And you know what teachers are like on a Friday afternoon, Mum. They're all out of school like a shot. The place was probably empty.'

'That is a gross exaggeration, young lady. You know very well that your father never gets home before you, even on a Friday. And that's with you meeting young Jamie for a coffee in town most afternoons before you come home.'

'How did you know about that?'

It was Sophie's turn to smirk. 'My spies are everywhere. Now let's get a move on. I think the clothes in that first shop are calling to me to come back for a second look. I don't want this morning to be a total wash-out.'

CHAPTER 13: WALKIES, CUDDLES AND MUESLI

Saturday, Week 2

The South Dorset Walkers' Club met every second Saturday, weather permitting, for a ramble around one of the county's many beauty spots or nature reserves. The members were primarily middle-aged and reasonably fit but preferred easy, chatty walks rather than the more strenuous treks of the other local rambling groups. That was how the secretary justified the club's existence in a county that already had nearly two dozen rambling groups.

'I suppose we're a group of gossipers who also like walking, rather than the other way round,' she would explain with a wry smile.

On this particular Saturday morning, just before noon, the motley collection of ramblers were on the penultimate leg of their walk. Having struggled around the windswept cliffs of St Aldhelm's Head, they were heading inland past Winspit towards a welcome refreshment rest at The Square and Compass in the picturesque village of Worth Matravers. John Wethergill slowed as he heard footsteps drawing alongside him. He half turned to see the attractive figure of the group's newest member coming level with him. He ran his hand through his hair, hoping that it wasn't too untidy. Maybe he should have worn a hat after all. 'Hello,' he said, trying to think of something witty and original to say, but failing.

'Hi,' she said. 'I'd better introduce myself. I'm Pauline Stopley.' She struggled slightly with a glove but finally managed to slip it off, holding out a slender hand.

John pulled off his glove and grasped her hand firmly. 'John Wethergill. Bit tired, a bit bored and looking forward to a pint.'

She laughed and wrestled with her glove, this time to get it back on. 'Maybe these are a bit small, after all. I wondered about buying the medium size, but vanity got the better of me.'

'It's a terrible thing, vanity, isn't it? But I think it has an important role to play in our self-esteem.'

'That sounds very impressive. Can I steal it from you?' She smiled at him, her dark eyes glinting mischievously in the midday sunshine.

'I think you must be our new member. Harriet said that someone new was coming today. Did she mean you?'

'I expect so. I just fancied the opportunity to see some of the countryside. I've only been back in Dorset a few months. Are you local?'

'Yes. I own a DIY shop in Dorchester. I've lived in the county most of my life, and so did my ancestors. Dorset born and Dorset bred, I suppose you could say.'

'I don't see anything wrong with that.' She looked around. 'Do we have much further to go? I could do with a pick-me-up. A gin and tonic would be nice.'

'About a mile, I think. I must warn you that you might get some disapproving looks over your choice of drink. This pub is known for miles around for the quality of its beers and ciders. They even brew their own.'

She looked coolly at him. 'I couldn't give a toss what people think. It'll be a gin and tonic for me no matter what.'

He held up his hands in mock surrender. 'That's fine. I just thought you ought to know.'

Her face softened. 'Sorry. I over-reacted there, I think.'

* * *

Once they reached the village, half of the group made directly for the car park, back to family and other commitments. Of those who did visit the pub, most had just a small drink and a hurried pie or pasty before heading off. Pauline and John soon found themselves alone at the table. They'd taken their outdoor jackets off, and Wethergill was casting surreptitious, admiring glances at the woman opposite. She had a good figure and her clothes were rather more stylish than those the ramblers usually wore. She'd obviously brushed her hair when she visited the loo, and its dark length fell to below her shoulders.

'How do you spend your time?' asked Wethergill.

'I'm a regional manager for the Arts Council, so I'm closely involved in fund-raising and the allocation of grants. I've recently got a promotion into the Wessex region, so that's why I've moved here, to Dorchester in fact. I've just bought a flat in town. Where is your shop?'

'Just off the High Street. I live above it. We're not rich but I make enough to pay the bills and live quite comfortably.'

'We? Are you married?'

'No, but I'm in a sort of relationship. I was married a long time ago, but that ended badly, so I've steered clear ever since.'

'Doesn't your partner like walking?'

'Not really. She's back in the Philippines at the moment, visiting her sister. She isn't due to return until next month.'

His words seemed to hang in the air for a few seconds. Did they beckon?

Pauline asked, quietly, 'what are your plans for eating this evening?'

'I was planning to order a Thai takeaway.' Another brief silence.

'Can I join you? I'm at a bit of a loose end.'

‘Of course. You’d be most welcome.’ He wrote an address and phone number on a beer mat and pushed it towards her. She slid it into her pocket without looking at it.

‘Thanks,’ she murmured. ‘I’d better be off. See you later. About eight?’

He nodded. He watched her shapely figure move to the door. He sat on for another ten minutes, finishing a second beer before getting up and making his way to the car park.

* * *

Wethergill looked around the flat. That should do nicely. It was only two days since his cleaner had made her regular Thursday morning visit, but he’d dusted and vacuumed throughout. He’d also washed the kitchen floor and cleaned the fridge. He’d cleaned the toilet with bleach and scrubbed the washbasin and the bath. He’d put a clean under-sheet on the bed and a fresh cover, in a pretty shade of lilac, on the duvet. He checked the bedside table drawer for condoms and paper tissues. He showered and washed his hair, and dressed carefully. An open-neck shirt in mottled grey, black trousers and freshly polished shoes. Everything was ready and there were still twenty minutes to spare.

Then he spotted the photo of Maralit on the shelf above the fireplace. Should he hide it? Or would Pauline expect some kind of photo of his partner? After all, he had been honest about it. The trouble was, it was an old photo, taken when she was still slim and attractive. If she saw the photo Pauline would assume that Maralit still looked like that, and might be put off. He could have swapped it for a more recent one, but he’d never bothered to get any framed since her skin had started ageing, her weight had increased and her personality had turned more waspish. He took the photo down and shut it away in a drawer.

He looked around again. Much better. Right, now for the music. He selected a CD of music by Gershwin. That would do nicely. He sat down and waited for the doorbell to ring.

Pauline was ten minutes late. Probably it was deliberate, thought John. He took her coat, ushered her through to the lounge and offered her a drink. She'd made up her eyes to look sultry, and her dark hair shone in the glow from the dimmed wall lamps. She was wearing a short black dress, shaped to fit her figure. It had an extraordinary embellishment: a gold zip, running from neckline to hem down the front of the dress. John's mouthed dropped open. Pauline tapped his lips with a finger.

'Sorry. You look so lovely,' he said. 'I'll get some ice for your drink. Maybe you could have a look at the takeaway menu. It's on the coffee table.'

He stood in the kitchen, trying to calm his racing thoughts. It wasn't just the dress; he'd spotted small, tell-tale bumps on her thighs. She was wearing stockings and suspenders. It was obvious he wouldn't meet with any resistance to his plans for later in the evening. Maybe he'd hit the jackpot at last. About bloody time.

* * *

The food was nearly all eaten. Pauline ran her tongue around her lips. 'That was delicious,' she said. She stretched out a long leg, ending in a shiny, black, high-heeled shoe. She took another sip of gin.

'Do you like black clothes for evenings?' John asked. 'They look incredibly attractive on you. Your dress is set off beautifully by the gold of the zip.'

She wriggled closer to him on the sofa. 'Would you like to give it a pull to see what happens?'

He leant forward and took the zip's pull tab, tugging gently at it. The front of the dress parted, revealing silky lingerie in black and gold. Her breasts gently rose and fell beneath the shiny fabric. She looked into his eyes. 'Go on,' she said. 'Touch if you want to.'

He pulled the zip further, then ran his palm across her breast. 'Take the zip down further,' she instructed. As he did so, she stood and shook herself free of the dress. She settled back onto the sofa, now so close that he could feel the warmth of her body radiating through the thin silk of her chemise.

She reached down to the waistband of his trousers. 'One good turn with a zip deserves another, don't you think?'

He gasped as her head followed her hand.

'You're wearing silk too. Naughty man.'

He could only manage a groan.

* * *

At eight the next morning she came padding through to the bedroom, carrying two mugs of steaming tea. She was still wearing her silk lingerie and stockings, and looked glorious. John stretched out his arms, and she slid into them with a laugh.

'I hoped you'd stay asleep,' she said. 'I was planning to wake you up by rubbing myself all over you. Then I was going to pass you your cup of tea and see how quickly you would be able to drink it.'

He shook his head, smiling. 'You know, you're amazing. I'd have never guessed on the walk yesterday that we'd be like this the next morning. I just can't quite believe it.'

She pushed her hair out of her eyes. 'Drink your tea, go to the loo, and I'll show you something that will really make your eyes water. It involves your wrists, my stockings and that bed-head. If it works right, we'll both come like express trains.'

* * *

'So tell me about your relationship, John. Should I be feeling guilty?'

They'd just finished a breakfast of muesli and toast and marmalade. Pauline had changed into a pair of trousers and a loose top. She'd brought in an overnight bag the previous night that Wethergill hadn't noticed. He took a sip of tea before he told her.

'Please don't feel guilty at all. I don't. I'm not sure where Maralit and I were going anyway. We needed a break from each other, which is one of the reasons why she decided to visit family back in Manila. It was all a bit sudden, though. She only arranged the trip at the beginning of the week. Apparently one of her sisters is seriously ill with cancer, so Maralit felt she needed to see her before it was too late. She doesn't live here, by the way. She has her own place on the other side of town.'

'So you don't have any children with her?'

'No, nothing as serious as that. She's not the maternal type anyway. She's a career woman. She works for one of the big pharmaceutical companies and earns about five times what I do. She says that children would have got in the way of her career. I suppose that's probably true for most women in the commercial world.'

'How long have you been seeing each other?'

He shrugged. 'About ten years? We were friends for a while before that. I've been worrying about where we were heading for some time now. Her personality seems to have grown harder in recent years. She's not the gentle person she was when we first met. She disagrees and says it's me who's changed. Human nature, I suppose. We always think other people are at fault, never us.'

Pauline nodded. That's my experience too. It was certainly at work in some of my early relationships.'

'Did you have children?'

She shook her head and laughed, grimly. 'The thought of giving birth always brought me out in a rash.'

'And you haven't got a wish to have any? You know?'

She looked at him. 'What do you mean, what do I know?'

He looked embarrassed. 'Well, time's ticking on. That's what I meant.'

'Why don't you say it then? Might I have a yearning for children in the few years of fertility I have left? That's what you meant, isn't it?'

'I was trying to be delicate and I made a mess of it. Sorry.'

'I suppose it's something all women in my position think about, having a child before it's too late. But for me, the age gap would be too big. Some women my age are already grandmothers, for God's sake. And I always end up thinking, what have I got to offer a child? I'm too bloody impatient. I know I am.' She checked her watch, then finished her tea. 'I'll help you clear up and then I'd better be off. I'm meeting someone for the afternoon and need time to get ready.'

'Should I be jealous?'

'Of course. Just to keep you on your toes. Maybe we can meet later in the week? Would you like to?' She carried their dishes to the sink.

'Yes. You know I would.'

'Call me. You have my number.'

'No, I don't.'

She looked at him coolly for a few seconds. Then she shook her head. 'Yes you do. You just haven't looked in the right place yet.'

She went to the hall, slipped her coat on, picked up her bag, gave John a soft, tongued kiss and left. He looked in the bedroom but could see nothing. She'd taken a shower before breakfast, so he checked in the bathroom. There it was, written on the mirror in lipstick: a telephone number followed by an xxx. He walked to the lounge window and peered out at the pavement below. But she'd already gone.

CHAPTER 14: AGAINST THE CUT

Saturday afternoon, Week 2

Despite her words to Jade, Sophie was invited, as a senior police officer, to be present during the child protection officer's visit. She thought about it and was about to turn the offer down but, before she could, Jade had a call from Asli. The two young girls wanted her to go to Asli's house.

'They want to talk things over with me,' said Jade.

'Well, that's probably a good sign, but she needs to be back home for the child protection team visit at two thirty. They'll want to speak to Safiyo to make sure she understands the meaning of the court order. I think you need to somehow convince her to go home. I think you'll need to explain what you've done in terms of seeking further advice, but in a way that doesn't scare her.'

'Can I tell her that I talked to you about it?'

'As long as you don't tell them who I am. That might scare the living daylights out of Safiyo, and we don't want that to happen. Just tell them that you told your mum. Okay? Maybe I'll go along as an observer after all.'

'Thanks, Mum,' Jade said. She still looked worried. 'I wish this had never happened. Why did Asli choose me to talk to?'

Sophie looked at her daughter. 'Probably because she thought you were the right person, Jade. It isn't just because you're running the campaign at school. I'd guess it's also because they like and trust you. It's something you need to get used to if you plan to be a doctor. This is what working life is really like for someone with those kinds of responsibilities. What do you think my job is like? I'm always having to make important decisions based upon what people say and do. All the time I'm thinking, have I made the right decision? Why did that person say that? What might the consequences of this course of action be? I could chuck it all in and work behind the counter in a dress shop, and then I wouldn't face these kinds of problems. But then I'd go round the bend with boredom. You are exactly the right kind of person for what you've chosen to do with your life, and it's those qualities that your young friends saw in you. As a prefect, you're in a position of responsibility, but they must also trust you. Otherwise they'd have chosen someone else to talk to. I'm proud of you, Jade. You've done exactly the right thing, so stop worrying about it.' She gave her daughter a hug. 'Now get round to Asli's house and take the two of them home to Safiyo's. There's no time to waste. I'll give you a lift. And you'll have a lot to tell Hannah when she gets home this evening. She'll be proud of you too.' She glanced in the mirror. The same soft brown cord trousers and tan ankle boots she'd been wearing in the morning. No time to change now. She unhooked her tan leather jacket from the coat-stand and followed her daughter out to the car.

* * *

The visit to Safiyo's home wasn't easy, but it went as well as could be expected. Sophie suggested driving to the house in a plain car rather than in a police squad car, so she ended up driving the slightly overawed uniformed constable across to Wareham from police headquarters near Wool. They met the child protection officer outside the house, and the three women approached the front door together, with Sophie hanging back slightly. 'If I can get away with saying nothing, then that's what I'd prefer to do,' she said.

Safiyo's mother opened the door, and stood with her mouth open when she saw them on her doorstep.

'Mrs Dalmar? We're here to talk to you about your daughter, Safiyo. I'm Cheryl Walker, the duty child protection officer from the council, and these two ladies are police officers, as you can see. May we come in, please?'

As soon as Cheryl explained the reason for their visit, Safiyo's mother burst into tears. Her husband came into the hallway to see what was going on. He looked annoyed.

'Maybe we could find a more comfortable place to talk?' suggested Fatima Sharma, the uniformed officer. 'It's rather crowded with us all in the hallway, and we will need to speak to Safiyo. Where is she, by the way?'

'She is in her room, with some friends,' the mother replied nervously. 'I will get her.' She looked at her husband. 'Take them through, please, Habibi?'

He ushered the women through to a front room. He followed them in and stood stiffly, as if to attention. There was a lengthy silence.

'Who are you again?' he said finally.

Cheryl repeated her introduction.

'I can see you are a police officer,' he replied, pointing at Fatima. He looked at Sophie. 'But you? Why are you not in a uniform like your colleague?'

'I'm just a police observer, Mr Dalmar. I'm from county headquarters.' Sophie indicated Fatima and Cheryl. 'These are the important people here.'

His wife entered the room, wringing her hands.

Cheryl coughed. 'We have reason to believe that you have been planning to take Safiyo out of the country in order for her to be circumcised. We must make clear to you that such an action would be illegal and would be treated as serious child abuse under UK law. We have with us a court order forbidding you from taking Safiyo out of the UK by any means until we are satisfied that she is not in any danger. Do you understand?' She looked at both parents in turn.

'It is not to do with me,' said the father. 'It is a woman's thing.' He shrugged and vaguely waved towards his wife.

'You would both be prosecuted if the cutting went ahead. Under the law, you share equal responsibility for the welfare of your children. If Safiyo is harmed in any way you will both share the blame. Do you understand? I must ask you both to make a commitment to keep her here and free from harm.'

'But it is a tradition,' said the mother. 'I had it done when I was her age.'

'It is a tradition that must stop, Mrs Dalmar. Everyone says so, all across the world. It does no good, only harm. Girls die because of it. Women can spend the rest of their lives in pain because of it.' She took the official order from Fatima and handed it across to the girl's father. 'These two police officers have witnessed that you have received the order. Safiyo must remain in this country until we review her case at a child protection hearing. You will both be invited to attend.'

Fatima Sharma added, 'Nothing has happened to Safiyo yet, so no law has been broken. There is nothing for either of you to worry about as long as you abide by the court order.'

'Will anything else happen?' asked the father.

'We'll inform the senior staff at her school, but not everyone will know. They will monitor her attendance and her wellbeing, as is their duty. Nothing will happen as long as you keep her here, and safe'.

Just then the door opened. Jade and two young girls came into the room. Jade was holding the hand of one of them, who held back, her hand at her mouth.

'Do you know why we are here, Safiyo?' Cheryl asked. The girl gave a small nod.

'We are worried about your safety, so we have given your parents an order so they can't take you out of the country. Do you understand?'

'Yes,' she murmured. 'Jade has explained to me.'

'Who are you? Why are you involved?' asked the mother sharply.

Jade said, 'I'm a prefect at the girls' school. They told me about their concern late yesterday. It was me that told the authorities.'

The father nodded. 'I am glad. It is better this way. It is wrong to live in a country like this and keep to old ways that do nothing but harm. I did not speak before, because it seemed to me to be a women's thing and I shouldn't be involved. But if my new country feels it is so wrong, then we must show respect to that. We will follow the order.'

'Are you happy with your father's promise, Safiyo?' Cheryl asked.

'Yes. If he has made a promise, he will keep it. He is the head of my family.' Safiyo smiled at her father. She let go of Jade's hand, ran across and flung her arms around him. Her affection for him was evident. 'I was so scared,' she said to him. He squeezed her tight.

Sophie looked across at Jade and smiled. A happy ending after all, she thought. Her phone rang. She took it from her bag and left the room, mouthing her apologies.

'Hi, Barry. Has something happened? . . . Okay. I'll be right in. Expect me in about half an hour.'

She poked her head back into the lounge, and mouthed to her two colleagues, 'got to go to Dorchester in a hurry.'

'I'll give Fatima a lift back,' Cheryl said. 'It won't be a problem.'

Sophie nodded to the Dalmars and left.

'Who was she?' asked Safiyo's mother.

'The Chief Inspector,' Fatima answered.

'She's not smartly dressed like you two.'

'I think she was off duty,' Fatima said.

Jade managed to keep quiet.

'Tight trousers and a leather jacket. Not right for a woman,' said Mrs Dalmar.

Now Jade's patience ran out. 'If she hadn't got involved, things might not have been organised so fast. You might have taken Safiyo away and got her cut. You'd have been prosecuted and probably put in prison when you got back. Safiyo and your other children would have been taken away from you. You should be grateful that she took an interest . . . Anyway, she's my mum and I'm proud of her. She'd never dream of hurting me, not like you, planning to have your daughter mutilated!' She turned on her heel and walked out of the house.

CHAPTER 15: DRAMA QUEENS

Sunday afternoon, Week 2

Dorothy Kitson sat three rows back, in the middle, exactly six chairs from the left. She deliberately chose this position to avoid drawing any attention to herself. Who would notice her anyway? And, even if they did, why would anyone bother to chat to her? She knew what she looked like: a thin, stooped, middle-aged woman, prematurely grey. She was extremely shy, and avoided speaking to anyone she didn't know. She rarely looked people in the eye. Dorothy folded her coat, placed it on the seat beside her and put her bag on top. Maybe her sister would attend this afternoon's talk, although she didn't hold out much hope. Her elder sister was a law unto herself. She always had been.

Dorothy took out the programme and scanned through the sparse details. The afternoon's activities were all to do with the campaign to reduce female genital mutilation, whatever that was. The way they described it, it did sound horrible, and probably ought to be stopped. It seemed to mainly involve people from far-away countries with exotic names. She wasn't particularly interested in any of these talks at the local Arts

Centre, but didn't like to admit it. Nobody asked her anyway. Because she came along to many of the Sunday afternoon events, people assumed that she must be genuinely bothered by goings on in the wider world. In reality, she only came because she had free tickets for the less popular events. She was a part-time cleaner at the centre, and this allowed her twenty free admissions per year. Her few friends were bemused by the events she chose to attend. They were even more bemused by the performances she didn't go to, some by well-known performing arts groups. If anyone bothered to think about it, they would have noticed that she never attended the evening events. Why would she choose to come out of an evening, with so much available at home on the telly? But Sunday afternoon was a different matter. It was a good opportunity to get out of her small flat.

Three people walked onto the low stage at the front of the room. She glanced at her watch and popped a peppermint sweet into her mouth. It didn't look as though her sister would make it after all. Nothing new there. She became aware of unexpected movement to her right as a figure squeezed along the row and sat down beside her. How typical. A choice between sliding to her seat in front of five people from the left aisle or ten if moving in from the right. Which would have the greater impact? There you go.

* * *

On stage, Hannah Allen went up to the microphone, introduced herself and gave a short description of the charity she represented.

'You'll only see me between speakers, you'll be glad to hear,' she said. 'They're experts and I'm not, and I'm so grateful to them for agreeing to talk this afternoon. It's the first time we've been to Dorchester. We're mainly based in London, but I grew up in Dorset, so I'm doubly pleased to be back in my home county, although I'm a bit nervous because my dad and Gran are here watching me.' She smiled and gave a small wave. 'Please don't think that the problem of FGM doesn't occur here in Dorset. I happen to know that only yesterday a twelve-year-old girl from a Somali family who live near Poole was saved from being flown out of the country to be cut. We must all be vigilant until FGM has become a thing of the past.'

Hannah introduced the first speaker and returned to her seat to one side of the platform. The stage was Hannah's natural home. She loved being there, having an audience in front of her, alive with anticipation. This was a very different kind of audience of course, assembled for a lecture, but it had still given her the familiar thrill. And she'd spotted Jade sitting next to her grandmother. She'd made it after all.

The two fifteen-minute talks were followed by a question and answer session, that Hannah chaired. Once that was over, the assembled company gathered around a table at the rear of the hall. Tea and biscuits were being served. One of the regular staff was ill, so Dorothy had volunteered to help. Not that there was much work involved. All she had to do was stand behind the table, pour teas and beakers of orange squash, put biscuits onto plates and push them towards anyone who approached the table.

Hannah broke away from her family and went over to the table to return her empty cup. 'I hope you don't mind me asking, but the woman sitting to your right during the lecture looked familiar. Do you happen to know if she was an actress at one time?'

Dorothy put her hand to her mouth. 'Oh, I don't know,' she said. 'No, I don't.'

'Not to worry. She arrived just as I was about to start speaking, so I waited for her to settle before I started the talk. I thought it looked as if you knew her.'

'Um . . . no.'

Jade came up beside her sister. 'Hi! I saw you in the café yesterday morning. I was with my mum. You left in a bit of a hurry. I wanted to tell you that you dropped your hankie. I spotted it, so Lily at the café kept it behind the counter. Did you realise you'd lost it?'

Dorothy looked frantically around, looking for an escape route. Why was this happening? Why were these two young women plying her with questions? Where had her sister gone? Why must she always panic when strangers started talking to her? And then, miraculously, Dorothy's sister appeared, as if from nowhere. She was smiling, ready to take control as she lifted a cup to her lips.

'Um . . .' Dorothy pointed to Hannah and managed to add the words, 'asking about you.'

'I hope you don't mind. I saw you from the platform as you arrived and I thought you looked familiar. It took me a while to put a name to the face, but are you by any chance Pauline Stopley, the actress? It's just that I'm in my last year at drama college in London and I've seen a couple of your photos from the nineties.'

Pauline lowered her cup, revealing a warm smile. 'Yes, that's me, although I no longer act. I work for the Arts Council now. I had to stop acting well over a decade ago because of a spell of bad health. It took me a long time to recover and I lost the motivation to get back on the stage.'

'I'm so sorry to hear that. I wondered what happened to you after I read about your acting career.' Hannah paused. 'Do you miss it? I hope you don't mind me asking.'

'Of course I don't mind. In your position, I'd ask exactly the same question. And strangely, the answer is no, not really. I do enjoy my current job, and I like the security it brings.'

'And my Gran thinks she remembers you. She saw you in a couple of productions at the Bristol Old Vic. She'd love to meet you, if you don't mind. She still lives in Bristol.'

Pauline smiled and nodded. Hannah beckoned to her grandmother.

'Gran, I was right. This is Pauline Stopley. Pauline, this is my grandmother, Susan Carswell. She's a great theatre-goer and is probably to blame for putting the idea of acting into my head when I was a teenager.'

While the women chatted, Jade looked back at the table. Dorothy appeared to have vanished.

'Where did that serving lady go?' she asked.

Pauline shrugged. 'No idea,' she said. She wasn't going to let on that the serving lady, as Jade had called her, was her younger sister. She was sure that Dorothy wouldn't have said anything either. Better not to have people wondering about their somewhat strained relationship. She was glad that she'd changed out of the short, gold-zipped, black dress and high-heeled shoes that she'd been wearing for her evening with John Wethergill. The outfit would have been just a little over the top for the crowd who'd turned up for this talk. Her conversation with these women wouldn't have gone so well if she'd been dressed as though she'd just come out of a nightclub. That man who'd come over with the older woman looked rather charming too. Pity he was wearing a wedding ring. Maybe she was being too greedy, thought Pauline. After all, she'd just had a very enjoyable night with the courteous, thoughtful and rather old-fashioned John Wethergill. She smiled brilliantly at the woman.

'I understand you saw me a couple of times at the Old Vic in Bristol. Can you remember which productions?'

Susan Carswell said, 'I was trying to remember after Hannah here mentioned your name. They could have been farces, possibly by Michael Frayn, but I can't be sure.'

'It's possible. I did several of those. At one point it seemed as if I was permanently on the road. It was great fun, but often I felt I was missing out on a stable, settled life. Once or twice I found myself wondering whether it was what I really wanted, after all. In the end the decision was made for me when I became ill. I pulled through but things weren't the same for me.'

'What was the illness, if you don't mind me asking?'

'Hepatitis. I was weak for a long time afterwards.'

'How sad,' Hannah interjected. 'Ending your career in that way. I find it such a thrill, being on stage. There's nothing like it. Did you find that?'

'Oh, yes. But life has to go on. And you find other things to do, other things to give you that rush of excitement and tension. It's not the end of the world, believe me.'

'Do you enjoy the work you do now?'

'Yes, I do. My job with the Arts Council takes me all over the place and I meet lots of interesting people. I'm quite heavily involved in theatre grants, so I haven't wasted all the years I spent acting. I don't approve of performing arts administrators who've never had any first-hand experience themselves. They can either be too harsh in their decisions or too . . . lovey-dovey.' She glanced at a clock on the wall. 'I have to be going, I'm afraid. It was lovely to chat to you all. Hannah, if you want to stay in touch, just call or email me. I'd be glad to help your career in any way I can.' She handed the aspiring actress a business card, then left.

'What a pleasant woman,' Hannah said to her grandmother. 'And she's right. The people in charge ought to have some first-hand experience.'

'I'm not so sure, Hannah,' Susan replied. 'Look at me. I'm the practice manager of a GP medical centre, yet I've had no formal medical training of any type. I've been on lots of training courses, and I think I do a good job. So do the doctors I work with. It's the motivation to do a good job that matters, more than anything else. That's what I think.'

Martin Allen nodded, trying to keep a straight face. 'I agree, Susan. Give me a sensible, well trained, dedicated person over a drama queen any day.' He winked at his mother-in-law.

Hannah's mouth opened, and then she realised that her father was teasing her. She gave him a sweet smile, and kicked his ankle.

'Dad, you're just an incorrigible mischief-maker.'

* * *

Dorothy Kitson stood outside, in the shadows at the rear of the building, trembling and drawing nervously on one more cigarette. Could she tell anyone? Should she? What would happen to her if she did? It was all too much for her, all of it.

CHAPTER 16: SOIL SAMPLES

Monday morning, Week 2

Rae was examining the brickwork. 'What do you think, sir?'

Barry Marsh directed a flashlight at the cellar wall and fingered the metal ring affixed to the brickwork. A single bulb lit this end of the cool, slightly musty room and few details could be made out. He guessed that this end of the cellar, away from the steps from the kitchen, had hardly been used over the years. The room was spacious enough to hold the junk that most families would throw into a cellar. There was no need to come to this end at all, with its dry soil floor. He was surprised that no one had bothered to split the vast room into smaller units, and fit shelves and cupboards. But then he remembered the garage, workshop and shed, all within easy reach of the back door and garden. Probably this room had never been needed.

'Well the boss has already asked forensics to take a sample of soil from over here, just as a precaution. It's not worth getting them to come back and dust for prints unless we find a strong reason for it.' The dim room had a different, eerier atmosphere than the rest of the building, and they were almost whispering. Maybe it had played a part in the events of twenty years ago.

'We need to trace every single previous occupant just to eliminate them from suspicion. I'm almost finished with the list. I'm just wondering, boss. We've only been tracing tenants. We may need to start on the landlords and owners next. The owners could well still have access to a key, couldn't they? They'd know when the place was going to be empty, or even when the residents were away on holiday. We can't discount them.' She peered into the dingy gloom of the cellar. 'This place gives me the creeps.'

'Until just now we couldn't be sure what might have happened, and what led to those two children being buried. But now? It's starting to look one way, isn't it? None of us have met this kind of thing before. It's why the boss went to London last week to see an expert she knows, just in case it turns out to be nasty. She was wondering about inviting him down, so that we're prepared for what we might discover. It's looking more and more as if he'll be needed. I keep wondering what that metal ring is for, sunk into the brickwork like that. I feel uneasy too.'

The two detectives climbed back up the steps to the kitchen door. Marsh locked the cellar behind him.

'Are there any other copies of the key?' he asked Philip Freeman, who was waiting in the kitchen.

Philip opened a drawer and took out a tin containing a single key. 'That's all we have,' he said.

* * *

Twenty minutes later Marsh and Gregson walked into the incident room and made their way to the information board. Marsh was adding a few words to the "cellar" strand on the display when he realised that Sophie and Neil Dunnett had joined them. He also realised that Rae had fallen silent. She was staring rigidly at the board as if in a trance. The atmosphere had become tense, and Dunnett did nothing to alleviate it.

'Good morning, Sergeant. And good morning to you, DC Gregson.' His voice was low. It almost slithered through the air, and the emphasis on the final phrase caused Rae to stiffen even more.

'Morning, sir,' said Marsh, trying to lighten the strained atmosphere. 'Good to see you here. An effective press release on Friday, I thought. It read well in the papers.'

Dunnett ignored him and continued to stare at Rae. 'How have you settled in, Gregson? Dorset treating you any better than Wiltshire?'

There was a pause. As she responded, Rae continued to stare straight ahead at the board. 'Fine thank you, sir. I believe so. I think I'm doing a good job.' Marsh and Sophie could both hear the tremor in her voice.

'Well, don't let the team down, Gregson. Not on my watch,' Dunnett said.

Sophie broke in. 'That's hardly likely, sir. I've already stated several times that I think Rae has done a first-rate job for us.'

'As long as that continues, I'll be happy.' Dunnett shook hands with Sophie and left.

Rae was trembling. She turned and hurried out of the room without a word. Marsh and Sophie stared at each other, then Sophie said, 'I'll check the toilets, you check the car park.'

Rae was nowhere to be found.

* * *

A full half hour later Rae reappeared, carrying a coffee that she set carefully down on her desk. She started to work on the Finch Cottage residents' list. Marsh looked at Sophie and raised his eyebrows, but she shook her head. The results had come in from the analytical chemists at Southampton University, so Marsh ploughed on. He finally gave up trying to decipher the rows of figures and the explanatory text that accompanied them. He took them to Sophie.

'Sorry, ma'am. It would help if I knew what we were looking for, but I'm completely lost, I'm afraid.'

'I guess you were just on the email address list,' she replied. 'It's really intended for Dave Nash, but I think I can explain. If the children were kept down in that cellar, tethered up and mistreated, there might be residues in the soil. That's why I requested the analysis. Urine leaves a high nitrogen content. Faeces leave phosphates. Blood leaves iron. None of it could have been leached away by rain, not there, so we're looking for unusually high levels. They took samples from three areas in the cellar, left side, right side, and near the rear wall, where you were looking at that securing ring. So let's look for differences.'

She spread the documents out on the desk and began reading.

'Look. This set of figures shows higher nitrate levels than the others. It's sample C, which is our position of interest, where that ring was fixed to the wall.'

Marsh read. There were slight variations in the nitrate figures for the other two samples, but the level here was significantly higher.

'Same for the phosphate, do you see? Though it's not as obvious.'

'So that means the children could have been there? And, if so, they were being maltreated?'

'It suggests the possibility. It could also be that someone stored some general fertiliser at that spot, and spilled some. We can't be sure what caused the increase. But look here. The iron shows no such level, indicating that there was no blood in the soil. We'll need to have a chat with Dave about all this, but I think my assumptions are right. It all adds to the picture, doesn't it? But it can't be counted as hard evidence. It simply adds weight to the possibility that the children were kept down there for a while, and maybe in awful conditions. But there could be other explanations. Maybe someone kept a dog tied up to the ring. It's all a mass of unknowns and we could get ourselves completely side-tracked by the various possibilities. We have to build up a reliable picture of what went on, and that is not going to be easy.'

Marsh pointed to the covering letter. 'They're asking us to contact their head of department, a Professor Wendy Millward. I'm a bit dim about all this detailed science, ma'am. Maybe it'd be better if you did it?'

Sophie was amused. 'It's a sign of the times, isn't it, when a bloke passes the scientific stuff over to a woman? Yes, I'll give her a ring later. Maybe she's found something else that's interesting.'

'So, what now?'

'I'll get Harry Turner to come down and talk us through it. If we're not absolutely clear, we'll find our minds are all over the place.'

Marsh paused. 'What about Rae, ma'am?'

'She should have calmed down by now. Have a word with her. See if she's willing to volunteer an explanation. I'm trying to recall the details of what I found out about our esteemed DCS when I had my first run-in with him a couple of years ago. I think he was in Wiltshire for a spell before he came here. I just wonder whether they've crossed swords before. It would explain why he said those odd things last week.' She tapped her fingers on the desktop. 'Don't push it, though, Barry. Let her take her time, and leave it if she's obviously not ready to do so. We can follow it up later, in the pub if necessary.'

Rae didn't look up when Marsh approached her desk.

'Hi. Do you want to talk?'

Rae kept her eyes fixed on the papers in front of her.

'Not really, sir.'

'That's fine. But I do need to know if the two of you have a history.'

There was a long pause. 'Yes, we do,' she whispered.

Marsh noticed the heightened colour in her cheeks.

'The boss and I need to know about it, Rae. We need to be kept in the picture if we're to help you.'

Rae nodded. Finally she raised her eyes. 'Okay. Maybe later, or tomorrow. I can't think straight just now.'

'Do you want to take a break and go home? We can afford to give you the rest of the day off.'

Her reply was sharp, bitter. 'That would play right into his hands, wouldn't it? That's what he'll be looking for, some sign that I'm weakening. It'd give him an excuse to start putting the knife in. No, I'll stay here. I'm alright, really. And thanks for your concern. I do appreciate it. Can you tell the boss that?'

'Pub later, after we finish here?'

Rae gave him a weak smile. 'Okay. Does that mean the boss'll give me the third degree?'

'I expect so. But don't worry. She has history with him too.'

* * *

Barry Marsh emerged from the bar area carrying a tray holding a few packets of crisps and nuts, the usual pint of ale for the boss, a gin and tonic for Rae and an apple juice for himself. He'd go for a drink in one of the Swanage pubs after he'd driven home if he needed it, but he suspected he'd feel too worn out.

'When he first appeared as a DCI in Salisbury, one of the DCs nicknamed him "The Swindon Tosspot."' Rae took a mouthful of her drink. 'That's what I was told. That was before I became a DC. I was warned about him almost immediately I joined the unit. They told me he sometimes seemed to be out of his depth and would explode into fits of rage at the slightest provocation. At first, things were fine. I think he recognised that I worked hard and didn't make mistakes, so I got off lightly compared to some of the others. But it all changed when I officially announced that I was transitioning. I followed the guidelines the personnel team gave me to the letter. But I found myself being left out of anything important. I was spending my time filing and on the phone, being asked to get the tea and coffee. I know someone's got to do those things, but that type of drudge job had previously been shared out. Now they were given almost exclusively to me. And I hadn't even transitioned then. I was still a bloke. I talked to my line manager, a DS, about it, but she just shrugged her shoulders. "What did you expect?" she said. "Complain to the boss if you don't like it." So I did. What I didn't realise was that it had all been a set-up. When I took my complaint to him he was ready and waiting. He told me I was a sordid little runt. According to him, I was ruining the camaraderie in the unit, everyone had complained to him about me. No one wanted to work with me, I had no real future in the police and I needed to find a different line of work. Of course, he said all this when there were no witnesses about, so I knew it would be my word against his if I made a complaint. I also guessed that's what he wanted me to do — make a formal complaint. I'd have initiated an action that could be used against me, so I could then be accused of all kinds of things. So I kept my mouth shut. Things just got worse, particularly when I went through my transition and reappeared as a woman. I was ignored completely, almost as if I didn't exist. I got most of my instructions through emails or written memos. I was side-lined completely. When I questioned this, unofficially of course, I was still ignored. Eventually one of my friends on the team told me what was really happening. It was all orchestrated by the Tosspot, and anyone who appeared to be on my side would find their own future in the unit under threat.'

'So what did you do?' Sophie asked.

'I soldiered on. I spent the better part of a year wasting all my training, doing menial, office work but I refused to give in. That's when I did the extra study that you saw on my CV, just to keep my hand in. Then I had several months off for my surgery, and when I came back he'd gone. The atmosphere was completely different, much more accepting. I tried to make a go of it but I felt I'd been let down by the rest of the team and I told them so. They could have shown me some support, but they'd chosen not to. They'd opted to keep their heads down and look after themselves rather than do what was right, and I couldn't forgive them for that. The only exception was my friend, Stevie, the one who'd tried to keep me in the loop about what was going on. How would I ever be able to work with people who'd done that to me? I thought the Tosspot had gone to county headquarters, so I decided to apply for a job here, in Dorset, just to get away from him. I had no idea he'd transferred here. It's a nightmare. I feel as if I've walked into some kind of trap.'

Sophie took a sip of her beer. 'I can see how it might look to you, but things really aren't as bleak as you think. Barry and I are your line managers, not the DCS. As long as you're working in this unit and doing a good job for it, you're safe. All he can do is to needle you, which is what he was doing this afternoon. And I must say you played right into his hands by reacting like that. He obviously spotted it. We can only expect more of the same, I'm afraid.'

'Sorry, ma'am, but I was totally unprepared.' Rae looked miserable. 'I didn't know how to respond.'

'Well, it needs to be better than that. Don't let him draw you out, which is what he'll be trying to do. My guess is that next time will be worse. He'll try to goad you into an angry response, knowing that I won't be able to protect you if you say something insubordinate enough. The key thing is not to speak to him without one of us being present. The trick with a bully, Rae, is to keep him on the back foot by taking the initiative yourself. You know the old expression "Know Thine Enemy"? You should. It's the essence of good detective work. Most important of all, leave any confrontations to me. I have the background and experience to deal with them.' Sophie turned to her sergeant. 'That goes for you, too, Barry. I don't want you sticking your neck out. Play it safe and let me handle any flak that he chooses to hurl our way. I can play dirty when I need to, and this might be one of those times.'

CHAPTER 17: A HAPPY LITTLE GIRL

Tuesday, Week 2

Surprisingly, given the previous day's aggravations, the morning's briefing proved to be very fruitful. It was largely based upon Rae's detailed findings about the residents of Finch Cottage.

'I've traced them back to 1980,' she began. She pinned a flow chart to the board. 'We start with Bill and Angela McKenzie, two school teachers. I think they may have owned the property, but I haven't confirmed it yet. They moved in during 1980 and lived there until September 1992. They then moved to Poole as far as I can tell. I have a probable address for them, in Poole, but only found it this morning, so I haven't contacted them yet. That will be my next job.'

'That could be before the dates we're looking at for the children,' Barry said. 'We still think about twenty years, so they would have left before that. Don't you think, ma'am?'

'It's not that clear. There could be a leeway of up to five years either way, certainly until we hear from the forensic dating experts,' Sophie responded. 'So they stay in the picture. Do we know anything about them, Rae?'

'Not yet, but it will happen.' She pushed a strand of dark hair behind her ear and continued. 'The next resident was Anthony Scrivener. He was Deputy Governor at the prison for eighteen months and lived at Finch Cottage for most of that time. I can't find any mention of a wife, partner or housemate, but that doesn't mean there wasn't one. He was the only person on the voters' roll, though. I think he moved out in October 1994. It looks as though the place might have been empty between the McKenzies moving out and Scrivener moving in, a period of about six months. Maybe there were some short-term residents, but I haven't found records of any yet.

'The next people to live there were called Camberwell, but the details are very vague. There's no record of first names, just the initial P. It's possible he, she or they were there for longer than the six months I have for them, but that's based on a single record only, so it may be wrong.

'After that, things get much clearer. Jessica and Bob Hart had the place for two and a half years, from May 1996 until November 1998. I've spoken to Mrs Hart and we know they rented. They were followed by two nurses, Andrew Lloyd and Verity Smith. They were in the house for ten years, from January 2000 to July 2009. They still work at the hospital and have confirmed that they rented the house. They're still together as a couple and have a house of their own now. Antonio Crella, a photographer, moved in during September 2009 and stayed there for a year, moving out in late August 2010. He was immediately followed by Hester Williamson, a lecturer in animal husbandry at the local agricultural college. She remained for two and a half years, moving out in March 2013. We know the next residents, the Freeman family. They moved in six months later. And that's it.'

'Thanks, Rae,' Sophie said. 'Let's talk this through before we move on. It's always possible, I suppose, that the children were buried during one of the periods when the house was empty. Maybe someone deliberately chose it because it was vacant. But if so, why put a shrub on top of the grave? It acts as a kind of marker in a way, so I'm inclined to think that it was part of the burial. If so, it was more likely to have taken place when the house was occupied, and carried out by whoever lived there. Anyone want to add anything?'

Marsh said, 'these are all probabilities. What you're saying is fine as long as we're aware that there might be other explanations for the burial.' 'I agree, but it gives us a start. So the people we are interested in are the McKenzies, Scrivener and Camberwell. Their occupancies span the period we're looking at. Once we get to the Harts, the odds start changing.' She stopped.

'Are you okay, ma'am?' Marsh asked.

'Yes, yes. It's the name Camberwell. It rings a bell somewhere in my head, some vague memory from decades ago. Can you go on, Rae, please? I'm listening.'

'Okay. The information I have about the owners is sparse. The McKenzies were owner occupiers. When they moved, the house was sold to a Dorothy Kitson who, it seems, never lived there. It's possible that she was only a joint owner for some of the time. It must have been her who sold it to the Freemans last year.'

Marsh sat forward. 'So this Dorothy Kitson was either the sole or part owner for all of the period we're interested in?'

'It would seem so. But I don't have dates at the moment and, as I said, there's no evidence that she ever lived there.'

Sophie was only half listening. 'Excuse me a minute,' she said. She took her mobile phone from her bag and made a call.

'Hi, Mum. Can you talk? Fine. The name Camberwell. Why should it seem vaguely familiar to me? Why do I somehow connect it with you?' She listened, ended the call and then sat, drumming her fingers on the desktop. Finally she announced, 'Doctor Li Hua Camberwell was a GP in a medical practice next to my mother's in Bristol. According to my mother, she died in a car crash more than twenty-five years ago. She was originally from Hong Kong.' She took a breath. 'I think it's possible that we've just made a breakthrough, though I'm not quite sure what it is.'

'If it was an RTA, there'll be a record of it, won't there?' Marsh said. 'Do you think we should find out the details? From the sound of it, she could have died at about the same time as the children. Do you want me to start now?'

'Yes. And, Rae, you get the details fleshed out, as far as you can, about these tenants and owners. But, before you do, contact that retired headteacher. See if he remembers the children's surname. I imagine he must have been mulling it over since you saw him last week. Don't give him the name Camberwell before he has the chance to come up with a name himself, but try it out on him if he doesn't remember. I'll see what I can find out about the doctor. Maybe after ten days of slog, when we seemed to get nowhere, our work has paid off. Let's meet again early afternoon.'

Sophie noticed a sudden look of horror appear on Rae's face.

'What is it, Rae?'

'Ma'am! I owe you such an apology. I feel awful about it. It was when you mentioned the headteacher. I suddenly remembered something he mentioned on Thursday. His name is George Bramshaw, and he thinks he might have taught you in Bristol when you were at primary school. I'm so sorry. I should have mentioned it on Friday but it slipped my mind.' Rae was blushing furiously.

'George Bramshaw? My goodness! Yes, I was nine or ten. I'm flattered he remembers me still.'

'He said he was only a couple of years out of college, ma'am.'

'I think I probably had a crush on him. Either that or I used him as a substitute father. Do you mind if I take this contact, Rae? I can't believe he still remembers me.' She checked the wall clock. 'I wonder? Call him, Rae, and ask him if he'll be in later this morning. Don't tell him it'll be me going to see him.'

* * *

At eleven o'clock Sophie pulled up outside the small bungalow in Salisbury. If Rae's prediction was accurate, the owner would be sitting in a window seat looking out at the road, ready and waiting. Sophie paused before opening the car door. Yet another influential figure from her past who'd helped her become the person she was, yet so long ago as to almost be in another life. Of course she had memories of that time. There was even a photo of her, sitting on a swing in the local park wearing pink trousers and T-shirt, and white sandals. It was her mother's favourite. It must have signified something important, although Sophie couldn't remember exactly what. Her birthday? It was so, so long ago. She'd been a small girl growing up without a father; a lonely, sometimes solitary child. No wonder I've turned out the way I have, she thought. But people like Mr Bramshaw had filled her mind with a longing for knowledge and understanding. He'd been a hero to her, really.

She checked her hair in the rear-view mirror, took her bag from the passenger seat, opened the door and swung her legs out. She smoothed down her skirt, stood and opened the gate. She could feel him watching. There he was, opening the door while she was still halfway down the path. I wonder what's going through his mind, she thought. Is he as nervous as me? He shouldn't be; he must meet ex-pupils often, surely?

'Well,' George said. 'I wondered. Remembering the kind of person you were, even at the age of ten, I thought you might come yourself. But then I told myself, no, she'll be too busy.'

'As you see, I did come after all. I'm in the process of re-discovering myself and couldn't miss this opportunity.'

He held out his hand, but Sophie came forward and gave him a hug. 'You deserve better than a handshake,' she said. 'You have no idea how much the little girl I used to be hung on your every word. I never felt the same for any other teacher. By the time I started secondary school, boys had entered the equation and things became more complicated.'

He smiled. 'You'd better come in. Coffee is ready, or tea if you'd prefer it. I want to hear your life story. Short version, of course.'

She followed him into the house. 'Coffee, please. Rae was complimentary about your chocolate biscuits, so I hope you still have some left. We'd finished the ones you sent by the next day.'

He led her into the sitting room. A tray of cups, plates and biscuits sat on a low table with a jug of coffee beside them. He poured two cups. 'Complimentary, eh? Did you choose that adjective deliberately?'

She sat in one of the easy chairs. 'You know I did. I still remember your lesson on pairs of words that can be easily confused. Homonyms? Which and witch. Villain and villein. Revue and review. Didn't you ask us to draw the witch and the villain? I think you put my effort up on the wall.'

'I expect the complimentary and complementary was just for you. A bit too hard for most ten-year-olds. So what happened after you left primary school?'

'I didn't change very much. I was still a swot, according to most of my friends. I became a bit wild in my middle teenage years.'

'Just a bit?'

'Well, that's what I've always told my family. I think my mother suspects, but she's never asked for the lurid details. To be honest, the wild spell didn't last long. I found it all a bit distasteful.'

He laughed. 'That doesn't surprise me. You always were very particular.'

'Anyway, I kept working hard through it all, and I went to Oxford to study for a law degree.'

He raised his eyebrows. 'Really? You did that well? But I shouldn't be surprised. I could see you had real potential, and your mother was very supportive, if I remember rightly. And then you joined the police?'

'Yes. Weird, isn't it? I went on the fast-track route, but still had to start off as an ordinary bobby on the beat.'

'Where was that?'

'London. I met my husband while we were at university in Oxford, and he got a job teaching in a big West End school.

I moved up through the ranks, but took some time off to have my family, and to do a masters degree. I went back and got a promotion to detective sergeant, then we moved to the Midlands where I was a DI in a big task force. The move to Dorset a couple of years ago suited us both.'

He nodded and sipped some coffee. 'But earlier you made a reference to re-discovering yourself. The way you said it sounded serious.'

Sophie took another sip of coffee. 'You might not have known it but there were just the two of us at home, me and my mum. No father. I always thought he had run out on my mum when he discovered she was pregnant. I don't know whether you can imagine how much that affected me. I rarely talked about it with mum because I could see the pain it caused, but I grew up secretly despising him, and that never changed, even when I grew up. If anything the hatred grew, and it really wasn't good for me. I had a loving husband, two beautiful and talented daughters, yet I had this cold, hard kernel of hate deep within me. Then, just last year, I discovered what had really happened to him. He'd been murdered by a criminal gang just because he'd happened to witness them committing a crime. They dumped his body down an old disused mine-shaft. It was only found twelve months ago. We discovered who did it and he'll stand trial later this year.' She sipped her coffee again. 'My dad never had a chance to find out that my mother was pregnant. The whole thing shook me to the core. I still can't get my head round it. All that totally misplaced hatred, for all those years. It shook my belief in who I am and what values I hold, and now I distrust myself. It's why I want to know what I was like in my early life, what people saw in me, what they thought of me. Does that make any sense?'

'Oh, I think so,' he replied. 'But remember, I'm no expert. I'm not a therapist or counsellor, so I can't say whether what you're seeking is going to be constructive or not.'

'I don't expect that from you. I've had enough therapy over the past year, believe me. But I want to know whether it showed, when I was small, what I was feeling inside about my father. Did it?'

'I don't think so. What I remember was a happy little girl of outstanding intelligence and insight. I was a little in awe of you, you know.'

Sophie laughed. 'Be serious.'

'I am being serious. I felt that you could have been anything you put your mind to: a surgeon or a top research scientist, or an academic of some kind. It doesn't surprise me that you ended up studying for a law degree at one of the world's top universities. But then it also doesn't surprise me that you've ended up as a senior detective. In some ways I'm happier with that than if you'd had a career as a city property lawyer or a financial tycoon. It's reassuring to know that you have such a socially worthwhile career. I can see how it fits.'

'I might still have a career in academia. I have an open invitation to complete a doctorate in criminal psychology in London where I did my masters, so that's what I plan to do when I've had enough of this job. I still keep in touch with my Oxford college, and we have an unofficial agreement about a role for me once I've got the necessary qualifications.'

His turn to laugh. 'Ah, the old boys' network.'

'Exactly. Rumours, handshakes and chocolate biscuits.' She took one from the plate and bit into it. 'This one's good. The thing is, I've realised that it's probably all false. It was all calculated and planned. I'm not the same person now, not since I discovered the truth about my dad. What I really want to do is go back in time, remove all of that misplaced hatred from my soul and replace it with admiration and love, because he was obviously such a good person. But how can I do that?'

'You can try to do that now, surely, in the present? Learn to love him?'

'No!' She almost snapped. 'I can't. It's easy to hate someone you've never met if you believe they've done you wrong. But you can't love someone you've never met. All you're doing is pretending to love a mental construction. It's false. Though

God knows I've tried. I've read his diaries and his poems, I've held his toys from when he was a boy. I've listened to his favourite music. I've tried to decipher the doodles in the margins of his lecture notes. But I get nothing except a sense of desolation. I can't get over the waste of it all.'

George said nothing.

'I was in a pit six months ago. Do you know how low I'd sunk? I was at a conference in London and allowed myself to be chatted up in the bar by one of the other delegates, a lecturer from Manchester. I decided, in a moment of madness, to go back to his room because he was staying overnight. We got as far as the lift. The doors closed and I looked at my reflection in the mirror. What was I doing, for God's sake? This was me, Sophie. I punched the button for the ground floor but we were already on the way up. I said to him, "no, this is all wrong." He got a bit angry. He put his arm around me, but too tightly so I hit him, quite hard. He was gasping for breath when the doors opened on one of the upper floors, so I got out and took the stairs down to reception. I walked out of that hotel, promising myself that I wouldn't let myself stoop so low again. And I haven't. But it scares me. I'm frightened to death of myself, and no one knows. I didn't even tell my therapist.'

'But you've told me?'

She nodded. 'Now I've told someone, I expect the tension of that episode will fade.' She finished her coffee. 'The thing is, how are the others coping? I'm not the only person who'll have been deeply affected by the truth about my dad's death.'

'How did your mother take it?'

'She cries. She pretends to be cheerful and upbeat, but I catch her sometimes, sobbing quietly to herself. It's such a waste. All because my dad was in the wrong place at the wrong time and he bumped into an evil bastard who was too trigger-happy. I looked into his eyes, you know, when we caught up with him. I thought I might see evil, but all I could see was desolate emptiness.'

'I don't know what to say. Is there anything I can say?'

'Of course not. But you've listened to my rant, and that's helped. And you know why I'm telling you this, don't you? Even though I hadn't planned it.'

He nodded. 'I was a substitute father figure for you? For that year?'

She nodded. 'I always knew I could come and find you, even though I moved into a different class the next year. The day I left to start secondary school you came to find me and told me that I could pop back and see you if I needed to. I never did, and I feel a bit guilty about it.'

'There's no need. And you've done it now. In a way I feel privileged that it's me you've chosen.'

'And I haven't asked about your life. Are you still married, or do you live here alone?'

He sighed. 'Alone. My wife walked out on me a couple of years ago. She went on holiday with one if her girlfriends, had an affair with a man while she was away and decided that I didn't match up. It happened just after I retired and we'd moved here.'

'I'm truly sorry to hear that. You must have been devastated.'

'It shook me, it really did. Maybe I took her too much for granted, but she did that with me. I was away on a singles cruise last week and that's why I missed all the news reports about the children's bodies. I had a bit of a romance while I was away, but it wasn't serious. I couldn't get Marie out of my head. Someone told me she's going through a bad time, so I've messaged her to suggest we try to patch up our differences. I haven't heard back yet.'

'I hope it works out for you. I always think of you as such a considerate person. Children? Grandchildren?'

'Yes. One lot are quite local, they're in Salisbury, which is why we chose to retire here. That and the fact that Marie grew up here and always wanted to return. I think she's in Brighton at the moment. She's in contact with the children but they're not particularly happy with what she did.'

Sophie reached over and patted his hand. 'I'm glad you're giving her the option of another chance. I hope that Martin would do the same with me if I did something totally barmy because of my mental state.'

'Life. It can be a mess, can't it?' There was a silence. 'Maybe we should talk about the real reason you're here. The surname was Camberwell. I remembered before Rae phoned. Another coffee?'

CHAPTER 18: HIT AND RUN

Tuesday afternoon, Week 2

'Your mother was mostly right, ma'am.' Barry Marsh was speaking to the detectives sitting around the central table in the incident room. 'She was a GP in Bristol. Li Hua Camberwell was thirty-six years old when she died. But it wasn't a straightforward RTA. It was a hit and run, and the culprit was never found. I'm still waiting for some of the details to arrive, but the bare facts are these. She died on the night of October the third, 1990, in the evening. She'd finished a round of house calls and she must have been crossing the road to get back to her car. It was parked a few hundred yards away from her last visit.'

'Wasn't it a bit odd, parking so far away?' Rae asked.

'Not in this case. She had two house calls close to each other and had parked outside the first. It looks as though she'd decided to walk to the second one rather than move her car. It's quite understandable. According to the coroner's report the impact of the collision suggests that the car was moving very fast, even though it was a built-up area.'

Sophie was watching Barry carefully. 'And?'

'She had two young children. No other details about them at present. So it looks as though you were right, ma'am. We have the breakthrough we were looking for.'

'And George Bramshaw has confirmed that the two children at his school for the 1995 spring term had the surname Camberwell. They were twins, Jasmine and Kenneth. There appears to be no record of them after they left. They vanished without trace, it seems. Well, we know why. They too died, four or five years after their mother. We need everything they have on that death, Barry. Can you visit tomorrow and collect it all?'

'Of course. But there's something else, ma'am. There was another Doctor Camberwell practising in Bristol at the same time. He was in one of the local hospitals, in orthopaedics. It could be a coincidence, but how likely is that?'

Sophie looked at her watch and did some calculations. 'Okay, we'll both go to Bristol and we'll do it now. You concentrate on the wife's death and I'll go to the hospital.' She looked around at the rest of the team. 'Unless anyone has anything important to add, we'll suspend the meeting right now and reconvene tomorrow morning first thing.' No one spoke, so Sophie stood up. 'Rae, do me a favour. Find out what you can about this second Doctor Camberwell. We assume he was related, but I don't want to end up trekking all the way to Bristol on a false premise. Be as quick as you can. I'll be ready to leave in about fifteen minutes.'

Rae soon found enough information to convince Sophie that she needed to visit the hospital.

The road to Bristol was surprisingly empty. Sophie dropped Marsh at police headquarters, and drove on to the infirmary. It didn't take her long to find the administration block and someone who could help her to trace records for a Doctor Camberwell. It was wonderful what a police warrant card could do. She was even brought coffee, just as foul-tasting as the liquid the police station supplied.

Richard Camberwell, as Rae's research had indicated, had been a specialist registrar in orthopaedic surgery. The records showed that he'd worked at the hospital from 1988 until 1994.

'Why did he leave?' Sophie asked. 'Do the records give the reason? A transfer to another hospital?'

Colin Peterson, the personnel officer, said, 'this record doesn't say, but I can check it another way. Just give me a moment.' He searched through the database. 'The problem is, it was such a long time ago. Data Protection regulations are fairly strict about how long we can hang on to personal data. Don't keep your hopes up.'

Sophie nodded. The year Camberwell had finished his spell at the hospital corresponded closely with the time when the two children were probably buried. It also fitted with the date that George Bramshaw had given her for when they started at his primary school — January 1995. Peterson could find nothing else in the records. Sophie would have to try and trace people who might remember the doctor. She asked him if he could identify anyone who had been employed at the hospital for twenty years or more and who might have had contact with Camberwell. This time the database yielded two names, a nurse and a sister.

'I'll go and get them,' he volunteered. 'I'd rather not have you wandering about the place trying to pin down people who might be anywhere. Give me a few minutes.'

He disappeared into an inner office, emerging several minutes later with a look of triumph on his face. 'Fortune favours the godly. They're both in this afternoon. I messaged them, and they can both give us a couple of minutes in a short while. Have another coffee while you wait?'

Sophie smiled weakly and shook her head. 'No thanks. I'm being careful of what's left of my stomach lining. Water would be good, though.'

Looking puzzled, he fetched a tumbler of water from yet another dispenser. What's wrong with good old tap water? Sophie wondered.

The two nurses arrived together, chatting.

'Why do you want to know about Richard Camberwell?' asked the sister.

'I can't tell you at the moment. It's to do with an ongoing investigation into a serious crime.' Sophie showed them her warrant card. 'I'd like to know where he went to from here, why, and where I might find him now. I'd appreciate anything you can tell me.'

'There's not much to tell,' replied the sister. 'He didn't go anywhere after here. He died in 1994.'

'What? How did it happen?'

'He tripped and fell down the stairs at home. Apparently he had severe head injuries that caused brain damage. He never regained consciousness and died the next day.'

'Did he have a family? What happened to them?'

'He left a widow and two children, as far as I remember. I'm afraid I don't know anything more about that side of things. She'd have been well looked after. There would have been a death in service lump sum, plus any life insurance that he'd taken out.'

'Do you know anything about the children? Could they have been twins?'

The sister shook her head. Her colleague said, 'I think they were a boy and a girl, but that's all I know. I seem to remember that he didn't talk about his family much, particularly to junior staff. He was a very thoughtful man, but kind of distant. We were both new here. I started about a year or so before he died. Weren't you the same, Bronwen?'

The sister nodded. 'Kept himself to himself. I never thought he looked particularly happy. Maybe it was just his nature.'

Sophie thanked them. 'If there's anything else you remember or if you think of someone who might be able to remember more, please phone me.' She handed over her card.

Bronwen, the sister, looked at the card. 'Dorset. And you're a DCI. Is it those kiddies' bodies in the garden? Don't tell me they were Richard's?' She put a hand up to her mouth.

‘I can’t comment, sorry. I’d like you to keep this meeting to yourselves, please. Any information that leaks out could put my investigation at risk.’

The two nurses nodded. They both looked shocked.

So, how does this alter things? Sophie wondered, as she drove into the car park at Bristol’s city police headquarters. Could it be true that the whole family had died within a few years of each other? First, Li Hua, the GP and possible mother of the twins. She’d died in the autumn of 1990, apparently in a hit and run incident. If the nurses’ recollections were correct, Richard died some four years later in 1994. Lastly the two children — if the bodies found buried at Finch Cottage were indeed the Camberwell twins. They had perished sometime in the spring of 1995. She’d have to wait to see what Barry had discovered, but it was beginning to look as if the case might be vastly more complex than any of them had imagined. The other interesting fact was that the sister was sure that Richard had left a widow. Had he married again after Li Hua’s death?

Sophie slid out of her car and made her way to the staff entrance.

CHAPTER 19: INFREQUENTLY WASHED KNICKERS

Tuesday evening, Week 2

Hannah Allen dropped her phone into her bag and walked through to her bedroom. She shared a flat with two other students. She had been in the only communal room, the kitchen, when the call from Pauline Stopley had come in. The former actress had explained that she'd been at an Arts Council meeting in the capital. It had finished early, her evening date had fallen through and so she had a free evening in London. Would Hannah like to meet her for a light meal and a few drinks? Hannah was excited and surprised by the invitation. It would be really useful to pick the brains of someone who'd done the rounds as a busy, working actress almost two decades ago. Pauline must have built up a wealth of experience and hearing her stories would be very useful to Hannah. Even if Pauline wasn't keen to talk about her past, Hannah would still gain something. She loved meeting people who had anything to do with the theatre, even carpenters or set designers. But she was puzzled. Had she really made such an impression on this woman?

Hannah rifled through the somewhat sparse contents of her wardrobe, finally settling on a pale blue dress decorated with small flowers in peach. A recent birthday present from her grandmother, it was simple but pretty. Ideal with those new peach suede shoes. Hannah went to the mirror. Maybe a hint of pink eye shadow? A little liner and mascara, a light touch of blusher and there she was, ready for an evening out. She slipped into her coat, picked up her bag and made for the door.

* * *

The Turkish restaurant in Bloomsbury was one of Hannah's favourites and she knew the staff well.

The manager looked concerned when she entered. 'You are not here with your young man. Should I be worried? Is it someone new you are meeting?'

'No, no. I'm meeting someone who used to be a famous actress,' Hannah replied. 'But don't say anything.'

She was shown to one of the better tables, close to an ornate shelf bearing vases of colourful flowers. She sat facing the door, looking out at the people streaming by outside. There were students, tourists and workers, alone or in groups, all on their way to an evening out somewhere. And there she was, Pauline Stopley. She stood out in the crowd even in this failing light. Hannah watched her stride towards the door, smile at the manager, then whisper to him as he took her coat. Hannah stood up ready to shake hands as she reached the table, but Pauline reached across and gave Hannah a kiss on the cheek.

'You look lovely,' she said. 'That's a pretty dress.'

'Thank you.' Hannah realised she was blushing slightly. 'You found the place alright? I was worried that my directions wouldn't be clear.'

Pauline smiled as she sat down. 'Bloomsbury, Covent Garden, Russell Square. This used to be one of my old stamping grounds. I couldn't get lost in this area. Now, let's choose some food and drink and then we can chat. This is my treat by the way. No arguments.'

She waved a finger. Very theatrical, thought Hannah. She wondered whether to comment on Pauline's dress, a beautifully cut, plain black shift, but thought better of it. They studied the menu, Pauline chose the wine, and the two women settled into a couple of hours of very pleasant chat about the ins and outs of an acting career. It was more than two hours later that they finished their coffees and Pauline paid the bill.

'Shall we go to a pub?' she asked. 'It's still early. My return ticket for Dorchester is tomorrow morning, so I'm in a hotel for the night and I'd just get bored going back this early. You must know some good bars near here if you're a regular. What about it?'

'Fine,' Hannah replied. 'There's a really interesting one just down the road. It has puppets on a shelf above the bar, but more importantly the beer is terrific.'

Pauline laughed. 'Beer? A slip of a girl like you?'

'It's something I inherited from my parents, both of them. My mum's just as keen on a good pint as my dad is. You wouldn't think so to look at her, but she keeps herself very fit. I try to do the same but it doesn't always work. On cold mornings I'm more likely to stay in bed than go out running.'

'Was that your father who was there on Sunday? He didn't say very much. Good-looking though.'

'I don't know whether I approve of that!' Hannah laughed.

'What does he do?'

'He's a teacher. He's assistant principal at a big secondary school and head of the maths department. He's great. I love both of them.'

They found a table and Hannah bought a beer for herself and a brandy for Pauline. They had a second drink, this time two brandies that Pauline bought. Hannah took a sip, looked at the glass and guessed it was a double. Did she really want to wake up with a splitting headache tomorrow? Why had Pauline bought them both so much drink? She took another sip and realised that her companion seemed to have moved closer. She could feel Pauline's thigh touching hers.

* * *

Hannah arrived back at her apartment just as her two flatmates appeared in the kitchen for breakfast. The three of them had been close friends at school and had decided to flat-share when they all found they were to be students in London.

'How did your evening go?' Marie, an economics student, asked. She still sounded half asleep.

'Well, it was interesting. Quite enjoyable really.'

Jess, more alert, nudged Marie. 'She's still in the dress she wore last night. She's only just got back in. Well, well, well, Hannah Allen. Sit down, have some tea and tell us all about it. We're all ears.'

'I thought you were meeting an actress?' yawned Marie.

'Yes, I did.'

'So did you meet someone else afterwards?'

'No.'

There was a stunned silence. 'Does that mean what I think it means?' asked Marie. 'I mean, I know I shouldn't pry, but . . . I don't quite know what to say.'

'Don't worry,' Hannah replied. 'I might be part lesbian, but I really don't fancy either of you two. I know how infrequently you wash your knickers.'

'Will you be seeing her again?' gasped Jess.

'Maybe occasionally, but she's a lot older than me. We both agreed not to make a thing of it.'

'Hannah . . . what was it like? I mean . . . For fuck's sake. Can you just swan in and tell us this? Well, you just have, so I suppose the answer to that is yes. Jesus, I would never have guessed.'

'I think I must take after one of my aunts. She's bisexual, though she doesn't spread it around. And to save you asking the question, no, this wasn't my first time. I don't think it'll be my last, either.'

'But what about Russell? I thought you two were an item. What happens to you now?' Jess asked. 'You know, this might be the first time I wish I'd opted to do behavioural psychology rather than engineering.'

Hannah shrugged. 'We'll have to see, won't we? Russell is not at the forefront of my mind just now.' She looked at the clock. 'Particularly since I'm due at a seminar.' She drained her cup, but sat on at the table. There was an awkward silence. 'I am a drama student, remember. Sometimes I just feel the need to rehearse.' After several moments Hannah broke into a smile and winked at her friends. 'Actually, despite the fact that she was very attractive, she was far too old for me.'

'You utter little tosser! I can't believe I fell for it,' Jess complained loudly. 'What did you actually do last night then?'

'Russell came to pick me up from the pub. What happened between then and now is strictly between the two of us.'

'Time for toast?' Marie asked.

'Thanks, but no. One thing I will say is that he cooks a brilliant breakfast. I don't think I'll be able to eat again until this evening.'

'The world will end before you miss out on lunch, Little Miss Greedy,' said Marie. 'One thing we do know about you is that your first love is food. It's also your second, third and fourth loves. Whatever else we've learned about you today, it will be a long way back in your affection rankings compared to a good nosh-up.'

Hannah paused at the doorway and laughed.

CHAPTER 20: CAMBERWELL BEAUTIES

Wednesday morning, Week 2

'So all four of them died, probably within four years of each other? It's mind-blowing, ma'am. I can't quite take it in.' Rae was commenting on Sophie's report about the two Camberwell parents.

The team were assembled around the central table in the incident room, along with five local detectives. Sophie was now in charge of a much larger squad. She'd decided that she couldn't afford to wait until the children's identity was officially confirmed. She would assume that they were the Camberwell twins and plan her strategy accordingly. The ACC at headquarters had agreed immediately, so all available resources were now being put at her disposal.

'We have to bear in mind that it could all be coincidence. There was never any indication that Richard's death was anything other than a tragic accident. It's also entirely possible that Li Hua's death was just a random hit and run, though the nature of the collision was suspicious, to me anyway. Barry and I visited the place where it happened, and we couldn't see why anyone would be travelling well in excess of forty miles per hour in a narrow suburban street like that. The unofficial guess was that the driver was doing at least fifty. It's possible it might have been someone high on drink or drugs, but it wasn't an area noted for that type of thing. And if it had been some local tearaway, the local bobbies would have expected to find the car fairly quickly, probably burned out on some nearby wasteland. It's never been found. Someone disposed of it very carefully.'

'Did they do a thorough search?' asked one of the local team.

Barry answered. 'Yes, I think so. The local crime unit seem to have done everything by the book. They even staged a partial reconstruction with a dummy body. They tried to find the car from paint fragments found on her coat but nothing turned up. It was dark blue paint from a Ford, a very common colour. If the car was dumped, it wasn't anywhere in the Bristol area. They did a check of local cars in that particular colour, but none had any evidence of front-end damage.'

'It implies careful planning,' Rae suggested. 'It fits with someone thinking this through very carefully in advance.'

'But what would the motive be? Why would someone kill her? She was a popular, highly regarded GP, a mother of two young children. What was to gain?' a local detective said.

Marsh replied, 'well, she might have been killed by her husband. We know from their headmaster that the children had a mother with them when they first arrived. She came to a couple of school events. So it seems fairly certain that Richard remarried. Li Hua's death freed him to marry again.'

Sophie was growing impatient. 'Let's not waste time speculating. We'll have to go back through the records to find out what happened before her death, and afterwards. Did he really marry again or was it merely hearsay? If so, how long afterwards? Who was she? We want to find out more about the relationship between Li Hua and Richard. When did they marry? Where? Were they happy? Let's try to trace any family and interview them. Leave the speculation to Barry and me at present.'

'One thing, ma'am. Can we be sure that Richard's death really was an accident?'

'I've thought of that, Rae. As I said, I'm keeping all options open. Maybe you could concentrate on that aspect. Find the post-mortem details if you can, and the coroner's report.' She turned to the rest of the team. 'If anyone finds anything interesting, let me know immediately. No delay. It must come straight to me. Is that understood?'

The group returned to work and a hush descended on the room. Barry Marsh was building up a picture of Li Hua's life. The picture of her that began to emerge was that of a dedicated mother, focused on her work and bringing up her twins. She had often referred to them as her "Camberwell Beauties," shockingly apt in the light of their burial place under a butterfly bush. Li Hua had been born and raised in Hong Kong and had gone to the local university. She met Richard there while they were both practising at a local clinic. They married and left for the UK several years before Hong Kong was ceded to China. Barry could find no connection with Bristol that would explain why they settled there. Rae was now researching his background.

Li Hua had come from a large family, so it shouldn't be difficult to find someone willing to give a DNA sample. He spent the rest of the day on the phone, attempting to make arrangements with the Hong Kong police.

Rae managed to track down the findings of the original investigation into Richard's death, along with the coroner's report. The house where the accident occurred was a tall, terraced property with steep stairways. It appeared that Richard had tripped on some children's toys left on the top step and had tumbled heavily to the bottom. His fatal head injuries were attributed to striking a protruding wooden window sill at the bottom of the stairs. This was sketched, and also shown in a photo attached to the report. The sill showed bloodstains where his head had struck it, and the wound was consistent with a collision of that nature. Richard had been alone in the house at the time. His wife, the second Mrs Camberwell, had returned from shopping with the children to find the body at the bottom of the stairs. There were no suspicious circumstances surrounding the death, according to the report. It had been accepted by the police, the pathologist and the coroner as nothing more than a tragic accident.

Rae looked again at the photos of the window ledge and the head wound. It was entirely possible that his head had struck the ledge after tumbling down the stairs, but didn't bodies tend to flatten out as they fell down a long set of steps, such that they slid down the last section? Could Doctor Camberwell's head still have been high enough off the level of the carpet to have struck the sill, a good two feet above the bottom stair? She took the file to Sophie.

'The problem is, ma'am, that no one doubted that it was an accident, in all these reports. His wife's whereabouts that afternoon were checked and there were witness statements from shop staff and neighbours, but I think there was enough leeway in the estimated time of death for some doubt to creep in. They've used the fact that his watch was damaged in the fall and stopped working to be the corroborating evidence for time of death. But what if had been deliberately altered then smashed separately? It's all too late now to do any checking of the scene. All we have is the records in front of us.'

Sophie nodded. 'We can bear it in mind. We need to find out much more about this second wife of his. Get onto it now, Rae. You're good at going through records and spotting things. We need to know what her name was before she married Richard, and where she is now. Do we have a first name yet?'

Rae nodded. 'Pauline. And that name matches the initial we have on our list of residents for Finch Cottage, a P Camberwell.'

'Good. We ought to get these photos of the head wounds checked by an expert. I'll ask Benny Goodall to recommend someone.'

CHAPTER 21: METICULOUSLY PRESSED TROUSERS

Wednesday afternoon, Week 2

Jill Freeman glanced at her watch for the seventh time in as many minutes. She felt nervous and tense, almost terrified, but remained in the hotel bar, sipping her gin and tonic. Where had her lover got to? The text message had been terse, merely stating a location (this hotel) and a time (fifteen minutes ago). Should she be doing this? Why was she doing this? What were her motives? She considered these questions for what seemed like the twentieth time that day. She came to the same conclusion. Yes, she should. She so desperately needed to. Anyway, who gives a tinker's cuss about motives when the emotions are as powerful as these? Her longing was so intense that it overran all reason. Jill was nothing but a quivering mass of desire. All other pressures were wiped away. In fact the extra pressures were part of the problem. After the discovery of those tiny, tragic bodies buried under the butterfly bush in her garden, it all became too much for her to cope with. She desperately needed to escape, if only for an hour or two.

Jill took another sip and glanced up in time to see the object of her lust coming through the door from reception, dressed in black, walking calmly and in control towards the bar, ordering two large gin and tonics, exchanging a quiet, relaxed few words with the barman, and finally turning towards her. Oh, that confident, reassuring smile. Jill felt her heart lurch.

'I've already picked up the key to the room,' she said, nervous.

'In that case I won't bother sitting down,' came the calm, assured reply as those long, sensitive fingers stroked out an errant fold in the fabric of the meticulously pressed black trousers. 'Shall we just go up? I want to get your clothes off with as little delay as possible so that I can worship that beautiful body of yours. It's been a tense and busy couple of days, and then to cap it all my train ran late.'

Jill rose from her chair, holding out her hand, and took the proffered arm. 'For me too. But I'm fine now you're here.'

* * *

It was nearly five in the afternoon when Jill Freeman, still slightly flushed, turned the key in her front door and let herself in.

'Anyone in?' she called. There was no answer. She'd chosen today for that very reason: both children would be in late. Karen was playing in an away match for her school hockey team and Paul would be at the after-school chess club. Neither would be back before five thirty. Jill had worked late on both of the preceding two days in order to gain the free afternoon. She went to the kitchen to make a pot of tea, then up to her bedroom where she changed into jeans and a loose blouse. She'd already showered at the hotel to wash off the smell of sex, so she dumped her bra and panties into the wash basket and returned to the kitchen to pour her tea. When Paul arrived home, excited from his first victory in the school chess challenge, she was sitting on the couch, feet tucked under her, sipping Earl Grey and apparently calm. Inside, her brain was still performing cartwheels.

'Have a biscuit and a glass of milk, Paul,' she called. 'Dinner won't be ready before six thirty, so you can probably get most of your homework done before we eat. Okay, sweetheart?'

She finished her tea, made her way through to the kitchen and started on a batch of ironing. Inside, she was still singing the Hallelujah Chorus, the music that had entered her head earlier that afternoon as she'd climaxed for the second time in an hour.

* * *

Dorothy Kitson telephoned Tony Younger, the church minister, telling him that she would be away for several weeks because a close family member was seriously ill. Would he be able to arrange a substitute cleaner? She then called the Arts Centre with the same message. She drew deeply on her cigarette, her fingers trembling. Maybe she'd keep on a couple of her household cleaning jobs. Those people wouldn't know much, after all. But that detective woman worried her, she and her nuisance daughter, always popping up in odd places and looking at her, trying to talk to her. That just wasn't fair. What had she ever done to deserve that kind of nosey intrusion? Nothing. She'd done nothing. It frightened her, especially after she'd seen the policewoman at the church on Friday morning. She hadn't expected that. She'd heard them talking, as if they already knew each other. Why? Was there something that she, Dorothy, didn't know? Had something happened involving the vicar? Had he called the police in? Why would he do that? What had the police found out? And most of all, what was her sister up to?

Her hand was still shaking. She poured herself a large glass of scotch and added some lemonade. She blew her nose noisily and lit another cigarette.

* * *

It was now seven forty-five. John Wethergill sat alone at his table in Dorchester's best Italian restaurant, disappointed and rather self-conscious. It would be obvious to the other diners, particularly the young couple at the next table that he was waiting for someone. He was sitting at a table for two and had not yet ordered any food. He was wearing a neat, well-pressed shirt and contrasting tie, and checked his watch frequently. She was fifteen minutes late, and this was a first date —outside his flat, that is. Did that night of passion count as a date? He sighed and idly pushed his small glass of beer around on the table, then started to play with his napkin. How much longer should he wait, and why hadn't she sent him a message? He looked up, and there she was, walking towards him with that seductive smile on her face. She slid out of her coat and sat down. She was wearing a shift dress in a delicate pink. She looked stunning. His throat became dry.

'Sorry I'm late. I've had one heck of a busy day. I've had a couple of days in London on Arts Council business, and this morning's session went over time. I rushed to get to my Waterloo train, and then it ran late. At least I managed to get a couple of hours' exercise this afternoon and a short nap. I was so tired after all the endless meetings. But here I am. You look shocked. Your mouth's open.'

John closed his mouth, then opened it again. 'Yes. I mean, no. Don't worry. It's not a problem. Was it an interesting couple of days though?'

Pauline gave him one of her disarming smiles. 'Yes, in a way. I had a charming evening out yesterday with a young woman from Dorset who is at Drama College in London. She was picking my brains about acting and then she told me all about her FGM campaign. We got a bit tipsy together.' She caught the attention of a passing waitress. 'Shall we order?'

They ordered and Pauline almost gulped her gin and tonic.

'What's FGM?' John asked.

'It stands for female genital mutilation. I'm surprised you haven't heard of it. It's been in the news quite a lot in recent years. Some cultures, mainly from Africa, practise female circumcision. It's a form of control, leaving the girl unable to enjoy sex. Her clitoris is cut out before she reaches puberty. There's nothing to gain from the practice and everything to lose, according to Hannah — she's the young woman I met. She called it totally barbaric. Many women are left mutilated and in pain for the rest of their lives. I met Hannah for the first time here in Dorchester, on Sunday. She was chairing a talk at the Arts Centre and we chatted over a cup of tea afterwards. That's when she found out who I was. I had a free evening yesterday so I contacted her to see if she was able to meet me.'

John looked a little puzzled. 'You said you were meeting someone on Sunday afternoon, so I thought you had another date. You meant the talk? You were just teasing me, weren't you?'

Pauline smiled mischievously. 'I went with my sister. But I did have lunch first, and that's all I'm prepared to say.' She paused for a moment. 'I did enjoy our time together at the weekend, John. I sometimes worry that I'm too pushy when it comes to the physical side of things, but it isn't forced. It seems natural for me to take the lead. I guess you'll just have to accept it.'

He smiled. 'It's not a problem. It was all new to me and I loved it.' He raised his beer and they touched glasses. 'Here's to us,' he said. 'Do you want to come back to mine again tonight?'

She shook her head. 'Sorry, John. I really can't make it tonight. But how about you coming to my place on Friday evening? I do a great pasta if you don't mind eating Italian again.'

'Of course. I'll look forward to it. I'll bring the wine.'

She leaned towards him and whispered, 'I've thought of one or two new things to try out. Wear your silk pants again. Okay?'

The young couple at the next table stared at them, wide-eyed. John was embarrassed, but Pauline smiled sweetly at them and winked.

CHAPTER 22: DREADFUL DEATH

Thursday morning, Week 2

'What's going on?' Sophie arrived at the incident room after a meeting with Jim Metcalfe and Neil Dunnett. The latter had been sullen and uncommunicative. Thank heavens for her good relationship with the ACC.

'It might turn out to involve us, ma'am.' Marsh held out some sheets of paper. 'An apparent suicide this morning, here in Dorchester. John Wethergill, owner of a local hardware shop. The cleaner found him dead in bed when she went in first thing this morning. It has all the signs of cyanide poisoning. The local uniforms were there pretty quick and the call to us came in just now.'

'Cyanide? Where in God's name would he get that? Did you say hardware shop? Even so, it's almost impossible to get hold of the stuff.'

'He could have had it for years, ma'am.'

'But why contact us?'

'Apparently they found something showing that he'd been the gardener at Finch Cottage many years ago.'

Sophie closed her eyes. How was this going to look to Dunnett? Checking for gardeners and odd job men was to be their next task. And now this. She gave Marsh a thin smile. 'Dunnett is going to have a field day with this. Okay, let's move. Get Rae, will you?'

* * *

Wethergill's flat was in a building that had once been a warehouse. A uniformed officer waited for the detectives in the flat's hallway. Another was sitting inside with the cleaner who had made the grim discovery. Sophie greeted the two constables and spoke quietly to the one at the door.

'What did you find that made you call us?' she asked.

He pointed to a framed photo on a shelf in the narrow hall. It looked fairly old, slightly faded and out of focus. It showed a man in his late twenties or early thirties, wearing gardening clothes and leaning on a garden spade. Sophie recognised the garden immediately. She could see Finch Cottage in the background. She turned the photo over and read the inscription on the back: "To John Wethergill, Finch Cottage gardener, 1986 - 1996. Good luck with the new shop."

Sophie nodded. She looked around her, waiting for Benny Goodall, who had pulled up outside just as the detectives were entering the building. The ceilings were high, with exposed beams in the kitchen and living room, but the bedrooms looked more modern. Not that the detectives had much desire to admire the decor in the main bedroom. The effects of cyanide poisoning were clearly evident.

'Not much doubt, is there?' Sophie said to the pathologist, who had finally caught up with them. The redness of the dead man's face said it all, along with the trails of vomit spread on and around the bed, evidence of severe seizures. 'He took it bad.'

Wethergill's body, still fully clothed, lay spread-eagled across the bed.

Goodall wrinkled his nose. 'Can you smell it? Almonds.'

'Yes. Is there any way it could have been accidental, Benny? Is that at all possible?'

'There's always a chance, I suppose. But why would anyone keep the stuff? It's so tightly controlled. If he did have some in the house, I suppose it could be taken accidentally, assuming it was potassium cyanide. It looks just like sugar. But realistically, how likely is that? Are there any hints of a motive for suicide?'

She nodded. 'Oh yes, most definitely. Once you get him out of here we'll start looking for more clues. For your ears only, Benny, he could have been the gardener at Finch Cottage.'

'Was the net closing in, then?'

'Not really, although he wasn't to know that. Anyway, it would have only been a matter of time. Rae has made a list of all the occupants and owners, so regular visitors and hired help would have been next. He would have guessed that. Time of death, Benny?'

'I'd guess sometime in the early hours. He's been dead about six or seven hours, so maybe between two and four this morning.'

Sophie nodded and looked at the empty glass tumbler on the bedside table. A small jar of white crystals sat beside the glass with its lid off, a teaspoon beside it. The aged label simply stated "Potassium Cyanide." A half-full bottle of whisky stood behind it, also open.

'We need to be careful with that stuff lying around,' she said. 'Whatever you do, Barry, don't put your fingers near your lips and mouth just in case you've picked up some grains of it without realising. Once we've finished our brief look we close the door until the forensic squad arrive. Dave should be here within twenty minutes or so.' She looked at Goodall. 'Do the full works, Benny. Everything you can think of. I'd like to get as complete a picture as possible of everything he did last night, and your findings will help so much.'

Marsh had been looking around the room. He picked up two framed photos lying face down on the nearby shelf. 'Ma'am, you ought to see these.'

He handed the first one to her. It was a picture of a young woman who looked Asian. The second showed two young children, a boy and a girl.

Sophie waited while Benny finished his cursory examination and the forensic photographer had completed her work. She left the bedroom, took off her forensic suit and went into the lounge. Rae was sitting with a pale, middle-aged woman with shocking pink hair.

'This is Sylvia McCabe, ma'am. She discovered the body soon after she got here this morning to do her weekly clean.'

'Hello, Sylvia. Have you been working here long?'

The woman nodded. 'About five years.'

'I'm the senior investigating officer on the case, and I'll need to ask you a few questions. Are you well enough to answer them now, or would you prefer it if we spoke later on today?'

There was a slight pause. 'Um. Now would be okay.'

'I'm Detective Chief Inspector Sophie Allen. Here's my warrant card. Let's start with some routine questions about your work for Mr Wethergill.'

The cleaning lady called at the same time each Thursday morning to clean the apartment and do some of the laundry. John Wethergill had always washed and ironed his clothes, but had arranged with her to do the bed linen.

'I don't wash it here,' she told them. 'I use the laundry down the road. It's quicker for drying the sheets and stuff.'

'Have you noticed anything unusual in recent weeks, Sylvia? In Mr Wethergill's behaviour? In the flat?'

'Not really, though I don't see him very much. He leaves me my money in an envelope on that shelf.' She pointed towards a bookcase by the wall. There was no envelope.

'Where is it today?' Sophie asked.

Sylvia patted her pocket. 'It's the first thing I do, find me money. There's no point in doing me cleaning and then finding it's not there, is there? That's the agreement. Me money has to be ready for me.'

'We'll need that envelope, Sylvia. It will have to be fingerprinted. That means we'll need your prints as well. No, don't you take it out. Rae can do it with a pair of tweezers.'

Sylvia watched. She looked anxious as the envelope containing her morning's wages was carefully extracted from the pocket on the front of her housecoat. Rae then opened the top flap and peered inside.

'Fifty pounds,' she said, depositing the small package into a plastic bag.

'S'right. When will I get it? I needs that money.'

'You'll get a receipt, Sylvia. If you're really short I can lend you some.'

The cleaner was quiet for a while. 'No, I s'pose I can wait.'

'Did you see anything else different today?'

'Me name isn't on the envelope. It always was before, but it's blank today. Maybe he couldn't find a pen, I dunno. And it's in smaller notes than usual. It's always two twenties and a ten. This morning it's four tens and two fivers.'

'There's a framed photo in the bedroom of a woman. She looks Asian. Maybe Indian? Do you know anything about it?'

'That'll be his girlfriend as was. Maralit or something like that, I think. She's not been around for a few weeks. He said she'd gone back to the Philippines or somewhere like that. That photo's always been in here before, not the bedroom.'

'And there's another, two young children.'

Sylvia shook her head. 'Probably Maralit's kids. I think they stayed back in the Philippines with their dad. He don't usually keep it out, only when Maralit's around and she's been away for weeks.'

'Can you walk round the flat with me, Sylvia? Just to see if anything else is out of its usual place. It won't take long, and we won't go in the bedroom. Then you can go. Okay?'

* * *

'So. Assuming the bodies were of the Camberwell children, have we been barking up the wrong tree?' Sophie asked.

'What if they were the two in this photo, somehow linked to Wethergill, who just happened to be the gardener at Finch Cottage at about the time they were buried? What if the mother is the woman in the other photo, Maralit or whoever, who's conveniently returned to the Philippines sometime in the past month or two? What I'm asking is, are we back to square one?'

Neither Barry nor Rae answered. They felt the same; despondent and angry with themselves. Sophie answered her own question. 'Obviously we switch our attention to Wethergill at the moment. We need to give his place the full works, and find out all we can about him.' She paused. 'But we don't bin the stuff we've already done on the Camberwells. It remains a possible avenue until I decide otherwise. Agreed?'

Her two juniors nodded.

'Fine. Let's get to work. Maybe a visit to the pub is in order tonight when we finish. Although I desperately want a shower and change of clothes to get rid of that foul smell. I think it's just my imagination. Reassure me please, Rae. You didn't come into the bedroom.'

Rae came closer and sniffed cautiously.

'It is your imagination, ma'am. Not a trace. You were both wearing romper suits, remember?'

'Sometimes those things do have their uses,' came the answer.

CHAPTER 23: FILM STAR LOOKS

Friday morning, Week 2

Dave Nash, the forensic chief with the film star looks, so breathtakingly handsome that he'd even give George Clooney a run for his money, stood opposite Sophie and scratched his ear.

'Dave, stop doing that. As it is, you've got half the women in the station watching you instead of getting on with their work. It gets worse when you actually move in some way rather than sitting still. You ought to go round with a hazard warning around your neck. Let's go through to my office where I can ogle you without any competition.'

Laughing, the forensic chief followed Sophie to her temporary office and sat down.

'What do you have for me?' Sophie asked.

'Well, remember that this is early days, so there'll be more to come. We've finished dusting the flat. There are two sets of prints that are all over the place, those of Wethergill himself and the cleaner. But we also found a third set in a few places, including the bedroom. We also found what looks like lipstick on the bathroom mirror, as if a message had been written there. It took a bit of time to reconstruct it, but it appears to be a phone number.' He passed across a photo of the mirror and a note with the number written on it. 'There are also photos of several Thai or Philippino women, so he may have been in contact with a dating agency of some kind, although they look quite old.'

'The photos or the women?'

Nash laughed. 'The photos. I'm not as sexist or ageist as people may think.'

Sophie smirked. 'I never thought you were. Can you confirm the presence of cyanide?'

'Yes. I've been in touch with Dr Goodall. Doubtless you'll be seeing him yourself, but it looks certain that it was cyanide poisoning. We took samples in order to analyse the contents of that jar, and it was potassium cyanide just as the label said. It's currently locked in a store cupboard in my office. There were also traces in the tumbler on the bedside table, along with some alcohol. Everything adds up, Sophie.'

'Anything else of interest?'

'We found his wallet on a shelf. It had a credit card receipt from an Italian restaurant in it, with Wednesday evening's date. Guessing from the total, I'd say he had dinner with someone.' He handed her a plastic sleeve containing the receipt. 'I have the cleaners in now, getting the bedroom back to some sort of normality. It's all yours from this afternoon onwards. I'll send you copies of all our videos and photos as soon as I'm back in my office. Is that all okay?'

Sophie nodded. She was serious now, the mischievous smile gone. 'Of course. You always do a brilliant job, Dave. I'm really grateful for the extra effort you put in, and I trust you completely.'

'But this isn't what you were expecting? Am I right?'

She shook her head. 'No. It came as a total shock. We were already well down another road entirely. Ah well. Such is life. I'll chase up the restaurant angle right now, then follow up on the phone number. We'll visit the flat this afternoon.

Did anything show up on the envelope of money that we gave you?'

'Lots of prints from the cleaner, as you'd expect. She obviously took the money out to count it, then replaced it. A couple of Wethergill's prints on the envelope and some of the notes but not all. And prints from a third person, not yet identified. Every single bank note as well as a single smudged print on the envelope. It's possible that whoever it was tried to wipe it off.'

* * *

'Well, here's an interesting one, Barry.' Sophie stood leaning against Marsh's desk. 'Ristorante Italia on the High Street confirmed that someone answering Wethergill's description was there Wednesday evening, dining with a woman. Apparently she was late, and the staff could see that he was getting restless. His date did arrive in the end, though, and she was well worth the wait, according to the manager. A middle-aged woman, very attractive and very well-dressed. He said they seemed very intimate with each other. I wonder if she's the person who left the lipstick message on the bathroom mirror? Shall we give the number a go? I want you to listen in on your extension.'

Sophie waited until Marsh was ready and dialled the number, that of a mobile phone. It was answered after two rings.

'Good morning. This is Detective Chief Inspector Sophie Allen of Dorset police. Who am I speaking to, please?'

The voice was cultured. 'I'm Pauline Stopley. How can I help you?'

'Pauline, did you visit the Ristorante Italiana on Wednesday night?'

'Yes, I did. Why?'

'Were you with someone?'

'Yes. I had a dinner date with John Wethergill.'

'And was it you who left this phone number in his flat?'

A short laugh. 'Yes. In lipstick, on the bathroom mirror. It was a bit of light-hearted nonsense after my visit at the weekend.'

'Were you in the flat on Wednesday night?'

'No. I'd had a couple of busy days of meetings in London and I was just too tired. I'll be seeing him tonight, though. He's coming round to mine. It's my turn to cook. Why?'

Sophie continued. 'Are you a longstanding friend or partner, Pauline?'

'Goodness, no. We only met for the first time on Saturday. I've seen him three times in total, but he's a really nice bloke. Can I ask why for a third time, since you haven't explained yet?'

'I really need to see you, Pauline. Would it be best if I came to you, or would you prefer to drop into the police station?'

There was a pause. 'This sounds serious. I'm at work at the moment, but I'm only five minutes' walk from you. I'll come over. Who do I ask for again?'

'DCI Sophie Allen. I'll have someone waiting.'

* * *

Pauline hurried into the foyer of the police station, looking anxiously around her. Marsh walked towards her.

'I'm DS Barry Marsh, Ms Stopley. If you'll come with me, I'll take you to the DCI's office. It will only take a moment.'

'Can you tell me what's happened? Please?'

Marsh shook his head. 'Sorry. That's for the DCI.' He led her through to the back of the station, where he unlocked an interview room.

'Would you like some tea or coffee?'

'A glass of water will be fine.' She looked tense and anxious.

Sophie came in, shook hands and introduced herself. 'Can I call you Pauline or would you rather I use your last name?'

'Pauline is fine.'

'I have some really upsetting news for you, Pauline. John Wethergill was found dead in his flat by his cleaner yesterday morning.'

'Oh, God,' said Pauline. 'But how? He seemed absolutely fine when I left him outside the restaurant. He only had an easy five minute walk to get home. What on earth happened?'

'We don't have the full details yet but the circumstances seem suspicious.'

Pauline put her hand to her brow. 'I can't believe it. How could it happen? Are you sure it's him?'

'Yes. His cleaning lady is certain. His appearance matches the photos in the flat, and one of my officers has been round to his shop. His staff were concerned when he didn't come in yesterday morning.' She paused. 'It may well be that you were the last person to see him alive, Pauline. With that in mind, I'll need a full statement about your date with him on Wednesday night. Would you like to do that now or some other time? I'd prefer to get it out of the way as soon as possible, while it's fresh in your mind. We'll also need to take your fingerprints since you've been in his flat, even if it was only once. Shall we change that water for a cup of tea?'

Pauline nodded, still looking dazed. The interview lasted another twenty minutes and when it was over Sophie mentioned that her daughter, Hannah, had met Pauline briefly at the weekend after the talk on FGM. Pauline nodded and said she remembered talking to her about the theatre.

Just after twelve, Rae returned to the incident room. She had been visiting Wethergill's hardware shop and the Italian restaurant that the couple had gone to on Wednesday. Pauline Stopley had just left, so the three detectives spent some time crosschecking her statement with that of the restaurant manager. Everything matched.

'One thing, ma'am,' Rae said. 'According to the manager there was another couple sitting at a table close by who may well have heard some of their conversation. It might be worth checking with them. They're regulars, so he gave me their details.'

'Good work, Rae. Go ahead. I just want to be reassured that nothing was said that might have tipped him over the edge. At the moment it looks like their date was free of friction, but all verification is good verification.'

The fingerprint check showed that the third set of prints belonged to Pauline Stopley. They were found in the lounge, kitchen, bathroom and bedroom. There were several sets on the headboard.

'We'll need to hear her explanation for those, won't we, ma'am?' Marsh said.

'Already done, Barry. We had a brief chat out of your earshot after she had her prints taken. She told me they'd spent Sunday night together in his flat. She said her prints would be all over the bedroom. Take that any way you want. I just find it makes his death a bit peculiar. He'd just found a new woman, a rather sexy one at that, so you'd think he would be feeling pleased with life. But instead he apparently commits suicide. Does it add up?'

'But the suicide was about something entirely different, wasn't it? It was about the bodies. Maybe he realised that sooner or later we'd get to know that he was the gardener at the time they were buried. He knew he'd have to face up to it sometime. Why not when he was feeling happy and fulfilled? Go out when you're on top?' Marsh shrugged.

Sophie frowned. 'Maybe. It just bothers me a bit. I still want us to keep digging into the background, Barry. The fact that the children died twenty years ago doesn't make the crime any less serious than one that happened recently. It was still an abhorrent act to put their bodies there, even if we finally decide that they died of natural causes. The fact that one of the people who was around then has topped himself doesn't change anything. I still want to know why and how it happened, even if it's hard to find the facts. Forensic science has moved on so much now. It can give us all kinds of leads that might not have been possible a quarter of a century ago. I still think that DNA profiling will be key to solving the case, but we've got to trace other family members for that.'

'I've asked for an inventory of the items kept by the Bristol police after Li Hua's death. The stuff will be in a box in some store-room somewhere, but the people I spoke to were pretty confident it could be found. The case is still open, after all. If we're in luck there might be something like a hairbrush that can be used. I should get the list tomorrow. It might mean that we don't have to wait until we find a family member before we can do a DNA check.'

Sophie nodded. 'That jar of potassium cyanide crystals at Wethergill's flat was very old, judging by the state of the label. It might well predate 1995, the year we think the children's bodies were buried. I just wonder if they were killed with the stuff. The problem is, I don't think there's any way of telling, not after so long. It would have leached out of the bodies and been broken down in the soil. It might be worth checking though. I'll get onto some contacts I have in the environmental chemistry world. They might be able to tell me whether it's worth testing the soil from around the bodies for residues. It's a long shot but it might help us to know what went on all those years ago.' She gazed out of the window. 'Twenty years ago I was in my first detective job, in the Met, working under Harry Turner. I'd just returned to work from maternity leave, after having Hannah. It seems so long ago. What were you up to, Barry?'

He pursed his lips. 'I was in middle school, about halfway through. I'd just lost my father. He was a farmer in Purbeck, and he died when a stack of hay bales fell on him.'

Sophie stared at him. 'Why on earth didn't you tell me this when we were in the middle of all that hoo-ha about my father? I was so bound up with myself, I could have done with someone reminding me that others have gone through similar tragedies in their childhoods.'

He shrugged. 'It's all in the past, isn't it? Get over it, that's what I tell myself.'

'Do you still miss him?' Sophie asked.

'Yes, I do. We were very close, him and me. Much closer than I was with my mum. The accident changed our lives completely. It made me decide not to stay in farming. One of the farm hands had stacked the rick really badly and my dad could see it was unsafe. He was trying to secure it when it happened.'

'That's awful. Did your mum get compensation?'

'Yes. Dad was well insured and the worker was found to be negligent. Mum sold the farm and we moved to Swanage. She bought a little café.'

Sophie looked perplexed. 'Why didn't you introduce us? We've been to Swanage often enough on cases.'

'She's not there now. She lives with my sister in Kent, and they run a café together. She moved away soon after I finished school,' said Marsh.

Sophie nodded, looking thoughtful, and then her mobile phone rang. She looked at the caller display and made a face.

'Hello, Neil,' she said, walking towards her office. 'Yes, it was unfortunate. No, I don't plan to scale things down right away.' She listened. 'I think I need to come and see you. We obviously need to talk, and the sooner the better. The problem is that I'm expecting Harry Turner to arrive soon. He's the retired expert on child murder I told you about.' She glanced at her watch. 'I'm meeting his train in about half an hour. Is it okay if I bring him with me? Or you could come down here for his talk if you want, whichever you prefer.' Another pause. 'Okay, we'll see you at about three.'

CHAPTER 24: SNAKE

Friday afternoon, Week 2

As the train made its way along the northern shoreline, Harry Turner looked out onto the mud-flats of Poole Harbour. Picturesque, he thought, particularly at high tide. Harry had his pocket binoculars to hand, and used them occasionally to spot some of the birds that rested on the marshy ground on their way to some distant breeding place. He glanced at his watch. Still half an hour to go before Dorchester. This would be the slowest part of the journey, winding through the Dorset countryside, with several steep inclines between Wareham and Dorchester. He took another sip of coffee and ate the last of his sandwiches.

He thought about the task awaiting him. How best to go about the session with Sophie's team? He decided to follow a question and answer approach. As long as he had his check list to hand it should be fine. A meal out in one of Wareham's top pubs was planned for the evening, and then on Saturday the activity he was most looking forward to: a day spent bird watching with Martin Allen at the Arne RSPB reserve. It was a top site he'd never visited before, despite many years of promises to himself. The problem had always been its proximity to Wareham, and the protégé from his working years. He had never dared risk a meeting with her. As it happened Sophie herself had broken the impasse the previous week when she'd phoned to arrange their meeting in the pub at Waterloo. So here he was, looking forward to what might be the most enjoyable weekend he'd had for years. He felt almost young again.

* * *

'So, now the introductions are over, you can start to tell us what you know, Harry. I think you know the background to the case. What might be relevant?' Sophie looked across at her ex-boss and gave him an encouraging smile.

Harry Turner leaned back in his chair. 'I'll give you an introduction to the main ideas, then you can ask questions. I'll try to be systematic. It'll help you to make sense of current thinking if I cover it in a logical way, but I'm also a pragmatist. I'll only include ideas that seem to relate to practical experiences and help to clarify things.

Who are the child killers? Let's go through the options, starting with those who are most closely linked. Parents, step-parents, siblings, half-siblings, step-siblings, uncles and aunts, other acquaintances, strangers. The emotional ties decrease in intensity as we go down the list. What this means is that the motives for child murder are likely to be very different in each case. We also need to make allowance for gender, both of the killer and the victim. A mother who kills her child will tend to have different motives from a father.

Why would a mother kill her child? The main factors include mental illness, absence of maternal feelings, severe emotional immaturity, abnormal power play, a distorted sense of reality caused by drugs or alcohol. Fathers? Well, inability to cope with the dramatic changes to life at home, excessive jealousy of the mother-child bond, and again drugs or alcohol. Financial hardship can also be a significant factor. Any of these can play a part, and if several of the factors are present then the indicators are strong. In addition, and for both parents, we must include the possibility of psychopathy.'

At the end of his talk Turner asked for questions.

Rae Gregson was the first to speak. 'You mentioned abnormal power play as a motive for a mother. Could you explain?'

Harry nodded. 'A woman, particularly someone of low social status and intelligence, might never have been in a position of power before. Never chosen as a prefect or monitor at school, never given a position of responsibility at work. She might not be in work. She's never had any power over anyone before. In fact, it's always been she who was the victim. And suddenly she is presented with a child who is totally dependent on her, particularly if she's a single mum. Most mothers respond amazingly well in such a situation, but in a small number of cases the mother expresses her insecurities through a mixture of cruelty and dominance. Each act might be followed with a show of love for the child.'

'So this particular reason probably wouldn't apply if the mother was high achieving? A doctor for example?'

'No. There the motives might be very different. For example, suppressed anger over an enforced career break, or something of that nature. It's important to realise that the mother herself will be unaware of these motives. They will be bubbling away in the subconscious. As we go down the list I mentioned at the start, the motives shift from ones that are primarily subconscious to ones that are more likely to be at least partly rational. You should all recognise a general truth. Child killers, as a rule, don't do it for a rational reason. Adults who are murdered are often killed for some type of gain, although emotion and temper still play a part. Few children are killed for gain. The motivations for their murders are twisted, and have been long suppressed. I'm generalising, of course. There are always exceptions. In the States for example, there have been cases where children have been murdered for insurance money.'

Barry Marsh said, 'there's a possibility that these murders were committed by the gardener who was employed at the house. Where would that fit?'

'He'd be an acquaintance. Let's build a possible scenario. He visits regularly, maybe a half day each week. He watches them playing. Maybe they tease him. Possibly there was a sexual element in his interest. Maybe he had a proclivity for young girls or young boys. That's where we hit the first problem. Usually it's either girls or boys, not both. Though if one of them witnessed something, both would have to be killed.'

'What might be the most likely method used to kill them?'

'Strangulation or smothering. They were only six, weren't they?'

'Not cyanide poisoning?'

Harry Turner frowned. 'That's highly unlikely, though there have been a couple of cases where a parent did use powerful poisons. It's too cold-blooded, too rational, and would require the children to drink or eat something laced with the poison. And, if it was the gardener, how would you hide it from the parents and the authorities? In fact, if it was the gardener, what kept the parents so quiet? Why didn't they call us in? It just doesn't follow. Or was a parent killed at the same time? Is there another body?'

Sophie shook her head. 'We think the parents were already dead a year or two before, though we're still waiting for the DNA profiling. We've had a sniffer dog in, and it didn't react in any other spot. We've used all kinds of ground-penetrating devices, and nothing else has shown up. If there is another body, and my gut feeling is that there isn't one, it's somewhere else. And you know what that means, Harry. You taught it to me. If there's no evidence of another body, don't waste time looking for one. It probably doesn't exist.'

Turner smiled. 'Absolutely right. It can be a real time-waster. Base your investigation on what you have, not what you might have.' He paused. 'Cyanide, eh? How would you go about finding that after twenty years?'

'Difficult, but not impossible. I spoke to a chemistry professor at Southampton University and she got back to me this morning. Apparently cyanide becomes untraceable in the body within a few days, but it's still there in a different form. It bonds very strongly to the iron in the blood, forming a complex. That's what she called it. Anyway, it's so stable that it stays around for ages. Years, even decades. I asked her if it can be identified in soil or fabric residues and she couldn't see why not, though it's never been documented in the forensic analysis literature. It will be much more difficult to carry out than a simple cyanide test, but she's willing to give it a go. Dave Nash, our forensic chief, is sending her some samples as we speak. Maybe we'll know by early next week. As far as the original cyanide is concerned, we're tracking back through records covering a quarter of a century. The gardener also owned a hardware store, so he may have had contacts that way. However he got it, assuming it was him, it should be recorded somewhere.'

Turner nodded slowly, and smiled. 'You haven't changed a bit, have you? There's only one person I've ever worked with that would follow things up in such detail, and I'm looking at her right now. You're totally relentless, and I say that in the best possible way.' He turned to Neil Dunnett. 'You do realise that you have a very special detective here, don't you?'

Dunnett smiled thinly and nodded. At the other end of the table, Rae visibly relaxed. She'd been dreading this encounter with Dunnett, but so far all was going well. She realised that another skirmish was being acted out in front of her eyes, and so far it was going in her favour.

Turner continued. 'Why do you think they might have been killed by the gardener rather than one of the parents?'

'We can't be absolutely sure just yet. We're awaiting DNA confirmation, but if it comes back the way we think it will, we have a problem.' Sophie paused. 'Our dilemma is this. If the children are who we think they are, then, as I said, their parents both died before them. And that begs a whole raft of questions. Who was the woman who looked after them for six months and claimed to be their mother at the local primary school? Why did they move here from Bristol, where both parents seem to have been doctors? Were the parents' deaths just coincidence? Was there some other link to John Wethergill, the gardener?' She looked at Turner. 'Those are questions for me to ponder, not you, Harry. But I would like to go a little deeper into his possible motives. You sounded just now as if you were unconvinced.'

'I wouldn't put it that strongly. And I did say that there could have been a sexual motive. But I would have thought that someone capable of killing two small children because of some pathological deviancy would have shown up on police radar well before then. Any signs of that?'

Marsh answered. 'No. Not a mention, and I've gone back more than thirty years. Not a whisper. The only possibility is that he was using an alias.'

'Which, of course, is always something we have to consider.' Turner ran his hand through his thinning hair. 'I just wonder whether it could have been accidental. If he had the cyanide for some reason linked to his gardening, and the children tragically ingested some. Could he have been confused and distraught enough to bury them and hide the evidence that way? It's a possibility, isn't it?'

'That's the way I'm thinking,' Dunnett interrupted. 'You've voiced my thoughts exactly. I think we need to scale things back, now that we have a strong candidate for their deaths. It was a tragic accident, he hid it for decades and took his own life on Wednesday night when he realised that the net was closing in. I'll think about it over the weekend and speak to the ACC on Monday morning with my recommendations. This is all costing time and money that could be better spent on other things.' Dunnett spoke as if his mind was already made up.

Rae was horrified. You utter snake, she thought. She was wondering what to say, when Turner spoke again.

'It's too neat and easy. I can see why Sophie is worried. At the moment there are a lot of loose ends and too many coincidences.'

'I made a promise,' Sophie said. 'To the children. When I saw their tiny skeletons laid out on those benches in Benny Goodall's lab. I made a promise to them that I'd get to the bottom of what happened, and see they got justice.' She paused. 'I always keep my promises. We need another week to collect all the information. It will look ridiculous if we start to close down, then have to reopen the case if something comes in that doesn't fit.'

Marsh remembered that she'd shut her eyes as she touched each tiny forehead. So that's what she'd been doing. 'I agree. Another few days should see us start to get information back in. Surely that's the time to make decisions like this, sir, not now?'

Dunnett didn't respond for several moments. Finally he said, 'you have until Wednesday morning. But you'll have to do without Gregson. There's an important job back at HQ that needs doing. Monday morning at nine, Gregson. Report to me. Don't forget, and don't be late.' He stood and walked out.

There was a stunned silence. Rae held her head in her hands. Barry could find nothing to say. Even Harry Turner was surprised. He looked at Sophie and raised his eyebrows.

'Meeting closed. Get back to work, please, everyone.' She hurried out of the room after her boss.

She caught up with him at the bottom of the stairs.

'Neil, don't do this. Trust me. The case isn't as simple as it looks. I need Rae to stay here. She's an integral part of my team.'

'My decision stands,' he said. 'The money's running out, and you're wasting what's left to no useful purpose.' He stared at her, and she could see the animosity in that look. 'As for Gregson, that decision stands as well. I want to see him on Monday morning.'

'Rae's a she, not a he. That's a fact in law. *She's* a member of my unit, and I need her next week.'

Well, Chief Inspector, I've given Gregson an order. And I've just given you one. I suggest you make sure those orders are followed. I don't really care what you think. You have too high an opinion of yourself and it'll do you good to have your wings clipped a little, just to remind you where you really are in the hierarchy. It's lower than you seem to think. You act as if the police service exists only to reflect your own grotesquely inflated ego back at you.' He turned away.

Sophie spoke softly. 'Don't do this, Neil. Take me seriously, please. The situation will develop differently to how you seem to expect. You'll regret it.'

He stopped, turned back and stood close to her. 'Are you threatening me? Do you think your influence extends that far? In case you haven't noticed, most of your allies have gone. You have much less power than you seem to think, you stuck-up bitch. You've picked a loser this time. I knew it when I saw Gregson's name on your unit's profiles. You know what makes me happy about all this? I'm killing two birds with one stone. And this conversation has never happened. It's your word against mine, and I'm the senior officer. You're nowhere, so get used to it.'

He turned and walked out of the door. Sophie nodded to herself, then slowly climbed the stairs back to the incident room. She beckoned to Turner and Marsh and walked to her office. As they reached the door she turned back and called to Rae to join them.

'It was a trap, Harry,' she said quietly to her former boss.' He had it all planned. And you know what really angers me? He couldn't care less about the case. As far as he's concerned the fact that those children died twenty years ago means they're not important. It's his way of getting back at me, and getting even with Rae.'

Marsh looked worried. 'We walked straight into it. I could kick myself. I couldn't think of anything to say. Where does it leave us now? And where does it leave Rae?'

Sophie gave a thin smile. 'Rae comes to work here on Monday morning, just as she would have done if that piece of nonsense hadn't happened.' Rae was standing behind them. 'Did you hear that, Rae? That's an order from me, your unit commander and the SIO of this case. This investigation proceeds as I outlined. Under no circumstances do we close the case until I say so. Wipe what you just heard DCS Dunnett say from your memory because it was of no importance whatsoever.'

Barry and Rae looked bemused. Harry Turner smiled and nodded, as if at some distant memory.

'He might have meant what he said to come as a surprise, catch us on the back foot,' Sophie continued. 'But I've been expecting something like it from him for some time. That's all I intend to say at the moment, other than that this evening's shindig at the pub is still very much on.' She glanced at her watch. 'Rae, you get back to work and Barry, can you look after our guest here for the rest of the afternoon? Take Harry through all the details we've discovered so far, and pick his brains. I have some entirely different business to attend to, so I'll be out of contact for the next hour or so. I have some favours to call in, so I don't want to be disturbed. Harry, can we have a few minutes alone? I think you can guess what I want to talk about.'

CHAPTER 25: AT FINCH COTTAGE

Saturday, Week 3

Saturday mornings in the Freeman household usually revolved around the two children. Karen attended a local "Young Musicians" group while Paul went to sports practice during the football season. This caused the usual problem: the activities occurred at opposite ends of the town and at overlapping times. Jill was adamant that parental responsibilities should not be related to gender, so on most weekends she took Paul to football, and waited to watch the match. Philip dropped Karen off at the music rehearsal. This weekend Jill had asked to swap roles. After parking her car outside Karen's music venue she walked towards the town centre. She was feeling restless and edgy. The euphoria she'd experienced in the middle of the week had faded. Like an addict, she was already desperate for another fix. But that wasn't likely to happen until Monday. Until then she was stuck with her dull husband and needy children.

She stopped, horrified. How could she think such things? Her children meant the world to her, and Philip was just the kind of caring and thoughtful husband that many of her friends would die for. What was going on in her head? If this was the effect a love affair had on her, maybe she should end it now. It had started as a fun experiment, but it had got out of control. It seemed to have created a void at the centre of her being in the place of warmth and family love. What was wrong with her? She knew the answer almost before she'd formed the question. Her newfound love life was making her totally self-obsessed, interested only in immediate pleasure. Wrong, wrong, wrong, Jill thought. But how gloriously wrong!

She wandered along the street, window shopping and seeing nothing she wanted to buy until she came to a small boutique. And there in the window was the most gorgeous lingerie set, a bra and panties in soft pink with pale blue polka dots, and at a reduced price. The price tag said that a matching camiknickers set was also available. Jill opened the door and walked in, turning to look more closely at the displayed garments in the window. The fabric was silky, even lovelier close up than from the pavement outside. Just the kind of underwear that her lover would appreciate. She smiled at the shop assistant and asked if there was a complete set in her size. Jill tried them on for a comfort check. She came out of the shop some twenty minutes later with a prettily wrapped package in her hand and made for the nearest coffee shop. There she sent a text message telling her secret lover about her purchase. Maybe a tryst could be arranged after all. She glanced at her watch and made her way back to the music venue. After dropping her purchases into the boot, she made her way inside, just in time to hear the ten minute performance that followed each Saturday morning practice. Karen looked happy, cheerfully chatting to her friends in the clarinet section of the wind band. She waved to her mother before the short performance started.

Later that morning the sun came out and it grew warm. Jill and Karen arrived home first. They hauled the barbecue unit from the back of the shed, searched out a bag of charcoal, a pack of firelighters and proceeded to set fire to the coals. When the men arrived home shortly after midday everything was ready to go. Jill knew better than to start cooking. The barbecue is an exclusively male preserve. Boys and fire. Women should not attempt to come between them. Jill had read that it was almost ritualistic, a return to prehistoric times. Apart from the beer, that is. But she had to admit, Philip was an extremely competent barbecue cook, and their lunch, out on the lawn, was very tasty.

The children wandered off and Philip asked, 'how was Karen this morning?'

'She was fine. I think she's back to normal. I called her tutor yesterday afternoon and she said that Karen seemed much more at ease this week. I think she's over the worst.'

'I'll be glad when the whole thing's over. It shook me up more than I'd care to admit. I can't say I'm over it. I can still see her holding that little hand. It keeps popping into my head when I least expect it.' He looked at Jill. 'Are you okay?' he asked.

'What do you mean?'

'You've seemed a bit distant recently. Not your normal self. I suppose we've all been under a lot of strain, but I thought I noticed it before all this started. Last month, before the weather started getting warmer.'

'Your imagination, Phil. Either that or I was just a bit off-colour.' Jill turned away and began to stack plates into the dishwasher so that he couldn't see her face.

'If you say so. But if something is troubling you, don't let it fester. Tell me and we can talk it through. Promise?'

She turned back to face him. 'Okay, promise. I'm meeting a friend in town this afternoon, by the way. I'll be back by six.'

She tried to sound nonchalant, but inside she was nearly paralysed with anxiety. She left the room quickly. She had a shower, put on her new underwear, slid into a dress, added a little make-up and ran down the stairs.

'Bye!'

The door banged behind her.

She took some deep breaths and made her way to her car. She didn't see her daughter watching from her bedroom window as she drove away. Karen walked silently to her parents' room and examined the discarded packaging in the litter bin. Jill drove across town to the northern outskirts. She parked in a quiet side street and walked to a gate in the shadows of tall shrubs. She looked up. The familiar face was smiling at her out of an upstairs window, a hand raised in greeting. How do you tell your husband that you're in the middle of a madly passionate affair that you never want to end? One with another woman?

CHAPTER 26: ON TENTERHOOKS

Monday morning, Week 3

Rae arrived in the incident room early on Monday. She was nervous about the conflicting directives she had received three days earlier. She noticed that Sophie was in her office so she hesitantly knocked at the door.

'Am I still okay to be here, ma'am? I mean, after what happened on Friday afternoon? I've allowed time to drive over to Winfrith if I need to.'

Sophie looked up from her desk. 'Sensible of you. But you're fine. The ACC, Jim Metcalfe, is now our overall commander, so you can relax. Things proceed as I outlined on Friday.'

'Thanks, ma'am. I'll leave you in peace.' Rae gave a nervous smile and returned to her desk. She looked and felt as though a monstrous weight had been lifted from her shoulders. She made herself a coffee and took a gulp before settling down. How had the boss done it? Something had happened over the weekend. Their evening in the pub on Friday had been muted by the afternoon's events, and no one felt like discussing them. Barry tried once, but Harry Turner had silenced him with a slight shake of his head. Turner and the boss had worked out some scheme that had obviously succeeded. Oh well, she'd find out before long. Rae had one or two contacts at police headquarters, and they'd let her know.

Marsh came in and made his way over to her.

'Are you okay, Rae?' he asked

'Yes, sir. I was on tenterhooks until just now. But it seems the ACC's taken control. That's what the boss's just told me. How did she do it?'

'I haven't a clue. It was obvious late on Friday that she was up to something, her and her Uncle Harry, as she called him. I just can't guess how they did it. I only found out first thing this morning when she texted me. Maybe we'll find out some day, but now we need to stay focused on the case. Even if the ACC is more amenable, he won't be happy with what's happened and he might well let us know it. The people at his senior level don't like the bureaucratic process being upset, so let's not waste time speculating. I must say I didn't exactly get my best sleep ever last night. You?'

Rae shook her head. 'I hardly slept at all. I feel almost lightheaded.'

'Well, finish your coffee and get stuck in. I bet the ACC'll come in at some point, so we need to make sure we're all grafting when he does.'

Marsh was right. The tall figure of the Assistant Chief Constable appeared in the doorway shortly after ten o'clock. On the few occasions when Barry had met Jim Metcalfe he'd been impressed by the senior man's relaxed and calm attitude, but today he was curt and watchful. He nodded to the people working in the incident room, glanced at the information board, then made his way into Sophie's office. He closed the door behind him.

"Good morning, Jim,' Sophie said, looking up from her desk.

He didn't respond immediately. Finally he said, 'The chief is not happy when this kind of thing happens. She feels manipulated and, like all chief constables, she hates that.'

'Why are you telling me this?'

'Because, figuratively speaking, it has your fingerprints all over it. Not that I told her that, of course. But she showed me the anonymous dossier that landed on her desk on Saturday morning and I had a look through it. Her first concern was how the authority had ended up employing someone who had lied on his CV, a person who was capable of treating junior female officers in that way, even if it was before he came to Dorset. How did he end up in such a senior role? But she was distinctly unhappy about the threat to go to the press with it. She may be the county's first woman chief constable, Sophie, but she's like everyone else who finds they've been boxed into a corner. She'll try to identify the person who put her there.'

'I don't know what you're talking about, Jim.' Sophie looked him in the eye. 'Your phone call last night, when you told me Neil was being suspended, took me by surprise. I hope he's coping okay. Would you like a coffee? Then you can meet the team and get an overview of how far we've got.'

'That would be very acceptable. I've said what I felt I had to say, so now we can get down to business.'

* * *

Sophie had been right in the prediction she'd made on Friday afternoon. As the morning wore on useful evidence and information started to trickle into the incident room from the various individuals and organisations contacted the previous week.

The first item to appear was an emailed list from Bristol Police. It summarised the items that had been retained after the unexplained hit and run death of Doctor Li Hua Camberwell, and included a hair brush. Barry replied immediately asking for the brush to be sent to him by emergency courier, for DNA analysis.

The next documentation was closely linked to this: the DNA profiles of the children's bodies, taken from residual bone marrow. The profiles reinforced several of the assumptions the team had already made. The children had been siblings and were part Chinese and part European. The results ruled out any Philippino background, which probably meant that a connection to Wethergill's partner was unlikely. If forensic experts could extract some DNA from hair follicles on Li Hua's hairbrush, they would be able to confirm or refute a possible family connection to the Camberwells.

The final item was a phone call that Sophie received from Southampton University late in the morning. Professor Wendy Millward had examined the rug fragments that had been sent to her laboratories. She reported that initial tests had failed to find any traces of iron cyanide complex. Further, more sensitive analytical work would be needed to confirm the result, but her most reliable technician was fairly sure that nothing would be found. Sophie was disappointed.

'But something else did turn up, so it's not all gloom. I don't know what to make if it, though.' Sophie waited.

'It follows on from the tests we did last week, on the soil from the cellar. You remember we had a chat about it?'

Sophie frowned, trying to remember what they'd decided. 'Yes. You wanted to do some more checks, if I remember right?'

'Exactly. We think there are traces of hydrocarbons in the cellar soil, but at a very low level.'

'What does that mean?'

'Well, the tests suggest paraffin residues. Obviously it was a long time ago, and all the volatile components have long since evaporated into the air. But there are traces of the heavier ones, probably adsorbed onto the soil particle surfaces. Maybe due to a spillage of some kind?'

'Thanks, Wendy. I don't know how relevant it will turn out to be, but it all helps us to build up a picture. I don't suppose you can work out how long it's been there? From the residues left, I mean. If it was paraffin then wouldn't it lose components at a steady rate? Given that it was cool in the cellar and at a fairly constant temperature?'

'There's an interesting thought. Personally I don't know, but I'll get in touch with one of my colleagues in environmental science. I think someone has done some work on evaporation rates from sand, but that was probably with crude oil rather than refined paraffin. I'll get back to you on it.'

Sophie walked over to Rae's desk.

'Have you got that list from the house clearance people, Rae? You know, the stuff they removed from Finch Cottage when it was sold?'

Rae scrabbled around on her desk and found it. Sophie moved a finger down the list and then stopped.

'There. Look. An old paraffin heater removed from the cellar. Rae, can you phone them and see if it's been sold yet?'

In the early afternoon Sophie received a text from Harry Turner, saying how much he'd enjoyed the weekend, and wondering how things had gone. Sophie told him of the sudden change in the command structure. She walked to the hospital to hear the results of Benny Goodall's post-mortem examination of Wethergill's corpse.

As she crossed the street Sophie caught sight of a familiar and very feminine figure turning a corner ahead of her into a side street. She filed the information away in her brain, already seemingly chock full of disparate observations and thoughts.

* * *

'My problem is this, Benny. If I stick only to the Dorset connection, I come to an obvious conclusion. There have been three deaths, the two children some twenty years ago and John Wethergill on Thursday. There is clearly some kind of link, and it leads us to suspect that Wethergill probably caused the children's deaths, and that he committed suicide as our net closed in on him. Two suspicious deaths and a suicide.

'However, looking beyond Dorset there have been five deaths, so the situation changes dramatically. We now include the rather unusual deaths of the children's probable parents in

Bristol. This gives us either four suspicious deaths and a suicide, or five suspicious deaths. If the latter, then we have good reason to think that the perpetrator might still be out there somewhere. Wethergill's death is key, you can see that. So, is there any sign that his death was anything other than suicide?'

'No. None whatsoever. Of course, that doesn't prove anything. There were no signs of a struggle and there were no other drugs in his bloodstream, other than alcohol. The amount of alcohol was moderate, so he wouldn't have been drunk.'

'So you can't tell me either way?'

'That's right. He was a fit man who looked after himself physically. All of his organs were fully functioning, and he probably would have had a long and healthy life ahead of him.'

'What type of alcohol had he been drinking?'

'I'd make a guess at something like Amaretto. Not the whisky on the bedside table, which is a surprise.'

'That's a bit of a giveaway, isn't it?'

Benny shrugged his shoulders. 'From your point of view, yes. Medically irrelevant though.'

Sophie's brain was whirring. 'I wonder if there were traces left in the glass on his bedside table. I'll ask Dave Nash.'

He nodded. 'I could arrange for some analytical tests just to confirm it, if you think it's worthwhile.'

'Yes. It's important. Amaretto in the stomach but an open bottle of whisky by the bed.'

He nodded. 'Almonds. Amaretto would disguise the smell and taste of the cyanide.'

'Exactly.'

She took her mobile phone from her bag and called her sergeant. 'Barry? Could you and Rae pay another visit to Wethergill's flat? Yes, right now. Can you see if there's a bottle of Amaretto or a similar liqueur anywhere? Even if it's empty? Look in the bins. If you find one, bring it in. Then see if there's any evidence that he was either interested in or wrote poetry. Collect any books on poetry that you find. Have a really good search for notebooks, scraps of paper or anything that has a verse of any type on it. Those strange verses that the vicar gave us weren't the work of an absolute beginner or someone with no knowledge of literature. I want to find out if we're being led a merry dance by someone.'

* * *

'So, nothing?'

Marsh shook his head. 'I looked for bottles of booze, notebooks or bits of paper, but I didn't find anything relevant. And I went through the place very thoroughly. Rae searched his books. Again, nothing.'

'The only ones he had were on gardening or cooking, ma'am. There were a few travel books and local maps, plus some Dorset guide-books. He had some general interest magazines but nothing literary at all.'

'Have forensics finished with his laptop?'

'Yes, I checked with them,' Barry replied. 'Stuff related to his business, general odds and ends, some files with dating sites, but otherwise the same kind of material as his books. Recipes and travel. There was nothing anywhere that was remotely connected to poetry.'

Sophie took the poems from the case folder and read them again. 'So it's looking as though he didn't write these. Maybe I should get them analysed by an expert. I've already said that I think they're the work of an amateur who knows how to use words and has some familiarity with literature. Am I wrong?'

Marsh shrugged his shoulders. 'I'm not into literature, and I don't think I could have written them.'

Rae disagreed. 'My degree was in engineering, but I can relate to them. I can see what a good therapeutic release writing something like that would be. I also think people are capable of much more than they think. They don't realise what they can do until they actually try their hand at something when they're feeling under pressure. I'm not saying that he did write them, and I know we've found no evidence for it, but I wouldn't discount the possibility. He might have got books from the library. Maybe he went to a couple of evening classes.'

Sophie thought for a while. 'We need to speak to the people who knew him. They might be able to say whether he had any literary abilities. I know we contacted his friends and family over the weekend, but maybe we need to talk to them again. Rae, can you do that now? Any headway with the paraffin heater, by the way?'

Rae shook her head. 'No luck, ma'am. It was in such a poor condition that they binned it. They said it was badly corroded and would probably have been lethal to use. Sorry.'

Sophie frowned. 'But that cellar was bone dry. Any corrosion would have happened before it was put down there, surely? Did they say where it was when they found it?'

'Just in the far corner. That's all he remembered.'

'Okay, but we need to think about this. Meanwhile, Barry and I need to spend a bit more time crosschecking the information we have on the Camberwell parents. We'll have a meeting first thing in the morning. We need to think through this Amaretto problem.'

Marsh shook his head. 'Why that in particular, ma'am?'

'Because Benny was sure it was Amaretto in his stomach. So if there was none in his flat, where did it go? Who took the bottle away?' She paused. 'Could you check with the cleaner that she didn't remove a bottle from anywhere?'

CHAPTER 27: SISTERS

Monday afternoon, Week 3

Dorothy Kitson's week had been so stressful that she'd made an appointment to see her GP. On Monday afternoon, having cancelled her usual cleaning job, she sat waiting for her allotted slot, still feeling as if her whole world might implode at any moment. Her sleep had been fitful at best and her appetite had all but disappeared. And that had been before the news about John Wethergill's death had reached the press, causing a tidal wave of gossip to engulf the town. The weekend had been like living through a nightmare.

She realised that she needed something to calm her down and help her to sleep. Her thoughts kept returning to the story in the local newspaper about the death of John Wethergill. In the seventeen years since the end of their on-off affair in the nineties, she'd hardly thought about him. And now he was all over the news. She'd heard the rumour that he'd probably committed suicide. People were asking why he would have done such a thing, less than two weeks after the children's bodies were found. Many of the locals knew he'd been the gardener at Finch Cottage for several years in the early nineties.

But no one could remember whether his time there had overlapped with any children living at the house. He'd been cruel to Dorothy, ending their romance with no explanation and taking up with that Asian-looking woman. Dorothy'd seen them walking through the park, arm in arm. That had really hurt. To think that he'd chosen someone from abroad rather than her. The problem had been sex, of course. With men it was nearly always down to sex, wasn't it? He'd wanted more from her than she was willing to give. When he whispered the things he wanted her to do, she'd felt sick with nerves. Why was that? Other women seemed to like sex, even her sister. Not that they talked about it much, but she knew what Pauline was like. When they were teenagers she'd hear Pauline creep in late at night. Dorothy would catch a glimpse of her as she passed her bedroom door, with that smug, satisfied smile on her face. Years later, she still radiated that sleek, self-satisfied look after a night out with some man. Not that she'd ever bothered to keep a man for very long, not Pauline. She just seemed to attract them, and she took her pick. Were all actresses like that? Putting on a show all the time?

All their lives people had been commenting on how different she and Pauline were. So marked was the difference that people were surprised they were even sisters. One glamorous, the other plain. One obviously clever, the other apparently stupid. One vibrant, the other dull. One brimming with confidence and the other timid. Yet sisters they were. And there was another, secret difference: one was full of empathy and the other was cruel. Dorothy was always taken as the elder of the two, when she was really two years younger. No matter what she did, she could never look as good as her beautiful and talented older sister. After her fling with John came to its abrupt end she'd given up trying. Of course, the smoking and drinking hadn't helped.

The doctor appeared at the door and called her name. She rose, slightly unsteadily, and went into the consulting room. Ten minutes later she came out, clutching a prescription for some tablets. Maybe this would sort out her problems. Perhaps she should go away for a few days. A short break would do her good, and it was only a quick bus or train ride down to Weymouth. She'd check her money when she got home and see how long she could afford. With the help of the tablets she'd get a decent night's sleep and then she'd feel much better. Maybe she'd even meet someone nice. Lots of people around her age visited Weymouth out of season. It might even be worth getting her hair done and looking for a new dress. Dorothy began to feel better.

* * *

On the other side of town, Pauline Stopley was meeting a client for lunch. He represented a large commercial manufacturing company in the area, and was planning to invest some money in local arts projects. Her regional boss had chosen Pauline specially for this task. Somehow she managed to get more grant money, and more frequently, out of potential sponsorship clients than almost anyone else in the organisation. He assumed that her acting skills were what suited her to the task, and he was right. Pauline saw it as a role. An impartial observer would note the seductive techniques she used on her clients and that it didn't matter whether they were male or female. They fell into the trap just the same.

Pauline left the meeting having secured a donation for a Dorset theatre group. She didn't feel like returning directly to her office. If John had still been alive, she would have popped into his shop for a chat and, if he'd been able to leave the place with his assistant, she might have lured him away to his flat for an hour or two. His death had put paid to all that. She sat on the low wall outside St Peter's Church on the High Street, took out her mobile phone and sent a short text message. She waited, watching people hurrying by in the rare April sunshine. She glanced at the screen, and pursed her lips in disappointment. One lover dead, and the other too busy to get away from work. There was no option but to return to work herself. Unless she could find someone else in the next few minutes. She'd wondered about her lunch client, but he'd been much too patronising. There was no need to hurry back to her office, so perhaps she ought to pop into the nearby Corn Exchange building to see her sister. Dorothy had a cleaning job there on Mondays. Pauline turned back down the High Street and saw that the main doors to the building were open. Workmen were moving barrels out of the entrance and into waiting vans and she quietly slipped past them into the spacious ground-floor room. Trestle tables and racks were being dismantled, and a smell of beer lingered in the air. There was no sign of Dorothy.

'Hello! Isn't it Pauline Stopley?'

She turned to face the tall, good-looking man who'd spoken to her. Well, things were beginning to look up. She gave him the benefit of her most brilliant smile. 'Hi. I hope I'm not intruding. I was passing by and was intrigued by what was going on, so I decided to take a look inside. It's decades since I was last in here. I hope I'm not causing any bother. Have we met recently? You seem familiar. Are you from round here?'

'No, I live in Wareham. We're clearing up after the weekend beer exhibition.'

'It's a beautiful building, isn't it? The restoration work has been done so well. So do you work here, or for the beer trade?'

He laughed. 'Hardly. I'm a teacher. Martin Allen.' He held out his hand. 'I'm on Dorset's real ale committee and the local group have just had their spring exhibition. They needed someone to oversee the clearing up today after the local person suddenly fell ill, so I foolishly volunteered. It's the school Easter holidays.' He paused. 'And we met last weekend, at the Arts Centre. My daughter Hannah gave the FGM talk.'

Pauline nodded. 'Now I remember . . . So that means that your wife is . . ?'

'Is what?'

'A senior police officer?'

'Yes, she is. Why do you ask?'

'No reason really. Well, there is. She interviewed me on Friday. So she hasn't mentioned me?'

Martin looked puzzled. 'No. She's not allowed to talk about ongoing cases. You seem worried about it.'

'No, no. Not at all.' The smile was back. 'It's just that I was shocked by the sudden death of someone close to me.' She paused. 'Well, to be honest he was my lover. It shook me up and I haven't got back to normal yet.'

'That's entirely understandable. It takes time to come to terms with sudden death. By the way, I should thank you for taking the time to meet up with Hannah last week and give her the benefit of your experience. I'm sure she appreciated it.'

Pauline looked disoriented again for a moment. 'It was a pleasure. I'm always glad to help aspiring actresses.' She glanced at her watch. 'Well, I'd better be getting back to the office. Work will be piling up. Goodbye.'

She turned and walked out. Martin watched her leave.

On her way back to her workplace, Pauline tried to phone her sister, but there was no reply. Not for the first time, Pauline wished her sister would keep her mobile phone switched on. Dorothy claimed the calls and messages made her feel nervous.

* * *

Martin mentioned his meeting with Pauline Stopley to Sophie and Jade at their evening meal. 'It was a bit peculiar,' he said. 'One moment she was all smiles and fluttering eyelashes, and the next she was giving guarded looks. It happened when I mentioned Hannah, too.'

'See, Mum,' Jade said indignantly, 'I said it was weird. She was definitely talking to that strange Dorothy woman from the café at the FGM talk, but she denied it.'

'Who denied it? Who are we talking about here, Jade?' Sophie replied, puzzled.

'Dorothy, the one at the café. She denied knowing this Pauline woman. But they were sitting together, and I know they were talking. And Dorothy had her coat on the seat next to her as if she was keeping it for someone. She moved it off when Pauline arrived. If they didn't know each other why did she do that? There were loads of empty seats, so someone coming in at the last minute would have chosen one of those if she didn't already know someone there.'

'Fine, Jade. I'll bear it in mind. Satisfied now?'

'Maybe I'll give Hannah a call this evening to see if she can enlighten me,' Martin added.

Sophie remained tight-lipped. She didn't tell her husband and younger daughter about the shift in mood during her own interview with Pauline Stopley. It had also occurred when she mentioned the actress's meeting with Hannah.

Later that evening Martin came into Sophie's study while she was tidying away some papers.

'I think I have the Pauline Stopley problem solved,' he said. 'Hannah was a little embarrassed on the phone, but told me what had happened. Apparently Pauline made a pass at her.'

Sophie gasped. 'What?'

'That was my reaction. I asked her if she could have been mistaken and misinterpreted it in some way, but she said not. Apparently they talked about it before they went their separate ways. Pauline probably felt understandably embarrassed by it when she met us. She must wonder whether we know.'

'Well, we do now.'

'The strange thing is, Sophie, before she realised who I was, she was really flirting with me.'

'How strongly?'

'Hand on my arm, her thigh brushing my leg. She stood so close I could feel her body warmth.'

Sophie giggled. 'Am I going to have to fit you with a tracking device? You're trying to get me jealous now.'

'Seriously. I was getting worried.'

'Okay. Noted. You get ten brownie points for loyalty and honesty. What does that equate to? A cup of tea in bed in the morning?'

There was a pause before Martin replied. 'Umm, how about some nookie tonight?'

Sophie looked at him critically. 'Martin Allen. Your seduction techniques have reached rock bottom. Is that the best you can do? I remember the days when you bought me roses, plied me with champagne and fed me fine food. Now you just feed me some yarn about how you nearly got picked up by an ageing actress with a hot flush.'

'So is that a yes, then?'

CHAPTER 28: CYNIC

Tuesday morning, Week 3

'So the DNA matches?'

'Apparently so. And with both of them, so there's no doubt about it.' Marsh sat back in his chair and stretched his legs out under the table. 'We didn't need the hairbrush after all. Both Kenneth and Li Hua had already been profiled because of how their deaths occurred. They were both on file. All the forensic expert had to do was compare them with the children's, and those were ready yesterday, as you know.'

Sophie nodded. 'So now we know that we're on the right track and we haven't been wasting our time. That's a relief, I can tell you. I've been worried since we saw that photo of the two Philippino children in John Wethergill's flat. We could have switched direction entirely at that point and wasted so much time. I'll let the ACC know once we've finished this briefing. So, we have a family of four, all dead within five years of each other and all, we think, in suspicious or accidental circumstances. What could we be looking at here?'

One of the local detectives spoke up. 'Sounds like some kind of revenge. A family feud? Maybe even a gangland payback. Could they have crossed one of the Chinese Triad gangs when they were in Hong Kong?'

'They were both doctors. Is it likely?'

Marsh said, 'we do have to think of all possibilities, ma'am.'

Rae added, 'Sean could be right with his first suggestion, though. What if it was some kind of personal revenge? Not necessarily Chinese. Could there be a clue somewhere in their past, do you think?'

Sophie nodded. 'Yes, you're right. We need more information about the parents first. I'm going to suggest we reconvene this afternoon after we've had another spell of digging into their background. Once we've learned more about them, we might be in a better position to speculate. And keep this quiet, everyone. We'll let people continue thinking that Wethergill's death was suicide and he was the twins' probable killer.' She waited until the local Dorchester detectives had returned to their work stations before speaking to Barry and Rae. 'It seems that every avenue we investigate brings us to the name Pauline. We need to know if it's the same one. Was the Pauline Stopley who was having an affair with Wethergill the same Pauline who married Richard Camberwell in Bristol after the death of Li Hua? Does she correspond to the P Camberwell on the residents' records of Finch Cottage?'

'If she is the same one, do we move in on her?'

'Not yet. It's all too circumstantial. And by the way, she turned up at the Old Cornmarket yesterday and chatted to Martin while he was clearing up after the local beerex. Would you believe it? But we have no direct evidence on her and I'll need something much more definite to work with before we bring her in. We need to keep an eye on her, though. Can you arrange that, Barry? Meanwhile, let's backtrack through Wethergill's activities over the past week or two. List where he went, who he met, that kind of thing. Rae, could you follow up that restaurant contact urgently, please? You remember, the couple who sat next to his table last week?'

'Already done, ma'am. They're coming in later this morning.'

'Good work. I'll see them. Meanwhile, you find out everything you can about Pauline Stopley. She might turn out to be the key person in all this. Put a photo of her up on the incident board. We need to let everyone know that she's a person of interest, even though there's nothing definite yet.'

* * *

Later that morning Theresa Jackson, the Freeman family's liaison officer, called into the incident room to let Sophie know that the family no longer needed to see her on a regular basis. From now on they'd call her if a visit was required. Theresa read through the information posted on the incident board. She hurried over to Sophie, who was perched on the corner of Barry's desk chatting to him about John Wethergill.

'Ma'am, you have Pauline Stopley on the incident board.'

'Yes. Her name keeps cropping up, but we're not sure how she ties in to any of the events. Why?'

'You remember that I saw Jill Freeman acting a bit suspiciously not long after the twins' bodies had been discovered? I saw her getting into a car with someone and I thought they embraced? You told me to run a check on the car but not to take it any further unless I thought it was linked in some way. Well, there was no obvious link so I didn't say anything. But I have to now. That car is registered to Pauline Stopley.'

Barry pursed his lips. 'Is there something going on between them? Is that what you're trying to tell us?'

'I don't know. But Karen, the daughter, is convinced there's something wrong between her parents. She told me this morning when I called in on my way to work. She asked if I could give her a lift to school instead of her getting the bus. It's the first time she's done that. I twigged that she wanted to talk about something, but thought it would be about the case. Instead she told me that she'd overheard some talk between her parents at the weekend and says that her mum is acting a bit strange.'

Sophie asked, 'did she say how long it had been going on?'

'Recent, I think. She says that she's only noticed it in the past couple of weeks. Probably that incident I told you about was the first. That's what made her suspicious. She's a perceptive young woman, considering the strain she must be under. I think she's really worried. She's been nosing about and says that her mum bought some sexy underwear at the weekend. She's worn it, but not with Karen's dad. At least, she doesn't think so. The poor girl is really worried. She was in tears. Of course, she won't suspect that her mum's having an affair with a woman. She'll be worried about her running off with another man.'

'Thanks, Theresa. We needed to know. Listen, would you mind if I got you seconded onto our team for the duration of the investigation? I know you've been keeping me updated, but we could use your insight into the family if there's something going on. What do you think?'

Theresa put her hand to her mouth. 'Oh, I'd love to, ma'am. But d'you think it would it be okay with my bosses?'

'Leave it with me. Go and waste time for five minutes. By the time you get back to your office I hope it'll have been cleared. I'll do it now. You'll be working for Rae over there but reporting to Barry. And you'll stay as the family liaison for the Freemans. Okay? Plain clothes, but keep them smart.'

Theresa was beaming as she left the office. Sophie turned to her sergeant.

'Well, what does this latest bit of news mean? Pauline Stopley's quite some woman, isn't she? And there's something else I should tell you that I was keeping quiet about. She's already made passes at two members of my family, Martin and Hannah.' Marsh looked confused. 'I'd better explain, hadn't I? From what I can tell, it's a wonder she didn't make a pass at me while I was interviewing her last week. Maybe I should be feeling disappointed.'

Barry's look of bemusement was still there after Sophie had finished her tale.

* * *

Sophie had chosen the most comfortable interview room in the police station, and had ordered a tray of coffee and biscuits.

'It's just horrible to think that he died that night after his evening out at the restaurant. We were sitting at the next table. He seemed such a nice man. How's his partner taking it? Or shouldn't we ask?'

'We interviewed her the next day and she was understandably upset. They weren't longstanding partners, though. They'd only met the previous week.' Sophie threw this in deliberately, to see the reaction. Barry Marsh leaned against a wall, watching.

'Gosh. That's really, well, surprising. I mean, they were obviously deeply involved with each other.' The young woman, Rachel, was blushing. She took a sip of coffee and a bite of biscuit to hide her embarrassment.

'I'll need to know why you thought that, Rachel. Nothing you say will go outside these four walls, don't worry. Okay?'

She nodded, then took a deep breath and repeated the conversation they'd overheard at the restaurant.

'So you'd say that the two of them seemed to be getting on well?'

'Yes, absolutely. And he was so obviously disappointed when she said she couldn't go home with him that night. But it didn't last long. He cheered up when she invited him round to hers a few days later. That's when we got embarrassed, wasn't it, Jordan?' Her boyfriend nodded but said nothing, nibbling at a biscuit. 'It was when she told him to wear his silk briefs again and expect some more adventures. She could tell we'd overheard, but she just smiled at us and winked. I mean, it was all a bit brazen.'

'Did they definitely go separate ways when they left the restaurant? They could have changed their minds, you see.'

Jordan spoke for the first time. 'Yes. They chatted outside the door for a few minutes, and then they went in opposite directions. Rachel couldn't see, but I could 'cause I was facing the door. He went into town but she walked away from it.' He seemed about to say more but stopped.

'Is there something else, Jordan?' Sophie asked.

'Someone might have been watching them from across the street. There was a figure in a shop doorway that I spotted a bit earlier. Whoever it was came across the road just after your couple parted.'

'You didn't tell me about it, Jordan.' Rachel sounded annoyed.

'Well, it wasn't important then, was it? And I can't be absolutely sure even now.'

'Which way did this figure go?' asked Marsh.

'The same way as the bloke.'

'Did you get a good look?'

'Not really. He came across at a slant, so he was sideways on. In a jacket with the hood up. Quite short.' He picked up another biscuit.

* * *

'What do you think, Barry?'

Marsh sat down on one of the chairs the couple had vacated. 'It proves nothing. Pauline could have called him and said she'd changed her plans. She could have turned up at his flat as a surprise. She could have even got there before him if her car was nearby and she drove. That restaurant must be a good ten minute walk from his shop and flat. It could have all been a deliberate plant, laying a false trail in preparation for when we started our questioning. As for this person who might have been watching, Jordan was a bit vague about it. As he said himself, he was in a lit restaurant staring out onto a dark street. It could have been anybody.'

'You're a cynic, Barry, particularly about our friend the actress.'

He laughed. 'Well, after what you told me, and added to Theresa's suspicions, I wouldn't put anything past that woman. She seems totally unscrupulous. To be honest, I can't get my head round this latest bit of information about her.'

'If it makes you feel any better, Barry, neither can I. Maybe we'd better get her in, although I'd prefer to wait until we get a few more facts in place. Did you post a check on her?'

Marsh nodded. 'It's not a full time watch, just at the times she's likely to be moving. She's at work at the moment, in the Arts Council offices.'

Sophie thought for a few moments. 'On second thoughts, I think I might pay her a visit this afternoon and have things out with her. It'll save us a lot of time if she opens up about her past, and her link to Finch Cottage. Do you want to come? Rae can take over from you now that we've got Theresa doing some of the donkey work. Our problem is that there's just no direct evidence against her and we'll need something definite before we can make an arrest. I think a steamroller approach is called for. Maybe we should rattle her composure a bit. Okay? Give me ten minutes to get my look right. This is the woman who's tried it on with two members of my family. I want to show her just what she's up against.'

CHAPTER 29: STEAMROLLER

Tuesday afternoon, Week 3

'Can I call you Sophie?' Pauline was sitting in her office, on one side of a coffee table, with the two detectives facing her. She'd wanted to remain behind her desk, but Sophie had asked for this arrangement, having noticed the low chairs. The sophisticated ex-actress versus his boss. Marsh smiled to himself, knowing that Sophie held all the cards. It would be no contest at all.

'No. DCI Allen will be fine.' Sophie gave her a thin smile and stretched her slender legs out in front of her, brushing an invisible speck from her immaculate skirt. 'Tell me about how you met John, Ms Stopley. Everything.'

'Well, it was on Saturday, a week and a half ago. It was my first outing with the walking group. John and I got talking and then had lunch together in the pub . . .'

She was about to go on, but Sophie stopped her.

'When I said everything, Ms Stopley, I meant it. You've already given me this short version, so I don't really need to hear it again. I want detail. Other members of the group said that you made a beeline for him, that you seemed to have your eye on him from the start.'

Pauline sat back slightly. 'That just isn't true. We didn't even start talking until the final mile or so. We must have been well past the three-quarter mark by then.'

'And was that the first time you'd ever met John?'

Pauline was about to speak but paused, seeming to weigh up her options. Finally she said, 'no. He had an affair with my sister a long time ago. We met briefly then, but only once or twice. He clearly didn't remember me.'

'Your sister being . . ?'

Pauline sighed. 'Dorothy Kitson.'

'I'll need to talk to her. Do you have her address? It would save us some time.'

'Of course.' Marsh took down the Dorchester address. 'But she's not there at the moment. I've been trying to contact her since the weekend.'

Sophie nodded slightly. 'Let's return to the morning of the ramble. You are adamant that you didn't talk to him until late on in the walk, so let me pose a different question. Did you know in advance that he would be there, on that walk?'

Again, a pause. Sophie gave Pauline another cold smile. 'Yes, I was aware that he would be on the ramble. His name was on a list that the secretary emailed to the group.'

'So you could afford to wait until late on in the walk, knowing that you could introduce yourself at any time. Would your name have been on that list as well? Why didn't he recognise it from all those years ago? Or didn't he know your name back then?'

'I don't know.'

'Did you have the same surname then?'

Again, a pause. 'No. I was Pauline Camberwell. I still am in a few historical records. Stopley was my maiden name, my stage name, and the one I've always used for work. And as I said, I only met John a couple of times, briefly.'

'Yet you remembered him very well. Isn't that a bit strange?'

'No, I don't think so. I have a good memory for names. I was an actress. I had to learn lots of names. I couldn't afford to get them wrong on stage.' She was sounding more confident. Marsh, notebook in hand, watched with interest as Sophie played along for a while, letting Pauline think she'd escaped.

'So, exactly when was this?'

'Probably some twenty years or so ago. Maybe longer. I was away a lot in repertory, touring around the country. I was even in the States for a while.'

'Have you lived in Dorchester before?'

'I grew up here. Apart from that, only for a short spell, when I was staying with my sister. I've always lived in Bristol or London when I've been in the UK.' Pauline smiled. She was visibly relaxing, back in control.

'Tell me about your life in Bristol, Pauline. Or should I call you Mrs Camberwell?'

Pauline's smile faded. 'Please don't. It has too many memories. I prefer to use Stopley.'

'Why's that? So you can keep acting? So you can keep spinning me along in your little play? You in the central role, with all of these other people orbiting around you, being charmed and entertained by you? What is it I read recently? "I live a spectral life, empty of meaning. I inhabit a ghostly world, vacant of substance." Or something like that. What do you think those lines mean?'

'Sorry. I don't know what you're talking about.'

Sophie nodded. 'Again, tell me about your life in Bristol.'

Pauline suddenly spat back, 'why should I? What's it got to do with you, any of it? Prying into my private life and my memories. What gives you the right? It's got absolutely nothing to do with my relationship with John, nothing. He was a lovely man who came to a tragic end, and I'm sad for him. I'm sad for me as well, because I thought at last I was on to something good, something worthwhile that might last. But now? It's all a mess, as usual.' Her eyes became moist.

Marsh wondered if the boss would soften, but he saw that her look was still icy.

'Cut the crap, Pauline. It doesn't impress me in the slightest. Tell me about Bristol.'

Pauline looked haggard. 'What do you want to know?'

'About your marriage to Richard, for a start. I want to know when and how.'

Pauline stared at Sophie bleakly. She finally spoke, quietly, with little emotion. 'Richard was the love of my life. We were sweethearts at school and I adored him. I always did. We had a stupid tiff and went our separate ways after we left school, but I never managed to get him out of my head and I always hoped we'd get back together. No one else ever came close, not really. We kept in touch, even when he went to Hong Kong for a couple of years. At least, I thought we'd kept in touch. How wrong I was. When he came back to Bristol, married, I was distraught, heartbroken. I didn't know what to do at first, but then I threw myself into my work and got through the next few years somehow. Then his wife gave birth to twins and I knew everything was lost. She was really pretty, a successful doctor and the mother of his children. What chance did I have? That's when I started going on tour for long spells, great for my career, but soul destroying for me.' She paused for breath, then sighed. 'Then I heard that Li Hua, his wife, had been killed in a road accident. It was awful for him, so I started visiting. I wanted to help him. I still loved him, for God's sake.' She looked across at Sophie, defiant. Her voice softened. 'It was wonderful. It all clicked back into place. We got married. I was worried about the twins and how we'd get on, but they were lovely children and they seemed to take to me. I was so happy, maybe for the first time in my adult life. It was like paradise. Even work was going well. I landed a couple of good roles in plays. My life couldn't have been better. Then I came home from a Saturday afternoon shopping trip with the children and found him dead at the bottom of the stairs. He'd tripped over some of the children's toys, fallen down the whole flight, and smashed his skull on a protruding corner at the bottom.' She was crying now. She looked at Sophie who answered her coldly.

'Go on. I want to know about the children.'

'I couldn't stay there, not in that house, not where he'd died. So I took the children and moved to Dorchester, where I was already part owner of a property with my sister.'

'Finch Cottage.'

'Yes. But things were difficult. I was offered a role in a play in New York that looked like it would last a year or more. My agent told me I would be mad to turn it down because it was really high profile. I thought about it for a long time, then took the decision to accept it. I took the children to Hong Kong to stay with Li Hua's sister, who was childless. She made arrangements to adopt them.' Pauline fell silent.

'So what happened to them?'

'I got a couple of cards from them, then everything went quiet, and I didn't get a response to my phone calls. I had a short break so I flew to Hong Kong to see them, but the house was empty. I checked with the neighbours and they told me that the husband's business had failed. He'd been declared bankrupt and they'd had to move out of their apartment. I couldn't find them anywhere. I was distraught.'

'So what did you do?'

'I went to the local police and reported them missing. They knew about the business going under, but didn't know what had happened to the family. I had to fly back to New York after a couple of days to resume my work, but I stayed in touch with the investigation. There was nothing. The family had vanished into thin air, taking Jasmine and Kenneth with them.'

Sophie stared across the table at the actress. She was looking bereft, tears streaming down her face.

'So how come their bodies ended up buried under a butterfly bush in the back garden at Finch Cottage?'

Pauline stared at Sophie with a look of horror. Marsh sensed a change in the atmosphere in the room. It seemed to become almost frigid. Either she really hadn't known or she was a consummate actress.

'What? That's impossible. It can't be them. It's got to be some other children. You must have made a mistake.'

'There's no mistake, Mrs Camberwell. DNA tests have proved the identity of those tiny corpses beyond any doubt. We know they are the children of Richard and Li Hua Camberwell. Who did you think those two bodies were?'

Pauline held her head in her hands, shuddering. Her words were barely audible. 'I don't know, but I knew it couldn't be them. The first press report I saw implied the bodies were teenagers. Anyway, my two were in Hong Kong, I know they were. I took them there myself. It's the truth.' She looked up. 'The Hong Kong police will know. They'll still be on record as missing, surely? Please check. Everything I've told you is the truth.'

'Oh, we intend to check it all, Mrs Camberwell. Everything you've said and plenty of things you haven't. Because, of course, John Wethergill was the gardener at Finch Cottage at one time, and he's now conveniently dead, so we can't question him. You knew he would be on that walk, you knew he'd had an affair with your sister, you knew he was the gardener at Finch Cottage and you picked him out deliberately and seduced him. Why? What were your motives? And why did you sell Finch Cottage soon after he left? All these questions point towards a picture that doesn't quite equate with the innocent self-portrait you've been painting. My job is to uncover the real picture and I intend to do so.' Sophie stood up. 'I want you to come to the police station with us to make a formal statement. Maybe you need to reflect on things before we get there, and consider whether there's anything else you need to tell us. The fact is, you could have volunteered all of this last week when we first met. It would have left me in a much better frame of mind than I'm in at the moment. I really don't like having my time wasted, Mrs Camberwell. I intend to see that those poor young children get the justice they deserve and your delaying tactics have not made it any easier. I also want your passport to ensure you don't leave the country. I can go through official channels to get it impounded, but you could choose to hand it over voluntarily. It might make me feel better disposed towards you. What's it to be?'

Pauline sat silently, then she said, 'I'll get it for you. It's at home.'

Sophie nodded. 'We'll pick it up on our way. There is one further thing, Pauline. You seem to have started a relationship with Jill Freeman recently. Why? Why her?'

The actress seemed to sink deeper into her chair. 'I can see how it might look,' she answered. 'But it isn't like that, really. I just need the softness of a woman sometimes. Is that so wrong of me?'

'Don't try to slide out of my question. I asked you, why her? I'm still waiting for an explanation.'

'It's entirely innocent. A few weeks ago I dropped Dorothy round there. She cleans for the Freemans. I stopped for a chat with Jill and I knew at once. The clues were there.' She looked at Sophie. 'I only hit on women if the signals are right. I don't go around throwing myself at every good-looking person I happen to meet.'

'Don't you? You can say that to me after trying it on with my husband a few days ago? And my daughter last week?'

Pauline gave a sly smile. 'That's bugged you, hasn't it?' She stood up. 'I think I'm ready to make that statement now. Shall we go and collect my passport?'

One small, final triumph, thought Marsh, in an otherwise overwhelming defeat. He looked at his boss. Her face was inscrutable. She glanced at her watch, then removed a document from her bag.

'Fine, Pauline. We'll arrive at about the same time as the forensic team. Here's your copy of the search warrant for your house.'

Steamroller was an apt description, after all.

CHAPTER 30: THE ADVENTURESS

Tuesday to Thursday, Week 3

Dorothy Kitson entered the hotel lounge and ordered a glass of white wine from the barman. He was the same ebony-skinned person who'd checked her in when she arrived earlier in the day. He was an older man with a few grey streaks in his hair who spoke with a soft Caribbean accent. He'd told her then that his job was to fill in wherever it was required, although he drew the line at cleaning the toilets.

Dorothy took her glass over to an armchair, then changed her mind and sat on a sofa. Maybe there was a nice single man staying in the hotel who might come and chat to her. She checked her reflection in the full-length mirror hanging on the far wall. Not bad. She primped her hair. It had been coloured and styled in Dorchester the day before she came away for her short break. She'd even had her nails done and had bought a new dress on her first day in Weymouth. She hardly recognised the person looking back at her. Not at a distance anyway. Close up, of course, her skin flaws would show but not all men wanted a sleek, glossy beauty. Some might welcome a woman who showed that she'd lived a little.

Her dress was beautiful. She stood up briefly and stretched so that she could see her full-length reflection. What a bargain. She'd spotted it in the window of a charity shop. Even the shop assistant had remarked how well it fitted. There was no way that she could have afforded a new dress of this quality, not after splashing out so much money on the five day break here. People would think she was mad, coming on a holiday to Weymouth when she only lived in Dorchester, a mere ten miles away. But it was a change for her, an adventure, and who could tell where an adventure might lead?

She heard footsteps behind her, and half turned as a man walked past her on his way to the bar. A businessman visiting the town? Someone approaching retirement, judging from the colour of his hair. She gave him a shy but friendly smile as he turned in her direction, glass of lager in hand.

* * *

Later in the evening she was strolling along the promenade, arm in arm with him, admiring the view as dusk fell. Lights twinkled in the calm waters of the bay. She was feeling excited but surprisingly relaxed. Colin seemed to be a real gentleman. He appeared to have accepted her stipulation that their first evening together should be just for getting to know each other. He'd nodded and smiled amiably at her. He was also planning to stay until Saturday. He'd come to Weymouth for a series of sales meetings at various local electrical shops. The absence of a wedding ring didn't prove anything of course, particularly since she could see a pale mark on the skin. He claimed to be a divorcee. Dorothy knew it was easy enough to slip off a ring at the start of a business trip away from home.

She stopped and pointed to a light twinkling on the horizon, far out to sea. 'Isn't it mysterious,' she said. 'Think of all the possibilities. It could be a tiny yacht sailing around the whole British coast with only two people on board. Or it could be a ferry on its way over to France, full of families off to exotic holiday locations. Or even a luxury boat on its way to the Spanish coast, with a dozen rich people on board, having a champagne party. We'll never know, will we?' She hugged Colin's arm even tighter. 'Maybe even a fishing boat coming in with the catch for tomorrow's market. We could be eating the fish for dinner tomorrow evening.'

'I won't be,' Colin replied. 'I had fish tonight. It'll be meat for me tomorrow night.'

He smiled at her. His face crinkled into a series of very attractive laughter lines. He really was very handsome, and he seemed so relaxed. Dorothy couldn't believe her luck.

'You've spoiled my fantasy now,' she protested, leaning in closer. 'I'm still going to have the fish and pretend that it might have come off the boat that's under that twinkling light.'

'We could go for a walk tomorrow afternoon if you like,' he replied. 'If I get started early enough in the morning, I might finish tomorrow's meetings by two. I could get back to the hotel, change, then meet up with you. What do you think?'

'That would be perfect. I'd love to.' Dorothy was wondering if she had enough money to buy another couple of dresses from the charity shop. Surely she could manage it? It wouldn't do to wear the same dress two nights running, not now she had a man to impress. Tomorrow was her birthday, so she ought to be able to treat herself. Thank goodness she still had her figure. Maybe she should go for one that was a bit edgier, a bit more seductive. A dress that would say to a man, yes, you're in with a chance. The type of dress that her sister would wear. She frowned, and tried to wipe the thought from her mind. This break was her treat to herself. Why spoil it with thoughts of Pauline and all the history that came with her?

* * *

The next day was sunny and mild. Dorothy left the hotel mid-morning, dressed in peach cotton trousers, a cream top and sandals. It was so warm that she carried her cardigan.

She'd switched her mobile phone off, having seen a series of missed calls from Pauline. She'd come away to escape the problems of her Dorchester life.

After a successful hunt around the charity shops she had a light lunch, then returned to the hotel in order to drop off her purchases well before two o'clock. She bumped into Colin in the reception area. He was looking harassed and anxious.

'Is something wrong?' she asked.

'Yes. I've had head office on the phone. There's some kind of problem and they want me back in Coventry. I tried to put them off until the end of the week, but they insist.'

'Oh, no. Surely you can wait? Can't you? Your booking's for the week, you said?' She laid her hand on his arm, tears in the corners of her eyes. Pauline wasn't the only actress in the family.

'Look, I'll try to be back as soon as I can. I still have another lot of meetings lined up for the rest of the week.'

'Please try. I was so looking forward to the rest of the week. It's not often I get on with someone as well as I have with you.'

Colin looked at her intently. 'I feel the same. I'll do what I can. I have your mobile number, so I'll call you. They've still got a few empty rooms here and probably won't need to re-let mine. With a bit of luck I'll make it back, maybe even late tonight.'

Dorothy leaned across and quickly kissed him on the lips, despite the man at the reception desk. He had served breakfast that morning, although he said that he was due the afternoon off.

'I'll make it worth your while,' she whispered in Colin's ear. 'I've bought a new dress and it's really special.'

'Okay. I'll do all I can.' He still looked worried.

* * *

That evening Dorothy squeezed herself into one of the dresses that she'd bought in the same charity shop she'd used the previous day. It was a fitted dress in mottled brown and gold. It shaped itself tightly around her buttocks and thighs, and lifted her bosom to new heights. There had been no message from Colin, so once her solitary meal was over she took a chance and phoned his mobile number. It was switched off. After some thought she phoned his home number, which she'd slyly read that afternoon from the checkout sheet on the reception desk.

'Hello?' It was a woman's voice. She sounded irritated.

'Can I speak to Colin, please?' Dorothy said, trying to sound confident and business-like.

'And why do you want to speak to him?' came the challenging reply. 'Who are you?'

Dorothy paused, thinking hard. 'I'm Dorothy, calling from Weymouth. We were due to have a meeting today.'

There was a snort. 'Ah. Is that where he's been? I get home from a cancelled business trip and he's nowhere to be found. I might have guessed he'd be somewhere along the coast, at the betting shops.'

'He said he worked in electrical goods, organising wholesale bulk sales to retailers.'

Another snort. 'Colin's a hospital porter from Poole, on a final warning from his bosses and from me. And the moment my back's turned he's at it again, spending my hard earned money on his gambling habit. No wonder he looked a bit nervous when he picked me up from the airport this afternoon. I knew he'd been up to something. I got to the answer machine before he could delete the messages. His supervisor had left one asking why he hadn't turned up for the early shift this morning. So who are you exactly?'

Dorothy terminated the call and switched the phone off. She started to tremble. Were all men such untrustworthy bastards? She walked to the bar and ordered a gin and tonic to calm her nerves. The same man was there again. She took a sip of her drink, and perched on a bar stool to chat to him. He seemed pleasant enough and didn't have any suspicious marks on his bare ring finger. He told her his name was Larry, that he finished his shift at eleven and had no plans for the night. She began to feel excited again and bought them both a drink. She wasn't imagining it, he kept looking at her cleavage, she was sure. She was determined to have a man in her bed tonight. Her sister wasn't the only one who could have adventures, and it was her birthday after all. She smiled at the barman and told him the reason for her buoyant mood.

'I know a great club where we can go to celebrate,' he said with a smile. 'A pal of mine runs it. We can get bubbly at half the normal price until the place shuts at two. Best of all, it's only a hundred yards away and tomorrow is my day off.'

She leaned forward, giving him an even better view of her cleavage.

'I'm up for an adventure,' she said. 'Let's do it.'

* * *

Dorothy woke late that morning. She stretched and yawned, then opened her eyes to see a mug of tea being placed on the bedside table. She turned and smiled as Larry walked back around the bed and slid under the covers.

'That's nice,' she said. 'I need it. I'm feeling a bit groggy. Are you okay?'

Larry smiled. 'Oh, yes. Great night. Good job I'm not needed again until the evening shift.' He leaned over and kissed her. 'Last night was brilliant. It's been a while since I've had so much fun.'

'Hmm,' she murmured, closing her eyes again. 'It was good, wasn't it?' She turned and faced him. 'What's the Caribbean like? I mean, would I like it there?'

Larry looked at her, then broke into a broad grin. 'Yeah, man. It's totally cool, and you'd love it. I go back to Jamaica in the autumn, when the tourists stop coming here. Why don't you come with me?'

Dorothy smiled happily. 'I might just do that. I'm fed up with this place. It jangles my nerves. I want to move somewhere warm and relaxed and, most of all, a long way from my bloody sister.' She looked into his eyes. 'Do we have to wait until the autumn? It's a long time away, isn't it? Can't we go now?'

CHAPTER 31: A DEAD END

Wednesday

Sophie stood in the pathology lab, looking down on the two small skeletons. 'Nothing else?' she asked.

Benny shook his head. 'That's the final lot of test results in. I organised some extra scans using a highly detailed machine that they have in Bournemouth, but nothing came up. There's no damage of any type on any of their bones, so there's not the slightest evidence of any maltreatment, or even accidental injury. What we have here are the remains of two seven-year-olds with near-perfect bones. Sorry. I know that wasn't what you wanted.'

'In a way, it's a relief. I know discovering some injuries would have made my job easier, but I'm glad for them. I know they could still have suffered in other ways, but if there was physical mistreatment it wasn't serious enough to break or scar bones, and that's reassuring. Though there could still have been emotional damage.' Sophie took her eyes off the skeletons and looked at Benny. 'You said the bones were in a good state. Does that mean that they'd had a reasonable diet? Maybe right up until the end?'

Goodall frowned. 'Until close to their deaths, yes. Any long term dietary deficiencies would have had an effect on bone density and size, and both were good. So if you want to pin me down, I'd say that they had all the nutrition they needed until a month or two short of their deaths. Maybe right up until they died, but it's impossible to make judgements about their final few weeks because we don't have any soft tissue to work with. The fact is, Sophie, we'll never know for sure how they were treated in their final days, not from the medical evidence. It's all too long ago. I feel bitterly disappointed that I can't be of any more help to you. What about forensics? Has our friend Dave Nash come up with anything?'

Sophie shook her head. 'Like you, nothing. Nothing in the soil from around the grave, nor anything unusual in the fabric remnants. It'll be people and their activities, Benny, that will take me there. It's like an old-fashioned case from almost a generation ago, before advanced forensics became so important. Killers were still brought to justice, though it took longer. I'll get there, don't worry.'

'I never doubted you for a moment. So what's your next move?'

'We're still digging into the complete tangle of their stepmother's life. She's still alive and she's heavily implicated.' She glanced at her watch. 'But first I have another visit to pay to Finch Cottage. All is not what it seems in the Freeman family, and I've been told that the mother is still at home this morning. A few words are called for.'

* * *

'Jill, you need to explain to me about Pauline Stopley.'

Jill Freeman collapsed onto the nearest chair and looked at Sophie, her eyes wide. She looked around her, as if she'd lost her sense of time and place. The two women were in the kitchen at Finch Cottage and Jill had been about to make a pot of tea. Sophie took over.

'Pauline Stopley. You need to tell me about her and what's been going on. And before you say that it's no business of mine, you need to know that many years ago she was part owner of this house. Probably at about the same time the children died. If you've ever checked the record of past owners, you might have spotted the name Camberwell. That was her married name.'

Jill looked ashen. 'Christ. Do you mean she might have had something to do with their deaths?' She shook her head, her dark hair swaying. 'No, that's not right. She's not that kind of person. She's thoughtful and kind.' She looked at Sophie. 'You must have made some kind of mistake. I know she has a bit of a lively streak but, then, she was an actress. I don't believe she's capable of anything criminal, let alone being involved in the deaths of two young children. It's just not possible.'

Sophie was watching her carefully, weighing up her words. 'How did you meet?'

Jill tucked her hair behind her ears. She spoke quietly. 'It was about four or five weeks ago. She brought her sister Dorothy round one very wet day. Dorothy comes every Tuesday morning to do the cleaning. She usually comes by bus but she had a bit of a cold and was running late, so Pauline gave her a lift. She brought her car right into the driveway as close to the front door as possible, but then got blocked in when the fishmonger arrived a few seconds later. He comes on a Tuesday too. Dorothy usually collects the fish from him and puts it in the fridge, but Pauline sent her straight into the house and took the fish herself. For once I was still at home because of a late meeting the previous evening, so I was in the kitchen when she came in. We got chatting and I guess something clicked between us.' She looked at Sophie. 'Nothing remotely like it has ever happened before. Please don't think I make a habit of this kind of thing. I knew things weren't quite right between Phil and me, but I couldn't put my finger on what it was. I'd been feeling for some time that something was missing, but it was something in me, not Phil's fault at all. All it took was one smile from Pauline and I kind of melted. And she spotted it. We chatted, and she left, but she stayed in my mind all day. I couldn't sleep properly that night. The next evening she phoned and asked me to meet her for a drink. The second time we met, a couple of days later, we went for a walk at Maiden Castle. Apparently it's her favourite place to get her thoughts in order. We had afternoon tea in a nearby café and continued chatting. And that was it. I felt a kind of magnetic pull and I didn't even try to resist.'

Sophie poured the tea and pushed a mug across to Jill. 'So you think it all happened quite by chance? That there was no pre-planning involved? Did Dorothy know that you might be there that morning?'

Jill shook her head, frowning. 'No. Even I didn't know until the evening before when my meeting seriously overran and my boss told me not to come in until mid-morning. I discovered that Pauline had given Dorothy a lift several times before, but had always dropped her off in the street outside. It just couldn't have been deliberate.' She took a sip of tea. 'Anyway, how could she possibly have been connected with the deaths of those children? Even if she did own the house then, it was being rented out to someone, wasn't it?'

Sophie nodded. 'Yes. But she was their stepmother, Jill. She says she was working in New York at the time of their deaths, and that seems to check out. She looks as upset as anyone would be, but she is an actress after all. We have several lines of inquiry, and people are checking them all out as we speak. I want you to stay away from her until we can be sure that she wasn't involved.'

'Their stepmother?' Jill whispered. 'God. That's unbelievable. But I can't see it, Chief Inspector. She's always been so sensitive and thoughtful. I really don't believe she has that level of duplicity in her.'

Sophie's face hardened. 'While she's been seeing you, she started an affair with a man here in Dorchester. He's now dead. I'm reallocating Theresa back to you. She's here as protection. Do you now understand my concerns?'

Jill said nothing.

'You also need to talk to your daughter. Karen suspects you've been seeing someone, though she doesn't know who. She told Theresa about it.'

A look of desperation swept across Jill's face. 'How did she know?' she whispered.

'Teenagers are more observant than they lead us to believe, particularly girls. You need to reassure her, Jill. She's only just getting over the shock of finding the bodies, and now this has landed on her. Spend some time with her. She's vulnerable.' Sophie got up to leave. 'By the way, don't worry about Theresa. She's totally non-judgemental and very discreet. I trust her totally, so you can too.'

* * *

It was late morning by the time Sophie got to the police station. She was preoccupied as she parked her car, and failed to notice the dark green four-by-four vehicle sitting in one of the reserved bays. She made her way up the stairs to the incident room. There was the familiar figure of Matt Silver slouched in a chair, his plaster-encased leg stretched out in front of him. She ran across the room and flung her arms around her boss.

'Ouch,' was Silver's first word, followed by, 'do I deserve this?'

'Hey, you! Just clamber off my husband, would you? He's already a physical wreck and can't cope with this level of excitement.'

Sophie turned and gave another warm hug to the curvy brunette who'd been talking to Rae Gregson. 'Tracy! You've no idea how relieved I am to see Matt in here with us.'

'Really? It looked pretty obvious to all of us onlookers. Get a grip, woman. Anyone would think he was important or something.'

'What are you both doing here?'

Tracy pulled a face. 'I'm here bringing him in for a visit, and he's here because he's driving me round the bloody bend. Working from home is fine when I have the place to myself, but it's a nightmare with him and his hangdog expression filling the house with gloom. So I thought I'd bring him in, dump him on you, and you can put up with him for a few hours. Meanwhile, I'm going out to visit a few bars to celebrate several hours of freedom.' She looked at her watch. 'Maybe come back for him at three? Can you put up with him for that long?' She dropped a number of carrier bags on a table, knocking files onto the floor in the process. 'Just a few nibbles to keep you going for lunch. Don't let him eat too much or he'll get a paunch and I'll be forced to divorce him. Then where would you be?'

Sophie laughed. 'Thanks, Tracy. Your timing is perfect, as always. We have quite a difficult briefing this afternoon and Matt is just who we need sitting in. We'll try not to tire him out too much.'

Tracy snorted. 'Bloody hell, Sophie, why do you think I brought him in? Tire him out all you want. Then he might not fidget so much tonight and I'll sleep better. Bye all!' She gave Matt a quick kiss on the lips and left.

Sophie, still smiling, looked at her boss. 'She doesn't change, does she?'

He grinned back and shook his head. 'No, thank goodness. She is who she is and I love her for it. She has a couple of appointments at the hospital.'

'I had no idea she was your wife, sir,' Rae said. 'I had a series of sessions with her a couple of years ago and she worked wonders on my voice. I knew her as Tracy Daunt.'

'That attitude of hers is all show,' Silver replied. 'She was already well-established when we met, and there aren't many speech therapists who've managed to get to her level of recognition. I can understand her wanting to retain her previous name for her work. Why change all that after marriage?' He turned to Sophie. 'You'd better look in the bags. I suspect Tracy's description of a few nibbles is somewhat wide of the mark.'

So it proved. One bag contained a tub of cold roast chicken legs, a tub of cold sausages and a box of baby-plum tomatoes, and another held a mass of smoked salmon sandwiches, all carefully wrapped in aluminium foil. A third contained a box of homemade, sliced fruit cake and several bunches of bananas. Sophie looked at the clock on the wall. 'Early lunch, I think. We can talk while we eat. Everyone in agreement?'

Sophie already knew that her hopes of building a case against Pauline Stopley had taken a severe knock. Earlier that morning, Barry Marsh had made a number of calls to the Hong Kong police. The liaison officer there had confirmed all of the important details of Pauline's story. The actress had flown into the city in April 1995 with the twins and records showed that she had flown back to Britain a week later, by herself. Children's Agency records showed that local officials had been aware of the children's transfer into the care of their aunt. Moreover, the Hong Kong police still had a record of Pauline's later visit in 1996 when she'd been unable to trace the two young children. A missing-persons' investigation had been set up, but the youngsters had never been found. Marsh had even spoken to an officer who had been involved in the search, and she had assured him that Pauline Stopley had been genuinely distressed by the disappearance.

Rae had been checking flight records dating back to the mid-nineties and had found bookings and flights that also corroborated Pauline's story. All the flights matched up with the account she'd given Sophie and Marsh. Moreover, Rae had uncovered a set of travel data from early 1996 that showed that Kenneth and Jasmine Camberwell had taken a flight back to the UK from Hong Kong. They were accompanied by a Jing Hua Chen, the aunt who had taken them in the previous year. Jing Hua had flown back to Hong Kong two days later, alone. Rae had double-checked with passport usage records and these gave further evidence to support the story. There was little doubt: the twins had returned from Hong Kong some ten months after leaving these shores. And there the trail went cold.

'I think you've done an outstanding job so far,' Matt Silver said. 'It shows you were right in sticking to your guns, Sophie. Is it possible to trace this aunt, Jing Hua Chen, and see what she has to say?'

Marsh shook his head. 'We can't. Hong Kong police finally traced some of her records last week and emailed them over yesterday. She died ten years ago. A brain tumour. And they haven't been able to find anyone else in the family. It's a dead end.'

CHAPTER 32: SCONES AND CLOTTED CREAM

Thursday

Sophie turned to Rae. 'What was it you discovered yesterday evening? I'm all ears.'

'The week of the hit and run accident that killed Li Hua Camberwell, Pauline Stopley was appearing in a Tom Stoppard play. At the Hippodrome. In Bristol. But not that actual night. It was a Monday so there was no performance. She had an evening off.'

'Not her again. Why does she keep popping up at every single twist and turn?' Sophie sighed loudly.

'Sorry, ma'am,' Rae said.

Sophie laughed. 'Don't apologise, Rae. It might turn out to be a vital piece of information. My problem is, I haven't found a way in behind her facade. Whenever I interview her I always find myself wondering whether what I'm seeing is the real Pauline. She was a first-rate actress by all accounts, and I keep wondering if she's putting on an act for me. Have I ever spoken to the real her or has it always been one of her characters? How do you fancy having a go? You might be able to find a way through. I'm due in Bristol this morning anyway.'

'If you want me to ma'am, but I'm not sure I'd be as perceptive as you.'

Sophie pondered. 'Yes, let's do it. I can't give it to Barry. She'd put on the seductive charm and he'd be mesmerised. You might well confuse her. I hope you don't mind me using that?'

'You mean the fact that I'm a TS . . ? I can see your reasoning, ma'am. You want me to deliberately give clues, is that it? To let it slip out?'

Sophie nodded. 'Pauline always plays on perceived masculine and feminine weaknesses. She has seductive strategies for both genders and uses them during conversation. It will be interesting to see how she copes with you.'

'Ma'am, I'll do it but only this once. I've put so much time and effort into being a woman that I'm not going to let it slip now. This is a favour to you. A one-off, and a thank you for all the support you've given me. When do you want me to see her?'

'There's no time like the present, is there? See her in her own office rather than bringing her here.'

Sophie began to wonder if she'd made a serious and unfortunate misjudgement but it was too late to back away now.

'Okay', Rae answered curtly. She picked up her jacket and left the incident room without saying goodbye to anyone. The door slammed behind her.

Sophie got the message, loud and clear. She put her hand to her head and thought, God, what have I done?

* * *

The request to try using more masculine behaviour — to revert — came as a shock to Rae. And it came from someone she had come to consider as her most understanding supporter. But the DCI could obviously set aside her principles when it was convenient to do so. Was she aware of the pain this might cause? Of course she was. Doubtlessly the desire for a possible breakthrough outweighed the sense of betrayal that she, Rae, would obviously feel, indeed did feel and all too strongly.

Rae began the interview.

'You were in a production at the Bristol Old Vic that week. I checked. Can you tell me about it?'

Pauline turned her head a little so that her face was slightly profiled. 'It was a long time ago. Do you really expect me to remember it all?'

Rae nodded. 'Yes. It would have been an important event for you in lots of ways. A starring role. In the city where your ex-boyfriend lived. The week his wife was killed. Of course you remember.'

She would normally have crossed her legs at this point, and possibly smoothed out her grey corduroy skirt, but she continued to sit upright with her knees slightly parted. She'd dropped her voice to a slightly lower register, and had omitted all feminine terms from her speech, although she'd found it hard to do so. She was trying her best to speak in the clipped tones that she'd spent months attempting to alter. Her mobile phone beeped and she glanced at the display. A message from the boss, marked urgent.

'I'll just have to check this,' she said, and read.

"Sincere apologies," it said. "I should never have asked you to do it in that way. I could kick myself. Please be your normal self. I promise never to ask you to do the same again. S."

Rae sighed, crossed her legs at the ankle, smoothed out a wrinkle where her skirt tightened against her thighs and relaxed into her chair. She looked at Pauline Stopley and gave her a slight smile. 'Please go on,' she said.

'I wasn't working that night,' Pauline said. 'It was a Monday. I was tired after the weekend so I spent the evening in my hotel and had an early night. I think I may have visited the bar for a drink after my meal, but I didn't leave the place.'

'And you didn't meet Richard at all? Not that night?'

'No. It was a temptation, I admit, but it would have been too difficult. Anyway, I was in the middle of a short fling with one of the supporting actors.'

'Did you spend the evening with him? It was a him, was it?'

There was a pause. Was the actress weighing up the chances of getting away with a lie?

'Yes and yes. We ate in the restaurant, had a drink in the lounge then went to my room. He stayed until late evening. I expect you'll want to know who he was?'

Rae nodded. The name was well known from his numerous television appearances.

'It went on all the time and probably still does. Meaningless flings between people on tour together. It's more to alleviate the boredom than anything else, and to help us come down after the highs of a performance. I'd be buzzing, with no other way of dissipating all that energy.'

'I'm not judging you, Ms Stopley. You don't need to justify it to me.'

'Oh but I do. It's almost impossible to explain to someone who doesn't regularly perform in front of audiences. The ups and downs, and the need for some emotional release. People in ordinary jobs and from ordinary backgrounds just can't begin to understand.'

'I think I can. My background isn't exactly ordinary.'

'Isn't it? Oh well, maybe I should stop making assumptions about people. I suppose everyone has a story to tell,' said Pauline.

'Did you see Richard Camberwell at any time that week?'

'He called me a couple of days later with the news about his wife. I visited him just to offer some support, and I ended up getting the children their tea. Everything just clicked into place for us. I didn't plan it, whatever you might think.'

* * *

'Did anyone ever seriously consider whether Li Hua's death was anything other than a simple accident?' Sophie was sitting in a small office in a police station a mile or so to the north of Bristol city centre.

Detective Inspector Polly Nelson took a sip from her cup of herbal tea, leant back in her chair and said very guardedly, 'what do you mean?'

'It became obvious pretty quickly that it was a hit and run. You probably all assumed that it was an accidental one, and that the driver panicked and kept going. But did you ever consider that her death might have been deliberate? That she might have been targeted by someone?'

Polly Nelson looked at her through narrowed eyes. 'Of course it was a possibility. The investigation was thorough. Are you implying otherwise?'

Sophie smiled at her. 'No. I'm not. But I'm aware of how much pressure can be brought to bear from above to get a case wrapped up quickly, particularly when there's no obvious counter-evidence.' She took a small mouthful from her own cup. How should she play this? It was obvious that she'd touched a nerve. 'Look, I'm not trying to stir something up here. It was twenty years ago, for goodness sake, and things were a bit different then.' She picked up the file that related to the incident. 'I just get the feeling that this is a shade on the thin side, and even the case notes that are in there seem padded out. To my mind it tends to pay only lip service to the possibility of a deliberately targeted act. Was her husband happy with the outcome?'

Nelson stared at Sophie. 'Yes, as far as I know. You have to realise that I was only a DC then. It was one of my first cases. I didn't meet her husband personally. I only saw him briefly at a distance a couple of times.'

Sophie nodded. 'It tallies with the recollections of his work colleagues. But they did say he seemed confused by it all, apparently broken-hearted and with two young children at home. He had no family to call on for help, so maybe he felt overwhelmed. The trouble is, Polly, that their marriage may not have been as happy as it appeared on the surface.'

'How do you know that?'

'I spoke to some ex-colleagues of Li Hua this morning. My mother is the practice manager of a neighbouring medical centre, and she got the contacts for me. Li Hua wasn't as popular at work as this record seems to suggest. She could be a bit of a harridan, apparently.'

'Why didn't you inform us? Isn't that unprofessional, to go behind our backs? I could make a formal complaint against you.'

'Let me explain how it looks from my angle. Li Hua is killed in a hit and run. Her husband remarries within a couple of years. Several years later he suffers a fatal fall down the stairs at home. Six months after that, the twins somehow die and are secretly buried in a garden. Within the last two weeks, and after the discovery of the twins' bodies, the man who was the gardener at the Dorchester house at the time this all happened is himself found dead from cyanide poisoning, looking like suicide. Come on. How does it look to you? You and I both know that coincidences happen. But all this? Absolutely not. So I'm going back to the first death in the sequence, and I don't like what I find in the files. It wasn't taken seriously. You know it and I know it. And I'm asking you about it. I'm not going to make an issue of it if that's your concern. I just need to know why it was just that wee bit slapdash.'

The silence lasted for nearly a minute. Finally Polly Nelson said, 'there was a change of command in the unit at about the same time. Someone new came in with his own priorities, wanting to make a mark, ready to shake us all up, changing all of our areas of responsibility. If you must know, I made waves about it. I said that more investigation was needed, and I nearly lost my job because of it. After that I just buttoned my lip and kept quiet.'

Sophie nodded. 'An all too common story,' she said. 'I've been there myself. A very junior woman detective dares to object to operational decisions made by some macho, self-obsessed, furrow-minded bloke. And gets an earful in response. Is that how it was?'

Polly nodded.

'Where is he now?'

'He's a chief constable but not here, thank God. Due to retire next year. He'll probably get a sheaf of honours. Look, in some ways he was a good cop and got results. That's why he is where he is. But this case was in limbo when he arrived and it just disappeared down the cracks during the transfer of power. There was meatier stuff going on at the same time, major crime initiatives and the like. As far as he was concerned it was a question of putting the resources where they'd have the greatest effect. What else could be done? We'd staged a reconstruction. We'd done everything by the book. He lost interest.'

'I can imagine. So assumptions were made on the basis of convenience rather than close scrutiny, and the whole team moved on.'

Polly nodded.

'What did you think?'

'The fact that the circumstances surrounding her death were never explained in a satisfactory way always bothered me. I didn't like leaving things in limbo. I still don't.'

'So if my boss asked your current powers-that-be to reopen the investigation, there's a chance that it could be looked into again? Would you be happy with that?'

The two women looked at each other. 'Yes,' Polly finally answered. 'I'd be happy to allocate someone if I get the go-ahead.'

They shook hands and Sophie left.

She glanced at her watch. There was time to meet her mother for lunch.

* * *

'It's been a worthwhile morning, Mum. It was so useful to be able to meet some of her ex-colleagues in the practice. Written records can tell us a lot, but there's nothing to beat a face-to-face with people who knew the victim.'

Sophie was in a Clifton café with her mother, who was reading the menu.

'It's all too ghoulish for me,' Susan replied. 'I'm proud of what you've achieved but I've never been sure where you got this obsession with probing into murder, violent crime and the like. It certainly isn't from me.'

Sophie laughed. 'You've told me that often enough. From my dad, maybe?'

'I don't think so, not from the brief time that I knew him.' Susan stared down at her plate.

'Sorry, Mum. Have I put my foot in it? I thought things were going well with Bill.'

'I don't know. He wants me to commit, to go through a ceremony of some kind. So I've hit the same barrier I always hit. I thought things would change after your dad's funeral last year, but clearly they haven't.'

Sophie reached across and put her hand on her mother's. 'Maybe you just need to give it more time, Mum. You're still grieving. I'm sure Bill understands. He's always come across as a considerate sort.'

Finally Susan spoke very quietly. 'I don't think things are ever going to change for me. I think I'm coming to accept that my emotional life was determined by that two-month period forty-four years ago. Is there ever going to be anything else? I wonder.'

'Mum, if you take that line you'll be fulfilling your own prophecy. You've got to take chances occasionally. If you really like and respect Bill, and I think you do, it's worth giving it a go. I hate to see you like this, so full of self-doubt. You're never going to feel the same level of overpowering emotion that you felt for Dad. It's impossible. You were a teenager, for God's sake, when everything is so charged. And added to that, you obviously felt something rare and special. I always felt strongly attracted to Martin, but I don't think I ever experienced it as powerfully as you've described with Dad. But over time even that level of passion fades away and is replaced with a much more comfortable kind of love. I'm only in my forties and, really, I'm not sure I'd want that level of overwhelming, aching desire running through my life now. It would just get in the way of everything and leave me a wreck.' She paused, choosing her words carefully. 'Mum, you've got decades of life still in front of you. You're fit and healthy. As far as I can tell, Bill is by far the most pleasant of all the boyfriends of yours that I've met. I know he stays over occasionally, and you do the same at his place, but it's not the same as living under the same roof most of the time, not for most people and probably not for him.'

Susan said nothing.

'Why don't you go for something fairly low-level to start with? Just a simple ceremony of commitment, like a blessing of some type? Or move in together on a trial basis? You won't know until you try it.'

'That's what he's suggested,' Susan murmured. 'He can't see the problem.'

'More than anything else, Mum, Dad would have wanted you to be happy. Surely you realise that? We've all told you so, including gran and grandad. You have everyone's blessing to move on finally.' She got up and walked around the table, crouching down to put her arm around her mother. She put a finger on Susan's forehead. 'Close your eyes and clear your mind.' A pause. 'I'm his daughter, his only child. I am what is left of him. He is in me, and he and I both need you to be happy in your life. Trust us, please. You must start to finally put him behind you.'

Susan started to cry.

'Would it help if you came to Wareham and stayed over this weekend? Hannah will be paying a flying visit on Sunday.'

Her mother nodded, unable to speak. The waitress hovered in the background, unable to decide whether to give the two women a few more minutes. Sophie smiled and beckoned her over.

* * *

Back in the incident room later that afternoon, Sophie had a review meeting with Barry Marsh, Rae Gregson and Theresa Jackson. Rae had brought in a tub of fruit scones that she'd baked the previous evening, along with a jar of raspberry jam and a pot of Cornish clotted cream.

'You wicked, wicked young woman,' Sophie said, spreading thick cream onto her second scone. 'This has to be a sackable offence. Why did I save you from the evil grasp of he who must no longer be obeyed if this is what you go and do?' She bit deeply into the scone. 'Oh, heaven! It's a good job I had lunch with my mother. She watches what I eat like a hawk and kept me to a slice of quiche, some salad and a solitary bread roll. My stomach was gurgling all the way back from Bristol.' She finished the scone and wiped her fingers.

'Right, let's get on. More and more I'm thinking that the key to all these deaths is the marriage of Li Hua and Richard Camberwell. Pauline Stopley says that the marriage was made in heaven, and the two doctors were deeply in love. That was enough to make me suspicious, and this morning I did a bit of digging. Sure enough, there were some signs of friction and a couple of suggestions that Li Hua did not have the angelic temperament we thought she had. Quite the opposite. Even at work she could be bad tempered and downright awkward at times. Someone even speculated that she'd trapped Richard into getting married by getting herself pregnant. This was one of her own work colleagues. They seem to have felt more sorry for Richard than her.'

'So Pauline told us the opposite of what was probably the case?' Marsh asked.

'Par for the course, don't you think?' Sophie smiled wryly. 'We've now got an ally in the Bristol Major Crime Squad and she's going to be doing a bit more digging from the inside. It's a DI Polly Nelson, so if she phones or messages, make a note of it and bring it to me. She admitted that the original investigation into the hit and run was a bit lax. I'll put in an official request for a collaborative approach via the ACC, but it might take days. Polly will try to make a start before then, if her workload permits. Meanwhile we dig into Richard Camberwell's history before he went to Hong Kong. Childhood, teenage years, university, everything. We know about his link to Pauline Stopley, but my gut feeling is that there's more. We can get started now, and continue tomorrow. We double check everything that our esteemed ex-actress has told us about her husband. Some of it will undoubtedly be true, but much will be false. The trouble is, we don't know which is which.

'Theresa, I know you're due to visit the Freemans when the children get home, but see what you can find out about John Wethergill from a local perspective. You're a longstanding Dorchester resident so you might be able to tap into sources that the rest of us don't know about. Find out what you can about his background, going back to his school days. Pick Barry's brain for ideas if you need to. Is that okay?'

'Of course, ma'am.'

'Rae, you spend some more time on the financial records. Wethergill and Camberwell.'

Sophie stood, deep in thought. Finally she said, 'there is something we need to follow up, isn't there? Wethergill was a Dorchester man. We know he had a relationship with Pauline's sister, Dorothy. Presumably they met while he was a gardener at Finch Cottage, when the two sisters owned the place. We also know that Pauline was in an on-off relationship with Richard Camberwell, dating back to their school days. Could those two men have ever met? Do we know where they went to school? Can you work on that, Barry? And remember, all of you, there's a possibility that someone followed Wethergill home from the restaurant the evening he died. If you come across anything that might give a clue about who it was, let me know right away.'

Rae was tracking back through financial records and bank statements from two decades ago. It hadn't been easy extracting such dated information from the various banks and building societies. John Wethergill's records in particular were a puzzle. He'd come from an impoverished broken home. He'd worked as a jobbing handyman and gardener for many years, yet somehow had managed to save enough money to set up a hardware store business. Rae could see that he'd secured a business loan from one of the local banks, but surely they'd only have awarded such a sum if convinced that he would be putting in a substantial sum of his own? And how would he have come by the kind of deposit required, considering his background? She pored through the reams of paper looking for an explanation, and found a partial one. He had had a deposit account containing twenty thousand pounds, opened in the winter of 1996, and left untouched, gaining interest, for almost three years. Where had that sum come from? She continued to study the statements. Nothing else came to light until the money was withdrawn towards the end of the decade. She walked to the desk where Marsh was sorting through a different lot of papers.

'Do we have a date for when Wethergill opened his shop, sir?'

Marsh took a sheet from one of the folders on his desk. 'Here's what Theresa has found out so far. According to her it opened just before Christmas, 1999. A good time to start, I'd imagine.'

'Okay. It matches with the withdrawal of money from a savings account of his that I've discovered, so I can see what the money was used for. But where did he get it? He could never have earned that much. Do you think he was left money in a will at about that time?'

'There's no evidence for that. Everything we've found says that his family had next to no money.'

Rae pondered. 'Where did he grow up?' she finally asked. 'Do we know? Was he born and bred in Dorchester?'

'Yes, as far as we know.'

'Any other family members still alive?'

Theresa had traced an aunt of Wethergill's, a resident of Blandford Forum. Marsh phoned her. She used to run a pub in Blandford, she explained, but had retired some years earlier. He asked her what she remembered about John as a boy. The young John Wethergill's life hadn't been a happy one. Beaten by a drunken father, in and out of trouble at school and too ready to mix with the "wrong sort." Marsh wondered whether the aunt was being over-judgemental. After all, Wethergill hadn't had a criminal record, not even as a youngster. Still, it was useful background information.

'Where did he go to school?' he asked. 'Did he live in Dorchester as a youngster?'

John had attended local schools, but had been hopeless at academic work apparently. Maybe he'd been a late developer. Marsh knew all about boys who failed to take education seriously until it was almost too late. He'd been a prime example of that. He thanked the aunt for her help and added the information to the file.

Rae had also been studying decades-old transaction details from Richard Camberwell's bank and building society records. They showed nothing of interest. There were no large sums unaccountably appearing or disappearing from any of the accounts. Where had Wethergill's lump of money come from? It had changed his life, and it had appeared in his account at about the same time as the twins had died. Coincidence?

CHAPTER 33: CHINESE WHISPERS

Friday evening, Week 3

'I saw that Dorothy woman again today, Mum, in Weymouth.' Jade was spooning fruit trifle into her mouth while studying some revision cards spread out on the table in front of her. A school chemistry test.

'In Weymouth? Are you sure? What were you doing there?'

Jade nodded. 'It was her, though she looked very different. Asli and Safiyo both play in the first year netball team and they had an after-school match against a Weymouth school. I went along to support them. We drove back along the front in the minibus so that some of the girls could get fish and chips and I went into the chippie with them. I nearly bumped into her when I was coming out. She looked very different. She had a new hairstyle and was wearing make-up.'

'Really? Could it have been someone else?'

Jade surveyed her mother gravely. 'You doubt me too much, Mum. Actually, I suppose I might be wrong, but I don't think so. Even though she was much better dressed she still had that nervous look. That was what I first spotted.'

'Did she recognise you?'

'I wouldn't have thought so. She didn't react, anyway. She'd just come out of the bookshop next door. She stepped back, then walked past and into the hotel on the same block.'

Sophie stared at her. 'A hotel? Are you sure?'

'Mum, I'm not totally stupid. I know a hotel when I see one, particularly when it has a big sign outside.'

'That's not what I meant, Jade, as you well know. She definitely went in?'

'Yes, as if she was staying there. And the bookshop was a small, antiquarian type of place. The kind of bookshop Dad likes.'

Sophie thought for a moment. 'I think I know where that hotel is. And you saw her come out of a bookshop? Thanks, Jade. Very observant of you.' Her mind went back to the search of Pauline Stopley's flat. A row of birthday cards had been displayed on a shelf. One of them was from her sister Dorothy, hand-made with a rhyme on the inside. That rhyme had been carefully crafted.

'Aren't you going to pat me on the head like you used to when I was little? I miss those motherly touches. They were an important part of my early childhood development.'

Sophie looked exasperated. 'Jade, you're four inches taller than me. I can't reach. And you're winding me up again, aren't you? Just you wait till Jamie comes round again. I'll get my own back.'

'That's the spirit, Mum. A bit of gentle teasing never hurt anyone, according to Dad. I'm immune to it after all the years. I'm surprised you fell for it just then. Didn't he ever tease you? When you were both much, much younger, I mean?'

Sophie narrowed her eyes. 'That's two provocations in two minutes. I'm not going to fall into your trap. Has he put you up to this?'

Jade didn't answer. She popped another spoonful of trifle into her mouth and shifted her attention back to her revision cards. Sophie phoned Barry Marsh, asking if they had an address for Dorothy Kitson.

'I think we do but it's back in the incident room. Trouble is, ma'am, Dorothy seems not to be around at the moment. Theresa reported that she has missed some of her cleaning jobs, not just the one at Finch Cottage.'

'But that means we might have some legitimate concerns about her wellbeing, don't you think? Busy at the moment, Barry?'

* * *

Within an hour, both detectives were standing outside the door of a small flat. It was one of ten in a shabby building in a back street west of Dorchester town centre. Dorothy's flat was on the second floor. There was no lift and the stairs were uncarpeted. Barry rang the doorbell. There was no answer.

'Check the flat next door, Barry. If anyone's in, ask if they have a spare key.'

Marsh dutifully rang the bell for the adjoining apartment. He was soon talking to a hard-faced woman who was clearly upset at being called away from her favourite soap on the television. Yes, she did keep a key for her neighbour's flat.

'We're concerned about her,' Marsh explained. 'Even her sister has been unable to contact her for several days so we need to check that she is alright. Would you like to accompany us, madam?'

The neighbour seemed about to reply in the negative, but then her programme's theme music sounded signifying the end of the evening's instalment. She said she would come with them but wait in the hall.

The single-bedroom flat was sparsely furnished but clean and tidy. They looked into the rooms but there was no sign of Dorothy, and nothing indicating where she was. The neighbour locked the door and Marsh and Sophie left the building.

'Weren't you tempted to have a closer look, ma'am?'

'Of course I was. I'm only human, Barry. But it's a legal minefield. We were there with the stated purpose of checking on her safety, with the neighbour as a witness. If we'd started nosing about, anything we found could be declared inadmissible in court. There are only two ways we can safely search someone's property: with their permission or with a warrant. Anything else might put the case at risk, and it's just not worth the gamble, not unless the stakes are high. Anyway, I had a good look round as I'm sure you did.'

'Some simple artwork on the walls,' he said. 'A few old photos, maybe of her and her sister when they were small, though it's difficult to be sure. Some books, mainly romance novels. A few magazines on a shelf in the lounge. A dark blue anorak hanging up in the hall.'

Sophie nodded. 'Well spotted. Also a bottle of Amaretto, along with a few other drinks, inside the glass-fronted cupboard in the kitchen.'

'Ah,' Barry said.

'Several small books of late twentieth century poetry on a shelf in the lounge recess. Including Ted Hughes. So.'

'So?'

She nodded slowly. 'It's possible we may have discovered our poet, though I'm not sure how important that might prove to be. In the 1960s Ted Hughes wrote a volume of poetry called "Crow." The poems were bleak in the extreme. That was the book I spotted back there.'

'Ah,' Barry said again. 'Er . . . so?'

Sophie laughed. 'Stop talking Chinese, Barry. Let's get back to Wareham. A couple of beers are required at this stage. Rae wants to meet up with us for some reason. It sounds as if she might be onto something.'

* * *

Sophie drained half of her glass in one swallow. Rae watched, her mouth open.

'Small glasses of white wine are fine in their time and place. But this isn't the place and the time isn't now. It's Friday evening. The beer's particularly good tonight.'

'Where did you pick up the taste for beer? Was it when you were a student?'

'No, oddly enough. When I was growing up in Bristol I had a rascal of a great uncle. My mum and I lived with him and Auntie Olive when I was a baby, and we stayed close to them even after we moved to our own place. They didn't have children of their own. Uncle Reggie was great fun. He used to tickle me, and would reduce me to fits of giggles. He taught me all the bad habits: how to swear, smoke and drink. He said he didn't want me growing up into a swotty little snob. Maybe he could see the writing on the wall, even when I was only eight or nine. Well, I never took to smoking. It made me sick. Even the swearing wasn't a great success from his point of view. I knew all the words but he said I sounded too intellectual when I used them. Anyway, he took up home brewing when I was about fourteen and I used to go round and help him with it. I suppose that was the start of my beer drinking. I took over the brewing when he had a stroke and couldn't do it anymore. I must have been about sixteen. I even put it on my university application form. The admissions tutor at Oxford asked me about it in my interview. He was particularly interested in the use of black treacle in my recipe for stout. He had a background in biochemistry, apparently. The law tutor was less impressed, but I had enough other stuff to win her over.'

Marsh spoke. 'I remember you telling us you were estranged from your mother's parents. Did you never meet them?'

'No. As far as I know, my mother never sought them out either. What I did discover quite recently was that she'd sent them news of me from time to time. A copy of my O level results, and my A levels, along with a copy of the acceptance letter for Oxford. My graduation photo. That was it. By the time I got my masters, they were both dead. My mum never stopped hating them. When she heard they had died her only comment was, "good riddance." I can understand it, considering what they did to her.' She sipped her beer. 'Let's get down to business. What have you found out, Rae?'

'It's Pauline Stopley, ma'am. Hong Kong sent a detailed report of her attempts to trace the children. Apparently she's been visiting every year since they went missing and she really pushed the police to keep the search going. She's never missed a single year. They would probably have given up years ago if she hadn't been there so often, making a fuss. It doesn't fit with the idea that she caused their disappearance, does it? One of their seniors wants you to phone him tomorrow, if possible, to fill you in on the details.'

'Okay, if it'll be useful. Maybe I've misjudged her,' said Sophie.

Rae nodded. 'If it was her who killed the twins I can understand she might make a couple of visits to play the grieving stepmother, but then she'd let them tail off, surely? She's a bit of a complex person, isn't she? Why wasn't she more open with us during her interviews if she had nothing to hide?'

'I couldn't begin to speculate. She's wrong-footed me several times. I just can't read her. It hurts, that. It makes a dent in my enormous ego.' Sophie laughed. 'We'll need to speak to her again soon. She and her sister might be the only two people who can enlighten us about a possible link between Dr Camberwell and John Wethergill. One of those two women must have known something about the sale of that Bristol house, surely? As I said to Barry, the elusive Dorothy might be in Weymouth at the moment. My eagle-eyed daughter, Jade, had a sighting. And several clues have come to light that could put her in the frame. So, Rae, you and I might have a day at the seaside tomorrow.' She looked at her empty glass. 'Your round, Barry.'

'Ah,' he said.

'So,' Sophie added, and smirked.

CHAPTER 34: WHATEVER MAKES YOU HAPPY

Saturday morning, Week 4

Pauline Stopley was feeling restless. She couldn't seem to concentrate on anything, and it worried her. She felt a deep sense of betrayal by people she'd trusted two decades ago, people who'd vanished or died during the intervening years. Her self-confidence had received a severe jolt. She was beginning to feel as if she were turning into her sister, with her super-sensitive nerves. It didn't help that she couldn't find Dorothy. She was the only person who might be able to explain the sequence of bewildering events that had been happening lately. Dorothy had always lived in Dorchester, so she might be able to shed some light on the key periods when Pauline had been away on tour or living elsewhere. How could she have been kept so utterly in the dark for so long?

She rose from her desk and walked to the window, looking down blankly on the street below. Who was she hoping to see? No one. There was no one left. Jill had called her earlier to say that their affair was off for the time being. News of it had got out and Jill needed to go into damage limitation mode. She might (might? Ha!) get in touch the following week if things settled down quickly. Now she needed time to work out what would be best for her and the family. Not much hope there.

John was dead. Unsophisticated, straightforward John, so convinced he was worldly-wise, but in reality a complete innocent when it came down to the nitty-gritty physicality of sexual liaisons. Dead. Did he deserve that? Pauline sighed. The problem was, she didn't really know. She didn't know where she stood with anybody any more. And what was more, she'd seriously antagonised the police. Why? Why had she acted in such an arrogant way? She couldn't possibly have selected two worse people to come on to. For god's sake, the husband and daughter of the very detective who was in charge of the case! What had been going on in her head? Now they'd be watching her every move. Was her phone bugged? Had a tracking device been planted on her car? Was she being tailed everywhere she went? She couldn't tell. Were they allowed to do such things in modern Britain? She just didn't know and wasn't in the right mental frame to find out. She needed a friend to talk to who would offer reassurance, but there was nobody. How deeply would the police probe? How far back would they go? Pauline sensed that a lot of hidden truths were about to be exposed, and her life would never be the same again. The whole messy business was out of control. Fuck that stupid, selfish sister of hers! Pauline had rarely needed to call on her for help, and now that she desperately needed to speak to Dorothy the self-obsessed bitch was nowhere to be found. Maybe she'd mentioned something to the church minister before she'd walked out on her cleaning job and disappeared from Dorchester. He might have some idea of where Dorothy had gone.

* * *

Dorothy Kitson couldn't believe her luck. Larry was a human ramrod. Despite the fact that he was in his early fifties, he could have sex twice a day, every day. He made her gasp, groan. She was delirious with pleasure, and it wasn't just the sex. He took her to small cafés and restaurants that he knew, relatively cheap but serving the most delicious food. He tipped rum cocktails into her, and he tickled her in the most sensitive parts of her body. Right now they were sitting on a promenade seat looking out to sea, and she could feel his fingers starting to move lightly into her armpit. She turned to him.

'Don't, Larry. Please. I'm far too full after all that food. You'll make me sick.'

He grinned broadly at her. 'Sure thing. You're the boss.'

She leant her head on his shoulder, breathing in the faint smell of pineapple that seemed to cling to his skin. Did he use a skin cream? How unusual was that for a man? 'What day is it today?' she asked. 'You've left me in such a whirl I can't remember.'

He laughed. 'Saturday. The weekend at last, but it's not a break for me. I'm back on duty this afternoon. It's our busy time at the hotel.'

'Oh, no! I'm due to go home tomorrow,' she wailed. 'What will I do?'

'You only live twelve miles away, you know. There's a bus every hour.' He tickled her stomach gently. 'You're nearly as nutty as my old mum.'

'So can I come and see you?'

'Of course, you sexy little mama. I'll be here the whole summer. And I can come and visit you. I know Dorchester well. Don't you worry, little darling.' His face crinkled into a broad smile.

'Have you been there often then?'

He nodded. The smile left his face. 'I was there for a year or two, a guest in a certain well-known local hostelry. Caught by the Weymouth cops distributing ganja, among other things. But that was a long time ago and I've been a good boy ever since.' He winked. 'Well, pretty good, anyway.'

Dorothy looked shocked, and Larry laughed and tickled her again. 'I was a youngster, Dottie. Life was different then.

I've steered clear of the stuff ever since just so's I stay out of trouble. I don't want that hassle again.'

She nodded. 'How come they let you stay here? Why didn't they send you back to Jamaica?'

'I'm as British as you, cheeky lady. I was born in Brixton. I have dual citizenship though. I go back to Jamaica each winter to see some of my family who stayed put. We have a place near the beach and I can really chill.'

Dorothy remained silent for a while. 'I'd like you to come and visit me, but . . . you might meet my sister. I'm scared I'd lose you.'

Larry sat back and looked at her. 'What do you mean?'

'She'll pinch anything of mine if it takes her fancy. Boyfriends, clothes, everything. She'd take one look at you and that would be that. You wouldn't stand a chance. She meets men all the time and just discards them when she's had enough. They follow her around like puppies. It's pathetic to watch. She used to be a famous actress. She still puts on a show if she's trying to impress someone. It makes me sick. How can men be so stupid?'

Larry shook his head, laughing. 'We're all shallow creatures. Is that what you mean? Well, you're probably right. My younger brother's a professor of biochemistry and he says that we're all ruled by our hormones. Men and women. I won't come and visit if you don't want me to — if you think I'll be a rabbit to your sister's foxiness.'

Dorothy giggled. 'I really don't want to go tomorrow. Is there any way I can stay?'

'Not in the hotel, there isn't. There's a hen party this weekend and it's booked solid.'

'Where do you live?'

He shook his head. 'I'm just in a room in the staff annexe. There's a small sitting room and a shared kitchen. It just wouldn't be any good for you to stay there, Dottie, not for more than a day or two.'

'So you don't rent or own a separate place?'

'I send money back to Jamaica. I have my place there. My cousins live in it and keep it clean for me. That takes most of my spare cash.'

She grasped his hand. 'I'll find a way. Maybe I'll move out of my little flat in Dorchester and look for a place here. What do you think?'

He nodded slowly, a smile on his face. 'Whatever makes you happy, little Dottie.' He poked a finger into her ribs, until she started giggling. He lifted his hand to massage her breast. 'Whatever makes you happy.' He paused, still smiling. 'How about going back to the hotel? I give a great body massage. You'll love it.'

Oh, bliss, Dorothy thought. To have discovered a man like this, and in her middle years!

'Yes, yes, yes,' she said.

Unfortunately she didn't get a chance to enjoy the feel of Larry's firm, soft fingers probing her flesh. Someone was waiting for her in reception.

Her sister, Pauline Stopley.

CHAPTER 35: WELCOME TO THE CLUB

Saturday afternoon, Week 4

Sophie spotted a parking slot opposite the hotel, pulled up against the kerb and switched the engine off. She looked across the road. A fish and chip shop, an antiquarian book seller. A hotel. All exactly as described by her daughter, Jade. She was about to open the car door when she saw a familiar figure come out of the hotel, pause, glance about as if to gain her bearings and slowly walk away eastwards, unsteadily.

'Well, would you believe it,' she said. 'Did you see her?'

Rae nodded. 'Our friend Pauline Stopley, ma'am. So was she telling us the truth when she said she didn't know where her sister was?'

'Who knows? She's one of the best liars I've ever come across. She's so smooth and controlled, you really can't tell whether whatever she says is the truth or not. I gave up trying over a week ago. I decided not to believe anything she told me. Now, with what we found out yesterday? I still don't know. But let's leave her be for the moment. She's not the reason why we're here. Can you get out of the car and try to see where she's going? She'll recognise me if she looks back and I'm not ready to talk to her again at the moment.'

Rae got out of the passenger door and stood at the kerbside. She craned her neck to watch the slender figure as it made its way along the esplanade.

'She's just stopped at a parked car. A red VW Golf? Isn't that hers? She's just got in. I think she might be crying.'

Sophie nodded. 'Okay. Let's forget about her for the time being and concentrate on Dorothy.'

From outside the Lake Guesthouse looked staid, even sombre, but the interior was much brighter. There was a light and airy feel to the reception area, and Sophie and Rae could see the modern furniture in the lounge. The hotel looked well-kept. A middle-aged man with a goatee beard and skin like smooth chocolate came out of a sitting room and walked towards the reception desk.

'Can I help you?' he asked. His voice was warm and friendly and he spoke with a pronounced Caribbean accent.

'We're police officers. We're looking for Dorothy Kitson,' Rae said, and held out her warrant card.

Concern flashed across his face. 'Just a moment,' he said. He came out from behind the desk and went into the lounge.

Sophie and Rae heard a murmur of voices. The discussion seemed to last longer than might be expected in such a situation. Finally the man returned.

'She's in the lounge. She's very upset by something another visitor has just said to her. Please treat her gently, won't you?' He looked at them, almost pleading, his gaze settling on Sophie. She smiled thinly.

'That will entirely depend upon the level of co-operation we get, Mr . .?'

'Waters. Larry Waters. I'm the assistant manager here and I've become rather fond of Dorothy since she arrived. She's a bit fragile.'

She nodded, looking at him closely. 'Are you in a relationship with her, Mr Waters?'

He nodded. Silently he pointed to the open doorway. The two detectives walked into the sunlit room, whose windows looked across the esplanade to an expanse of blue sea beyond. There was only one occupant. She was sitting in an easy chair at a window table, staring out to sea. Her fingers were nervously clutching at the sleeve of her dress. As they approached they could see red blotches on her face and tears in her eyes. She glanced up at them, and her eyes rested on Sophie. She looked frightened and vulnerable.

'I know who you are,' she whispered. 'I knew you'd find me, ever since I saw you talking to the vicar in the church.'

'We spotted your sister leaving. It's just a coincidence that we came at the same time. We hadn't arranged it.'

Dorothy nodded slowly. 'I've never seen her like that, not ever. I've never seen her cry like that. I've seen her in every other mood. She's been livid with anger, upset, disappointed, frustrated, happy, elated. All those, but never so shocked. I couldn't calm her. She kept hitting me.'

That explains the bright red marks, Sophie thought. 'What's your background, Dorothy?'

'According to my sister I'm a waster who ruins things. I ruin everything, and she's right. Everything I'm involved with goes wrong and falls apart sooner or later. Jobs, education, marriages, relationships, everything. I couldn't stick at any jobs I got. For a long time I've just done cleaning jobs.'

'Did you have plans to be an actress too?'

Dorothy shook her head. 'I wanted to be an English teacher, but I failed my university exams and had to leave.'

Sophie nodded. 'Why does Pauline think you ruin things?'

'You know why. You know what I've done. Pauline never knew about the twins until you told her. I kept it from her. I was terrified of how she'd react if she found out. Even when you found the bodies I convinced her they were some teenagers. I may not like her very much but she is my sister, and she's never done anything truly evil. Not like me.'

'How did it happen?'

There was a long silence. 'John and I were together then. We were happy. But when the twins came back they changed everything. It was too sudden and I couldn't cope. When they were naughty I used to lock them in the cellar. Then winter came. The cellar was freezing and I lit an old paraffin heater so they'd stay warm. I found them the next morning.' She began to sob. 'I never meant it to happen. I was frantic. I called John and he went berserk. He told me he'd deal with their bodies but it was finished between us.'

'But why? Why didn't you just call the police or an ambulance?'

'What good would an ambulance have done? They were dead from the fumes. John said it must have been carbon monoxide and I should never have used a paraffin heater in such a poor state and I'd been totally negligent. Anyway, no one knew they were here. When they came I just got a phone call at my flat telling me to be at the bus station at a particular time. No explanation. And there they were. No one with them. Someone had brought them back from Hong Kong, brought them to Dorchester and abandoned them in the café. They told me it was their aunt and that she was already on her way back to Hong Kong. So I brought them to Finch Cottage. It was empty at the time and my flat had no spare room. I didn't know what to do. I was waiting for Pauline to get back from the States because I just couldn't handle them. I've never been any good with children.'

'So you locked them in the cellar? Often?'

'No. Only a couple of times. It was what our parents used to do to Pauline and me if we were naughty.'

'There was a metal ring set into the wall at the far end of the cellar. Did you ever use it? Did you tie the children to it?'

There was a silence that seemed to last for minutes. Dorothy's voice was a whisper. 'I couldn't let them run around down there, could I? There was all kinds of stuff that could have been dangerous. It could have harmed them. It was only a few times. They could have hurt themselves otherwise.'

Sophie closed her eyes, thinking hard. Rae still had her mouth open in shock. Finally Sophie spoke. 'Dorothy, you'll need to come back to Dorchester with us. You need a solicitor and I'll need a signed statement from you. Do you understand that?'

Dorothy nodded. She looked at the detectives through her tears. 'Maybe it's time. I've hated myself for twenty years. I couldn't go on any more, not once Pauline found out.'

'Did you tell her what happened?'

There was a nod. 'She didn't say anything after that. She just started crying and she stared at me. I tried to hug her but she just pushed me away and kept hitting me. She hates me. She'll hate me forever.' She paused. 'I deserve it all. I don't know how I've managed to live for twenty years after what I've done.' She sank back into the chair, her head dropping onto her chest.

'What about John Wethergill, Dorothy? Can you shed any light on his death?'

There was no answer.

* * *

Late in the afternoon Sophie and Rae finally made the drive to Maiden Castle. One of Europe's largest iron-age hill forts, its brooding presence dominates the land to the south west of Dorchester. And there, parked under the shoulder of this monstrous structure, was a bright red Volkswagen Golf.

'Thank goodness,' Sophie muttered. 'I was starting to worry, wondering where she was and what she was doing. Then I remembered what Jill Freeman told me.'

'But the place is huge, ma'am. She could be anywhere. Shouldn't we just wait here? She's bound to come back, isn't she?'

Sophie frowned. 'To tell you the truth, I'm a bit worried about her. I think I may have misjudged her. I want to have a look around just in case, but you stay here.'

Sophie got out her pink wellies from the car's boot and slipped her feet into a pair of well-worn, bright pink socks. Rae smiled.

'Chosen by Jade when she was twelve,' Sophie explained. 'I need a new pair of socks but I'll need to plan the changeover like a military strategy. She used to view these socks and wellies as the most important symbol of our mother-daughter relationship. Dare I suggest a new pair for my birthday?'

'I noticed that Barry tends to be a bit nervous around Jade,' Rae said.

'He has every reason to be. She can floor any man with one withering comment, if she chooses. God knows where she got that particular skill from, certainly not from me. Martin has taken her to too many Shakespeare plays, I expect.' She paused. 'If Pauline arrives back here before me, don't let her go. Here're my car keys. Block her in if necessary. And if any Jobsworth arrives to lock that gate, threaten him or her with a night in the cells for obstructing the police in their duties.'

Sophie pulled her coat more tightly around her and set off in an anticlockwise direction, guessing that most people did the circuit the opposite way. Not that there were many other people. The afternoon had become overcast. It would be raining soon, she thought, and the wind will start to pick up. She chose the top rampart: from there she should be able to see the lower sections and, with luck, would be able to spot Pauline Stopley. The views were spectacular, despite the cloud cover and the gradually dimming light. Sophie promised herself a visit on a sunny day. She walked on, occasionally meeting small groups of people coming around the site in the opposite direction, but even these grew less as time wore on. Where was the woman? Twenty minutes had passed. That meant that she was about a third of the way around the huge site. Assuming Pauline was walking clockwise, and had at least a twenty minute start on her, she should have met her by now. Maybe she was one of those awkward people who always perform circuits in the unexpected direction. In that case she'd already be back with Rae.

Sophie stopped to gather her breath, ready for the next part of the circuit. Then she saw someone sitting on an outcrop below her, half hidden in shadow. The person was wrapped in a dark blue coat, of exactly the same shade that Pauline had been wearing earlier in the afternoon. Sophie stepped down the grassy bank. The actress heard her footsteps and half turned. She moved to one side, making room for Sophie to sit beside her.

'I saw you earlier,' Pauline murmured. 'Back in Weymouth. I was in my car but I couldn't drive because I was shaking so much. I got out again and that's when I saw you, just as you entered the hotel. I needed some air, to be alone with my thoughts. So I came here.'

Sophie nodded. The view to the west stretched out in front of them. Miles of undulating countryside under a sky of darkening, scudding clouds.

'You know, I guess. She told you?' Pauline's voice was thin, as if she was having trouble forcing the words out.

'Yes. She's in custody. We've charged her with murder, but if what she says is found to be true, it might drop to manslaughter. That won't be up to me. The prosecution service will decide.'

'I can't get my head round it. I just can't comprehend it. For twenty years she's been holding on to that secret. My lovely twins. I know you and everybody else are going to say that they weren't mine, I was only their stepmother, but in the years I had them they became mine. Do you know what it's like to lose children like that? To realise that you'll never see them again? Do you?'

Sophie slowly nodded. She answered quietly. 'I lost a baby twelve years ago, halfway through the pregnancy. He would have been my only son because we already had two daughters. When I lost him I howled the place down for hours. One of the student nurses thought I might be in need of a psychiatrist. The older and wiser staff took her aside and told her to leave me alone and I'd get over it. I did get over it, after a fashion. But I still miss him. Every day I miss him. He was my own flesh and blood. My only son. But it's true. The pain does lessen with time. What was razor sharp and could shred my emotions like tissue paper has changed to a dull ache.'

Pauline looked at Sophie. 'I checked with the Hong Kong police every three months to see if they'd been traced. Did you know that? For twenty years. And they were here all the time, in a hole in the ground, put there by my own sister.' She shook her head from side to side as if to clear her brain of its terrible thoughts.

'I know. We were in contact with the Hong Kong authorities yesterday and they told us. They also told us that you'd visited at least once a year, every year since the twins vanished. I spoke myself to the officer in charge this morning. What can I say?'

Pauline burst into tears so suddenly that Sophie was taken aback. She put her arm round the other woman's shoulder and felt the great heaving sobs that racked through her body. 'Life can be a totally fucked up experience for some of us, Pauline, and not due to our own actions. Christ, don't I know it. All I can say to you is, welcome to the club.' She sat in silence for a while, her arm still around Pauline's shoulder. 'We need to know it all, Pauline. Not just what you know happened all those years ago, but what you suspect happened. You, Dorothy, Richard, John and Li Hua. We need to get to the bottom of it. Do you want to tell me now or come back to the station with me? Either way, it's time to be honest. Were you having an affair with Richard before Li Hua died?'

Pauline turned to face Sophie, tears still running down her pale cheeks. She nodded slightly. 'He was so unhappy at what she'd become. She'd turned into a first class bitch, he said. She'd changed completely from when they first married. She treated him like dirt and the children not much better. He couldn't put up with it any longer.'

'So what happened? Was it him in the car that night?'

Pauline turned to face the dark clouds, scudding in from the west. 'We never talked about it. Just the fact that she was dead made everything right for us. Why would I want to find out the gory details? And he didn't want me involved, I could sense that. If I came to know anything I'd become an accessory, so I didn't ask and he didn't tell.'

'But you picked up clues? You guessed it was him driving the car that killed her?'

Pauline took Sophie's arm away. She seemed to draw herself together and stared coldly at her. 'Do you really think I'm going to tell you anything that would confirm that my only true soul-mate was a murderer? Do you really think I'm that feeble-minded? I loved him. I still love the memory of him. I loved those two children of his. That's all you need to know, and that's all I'm telling you. If you want to interview me under some kind of caution then that's your choice. But don't expect me to surrender up my pride either in myself or the man I adored. Because that's all I'm left with, and I'm not letting it go.'

There was a long silence. Sophie asked, 'what happened that night last week between you and John after you left the Italian restaurant? Is there anything you want to add to what you told me last week?'

Pauline took a breath. 'John finally realised who I was. We'd been talking about our backgrounds. He already knew I worked for the Arts Council, but no more than that. I let slip on our way out that I used to be an actress. It took him a moment or two to twig. I was amused that it took so long. We'd spent a couple of hours or so together when we first met on the walk, I spent the night with him at his flat, we'd just spent a couple more hours talking at that restaurant, and he still hadn't caught on. I thought I was famous. Clearly not. Well, not among hardware shop owners, anyway.'

Sophie was exasperated. 'Why didn't you tell me this at our last interview? I could charge you with wasting police time.'

'But you won't, will you? Because you, Detective Chief Inspector Sophie Whatnot, are too much like me. Manipulative and devious maybe, but not bloody-minded, not evil. I wish you were the sister I never had, not that selfish, murdering, child-killing waste of space, Dorothy fucking Kitson.'

Sophie stood up. She was beginning to feel cold and the air was becoming misty. They'd need to start walking back to the car park soon. 'So you did target John deliberately? Despite your denial last week?'

'I wanted to find out what had been going on at Finch Cottage. I wanted to know whose bodies they were, and what had been going on. He'd been the gardener there for yonks, for Christ's sake. The first press reports didn't say they were children, just that bodies had been found.'

'Why didn't you ask your sister? She still had a connection because of her cleaning work.' Sophie held out an arm and helped Pauline to her feet.

'I did and she told me she'd heard they were the bodies of two teenagers, probably tramps. Anyway, it's been an absolute rule of mine since we were children. Never ask Dorothy for a favour of any kind. It'll just get thrown back in your face when you least expect it. Never ask her for information. It'll be twisted and bent. I wish I'd spat in her ugly face back there in Weymouth, but I was just too shocked by it all.'

Sophie took out her mobile phone and called Rae. 'We're just starting back,' she said. As the two women climbed back up to the footpath, a light rain began to fall.

CHAPTER 36: MONEY MATTERS

Monday, Week 4

'The facts are, Barry, that both sisters did very well financially at that time. Pauline would have inherited the property in Bristol after her husband died. Assuming he had life insurance, she'd have no mortgage repayments to make, so she'd have got the lot. She and Dorothy jointly owned Finch Cottage which was sold soon after our assumed date for the death of the twins. Pauline had also completed a long stint on Broadway which would have earned her a tidy sum. They'd have been swimming in money. And this was at the time that Wethergill got this mysterious deposit in his account, the one that allowed him to buy his shop. But it doesn't stop there. That flat of his was worth a lot and if you think about the quality of the furniture and fittings, it doesn't add up. His shop wasn't doing that well, not according to the figures I've seen. And we've been puzzling for days about how he got the money to start up his business.'

Rae looked at her boss. 'What are you suggesting, ma'am?'

Sophie tapped her fingers on the desktop. 'I wonder if he was blackmailing Dorothy, and over a long time period. She's not got a huge amount in her bank account and her home is very threadbare. What did she do with that cash? It's not obvious at the moment.'

'So Wethergill seems to have much more disposable income than he should have, and Dorothy had much less? And blackmail would give Dorothy enough motive for killing him, if that's what you're suggesting? It's a highly plausible theory. But do we have any evidence for it?' Marsh was being his usual pragmatic self.

Rae shook her head. 'Not yet. But once we get her financial records sent through, we should find out, one way or the other. But if it did happen that way, ma'am, shouldn't something have turned up at one of the flats, either Wethergill's or Dorothy's? Or even at both? I mean something that suggests murder rather than suicide?'

Sophie nodded. 'So let's go back over everything to see if we've overlooked something vital.' Her phone rang. It was Dave Nash. She listened to his message with barely concealed excitement.

'Thanks, Dave. Very timely.'

She sat back in her chair, eyes closed, making the most of the warm glow of satisfaction that spread through her body.

'Don't keep it to yourself, ma'am. You look like the cat that's got the cream,' Marsh said.

'That's exactly what it feels like. Those bank notes? The ones that Wethergill supposedly set out for his cleaner's wages? They've got Dorothy Kitson's prints all over them. Do we have a list of all her cleaning jobs somewhere?'

Marsh nodded. 'I think it's complete. She worked in about half a dozen places.'

'Okay. We have some checking to do. One of the fivers is defaced with a "Free Palestine" message. It's fairly noticeable, according to Nash. Let's go through the list and check to see if any of Ms Kitson's employers remember it.'

It was almost inevitable that it would be Tony Younger, the vicar of St Paul's, who could identify the banknote in question. He knew the banknote instantly when Rae phoned him about it.

'It was the only five pound note I had available at the time,' he said. 'I felt a bit guilty about passing it on like that but decided not to tell her in case she made a fuss about it. She can be a bit awkward at times. I'd have changed it later if she'd had any trouble using it. Is she alright, by the way? I'm a bit concerned about her heading off like that. She seemed very anxious about something when she told me about her break on Monday, but she wouldn't offer me any explanation.'

'She's safe, Mr Younger. I think you'll have to speak to the DCI for more information about her. It's all a bit sensitive at the moment. Shall I ask her to call you?'

Rae then put a call through to the IT forensic team, asking for the examination of Dorothy's laptop to be upgraded to top priority. Things were beginning to come together rather nicely, she thought.

CHAPTER 37: FUNERAL

Friday, Week 4

St Paul's Church was packed. Sitting silently in the pews were neighbours, current and past, medical staff, police officers, past Finch Cottage residents, staff from the school the twins had attended all those years ago, and Dorchester residents, confused and ashamed that such a thing had happened in their town. The two small coffins, layered with wreaths of every colour, were carried in and set down in front of the altar. The Freeman family sat in the front left row. The front right seats were occupied by Pauline Stopley, sitting alongside Sophie, Barry Marsh, Rae and Theresa. It was rare for police officers to find themselves so prominently on display at a victim's funeral, but the twin's stepmother had insisted. She had no one else to sit with her.

Tony Younger looked around him as he spoke, seeming to fix his eyes momentarily on each person in the audience as if he acknowledged the part each had played in uncovering the tragic story. This included at George Bramshaw, during the introduction to one of the music items chosen: an extract from Mozart's flute sonata in C Major, the very piece played by the twins in that school assembly of so many years earlier.

* * *

The drive to the local crematorium, situated ten miles away in Weymouth, passed in silence. Only Pauline, Sophie and Tony Younger were in the official car. As they entered the reception hall they were unexpectedly joined by a fourth figure who'd driven, unseen, behind them on the short journey from Dorchester. She slipped into the seat beside Pauline and held her arm tightly during the committal, then led her outside once the short ceremony was over. Sophie saw Jill Freeman embrace her ex-lover, weeping openly as she pulled Pauline's head close. Tony Younger stood by, looking awkward as he waited for his lift back to Dorchester.

Sophie stepped forward and touched Pauline's arm. 'Time to go,' she said.

Pauline stood back, and then smiled at Jill. 'I'm okay,' she said. 'You should go back to your family. They need you.'

Once Jill Freeman had left, Pauline breathed deeply, then turned and slipped her arm through Tony Younger's. 'That was a wonderful ceremony,' she said. 'You judged it just perfectly.' She paused. 'Do you fancy a meal out this evening? I just couldn't bear to be alone, not after this.'

The minister nodded, a look of mild surprise on his face. 'That's understandable. Why don't you come over? I cook pretty good casseroles.'

'I'd prefer to be out, if you don't mind. I don't want to brood inside a house, even if it's yours. Maybe you can cook for me next week? When I'm feeling a bit more human? It'll be my treat tonight.'

He smiled gently. 'Of course. Whatever you prefer.'

Sophie was dumbfounded. Pauline was just amazing. Would a mere vicar be able to cope with what might be in store? Then again, maybe he could provide some stability, an answer to the actress's constant emotional restlessness.

CHAPTER 38: LICKED LIPS

Friday, Week 5

The atmosphere at Finch Cottage was tense. Jill had told Philip about her short, torrid affair with Pauline Stopley. He'd been shocked at first, but once he'd taken the time to think things through he'd decided to stick by her, to give their marriage another chance. Both knew that it wouldn't be easy. From Philip's point of view he'd been made painfully aware that there was a side to his wife's sexuality that he could never satisfy. Jill was now aware of a hitherto unknown kind of pleasure. Could she forget it? Only time would tell. Jill had also sat down with Karen and tried to explain something of the emotional whirlpool that had swept her along in its flow. The girl had claimed that she thought she understood some of what her mother was telling her, but Jill was doubtful. Jill didn't fully understand it herself. The good thing was, though, that the family was still together, and there had been no vicious arguments. There was total family agreement about one thing: the need to move away from Finch Cottage.

* * *

Theresa Jackson relayed this information to the team of detectives while they were marking the closure of the case with a celebratory pub meal in Dorchester. The key investigators were joined by Matt Silver and Harry Turner, who had come from London for a second visit. The atmosphere was more muted than that of past celebrations. Sadness at the children's fate still hung over the team.

'Did you ever discover where the jar of cyanide came from?' Turner asked.

'It was decades old,' Sophie replied.' We think he had it in his possession for a long time, probably back before his time as a gardener at Finch Cottage. We don't know how he'd avoided having it logged on a poison register somewhere. Clearly he'd obtained it illegally, but for what purpose we don't know. What has become clearer is that our speculation about possible blackmail is looking stronger as each day goes by. We've got more evidence piling up that shows large sums of money leaving Dorothy's account and being deposited in his.'

'So she's been living for twenty years in fear of discovery?' Turner said. 'No wonder she was a bag of nerves. And once you discovered the twins' bodies, she knew that time was running out.'

'Maybe he let slip at some time that he kept cyanide somewhere, or she spotted it.' Rae added. 'It gave her a neat solution to the problem, didn't it? Removing her co-conspirator, her blackmailer and throwing suspicion onto him because it looked like suicide. All in one go. You've got to give it to her, she was clever. The only problem for her was that she'd left the record of her search history on her laptop. Loads of stuff on cyanide poisoning, telling her everything she needed to know. And us.'

'Do we know how long it will take for the Bristol team to reinvestigate the hit and run that killed Li Hua?' asked Marsh.

'Don't hold your breath,' Sophie replied. 'My guess is months rather than weeks. Polly phoned and said they were snowed under at the moment. She'd have pushed for an immediate start if it could provide vital evidence in our case, but now we're largely wrapped up there's less perceived need to hurry. I'm afraid it means that we haven't seen the last of Pauline Stopley. There are still too many unknowns. But she's out of our hair for a while. I hope.'

* * *

On the other side of town Pauline was ringing the doorbell of St Paul's Church manse. Underneath her coat she was wearing a short black dress with a full-length gold zip up the front. Her shoulder bag was rather larger than might be expected for a simple evening visit. She breathed deeply, savouring the cool evening air. Tony Younger opened the door and invited her inside, the smell of venison and red wine casserole drifting out into the night air. Pauline licked her lips in anticipation.

THE END

ACKNOWLEDGEMENTS

The Beaumont Society (www.beaumontsociety.org.uk) is the UK's leading support organisation for transgender people. The society has a network of voluntary "Regional Organisers" across the country who can help with problems. The author wishes to thank members of the society for their help with parts of this novel. Similarly, the author would like to thank Bailey at the NTPA (the National Trans Police Association) for her help in supplying background information about the experiences of police officers with gender identity issues.

Female Genital Mutilation (FGM) is still a serious problem throughout the world. For more information visit the websites of these three charities: 28 Too Many; The Orchid Project; Desert Flower. I would like to thank Alice Newton-Fenner for increasing my awareness of the mutilation of young girls from some ethnic communities living in Britain today, and for showing me where to look for information.

Thanks to Anne Derges for her
painstaking editorial work.

CHARACTER LIST

Detective Chief Inspector Sophie Allen is Dorset's acknowledged expert on murder and violent crime, newly appointed to run the county's Serious and Violent Crime Unit. She is 42 years old as the series starts, and lives with her family in Wareham. Sophie has a law degree and a master's in criminal psychology. Sophie may appear at first to be somewhat of a 'cold fish,' over-intellectual and too clever by half, but conceals a dark past.

Detective Sergeant Barry Marsh is in his early thirties and in Dark Crimes, the first novel, is based at Swanage police station. He's quiet, methodical and dedicated, the perfect foil for Sophie's hidden fragility.

Detective Constable Jimmy Melsom is also based in Swanage. He has only recently joined the CID, and is a little gung-ho in his attitude to crime investigation.

Detective Constable Lydia Pillay is a talented young officer based with DCI Allen at Dorset County police HQ.

Detective Inspector Kevin McGreedie is attached to the Bournemouth and Poole division of Dorset police. His assistant is DS Bob Thomson.

Detective Superintendent Matt Silver is Sophie's immediate boss. He helped to appoint her to lead the Violent Crime Unit but, to his regret, has a largely administrative role in the county police hierarchy.

Detective Chief Superintendent Neil Dunnett is the overall commander. He clashes with Sophie several times in Dark Crimes. The source of the antagonism is not clear.

Martin Allen is Sophie's husband. He is head of the mathematics department at a large secondary school in Dorchester. Martin has a minor, but very supportive, role in the novels. He and Sophie met while at university. He has a more prominent role in later novels in the series.

Sophie and Martin have two daughters. **Jade** is fifteen in the first novel, and appears in all the subsequent stories. She has a lively and very quirky personality. **Hannah**, the elder daughter, is a drama student in London. She is quieter in her approach to life. She appears as a minor character in the first novel, but has a more important role in later books.

THE JOFFE BOOKS STORY

We began in 2014 when Jasper agreed to publish his mum's much-rejected romance novel and it became a bestseller.

Since then we've grown into the largest independent publisher in the UK. We're extremely proud to publish some of the very best writers in the world, including Joy Ellis, Faith Martin, Caro Ramsay, Helen Forrester, Simon Brett and Robert Goddard. Everyone at Joffe Books loves reading and we never forget that it all begins with the magic of an author telling a story.

We are proud to publish talented first-time authors, as well as established writers whose books we love introducing to a new generation of readers.

We won Trade Publisher of the Year at the Independent Publishing Awards in 2023 and Best Publisher Award in 2024 at the People's Book Prize. We have been shortlisted for Independent Publisher of the Year at the British Book Awards for the last five years, and were shortlisted for the Diversity and Inclusivity Award at the 2022 Independent Publishing Awards. In 2023 we were shortlisted for Publisher of the Year at the RNA Industry Awards, and in 2024 we were shortlisted at the CWA Daggers for the Best Crime and Mystery Publisher.

We built this company with your help, and we love to hear from you, so please email us about absolutely anything bookish at feedback@joffebooks.com.

If you want to receive free books every Friday and hear about all our new releases, join our mailing list: www.joffebooks.com/free-books

And when you tell your friends about us, just remember: it's pronounced Joffe as in coffee or toffee!

Printed in Great Britain
by Amazon

55207105R00158